# DARK DREAMS

Ann Thorsson

To Lucy –

*The lovely wee lassie who gave me a bad dream.*

# What the people say about Dark Dreams:

*"From the beautifully crafted sentences to the simple but powerful ingredients, Thorsson turns the words into a film playing in your mind. She knows how to make the characters jump off the page!"*

**Lisa G Shannen,** *Freelance Writer and Author.*

*"Highly authentic for the time period and characters that conjure every emotion in the reader. The unpredictable, dark and even ghostly events make this twisted tale a must-read."*

**Gemma King,** *Paranormal Author. (Five-star review)*

# Other books by Ann Thorsson

A gritty drama set in the North of England during the 1980s and 90s. This is no ordinary boy-meets-girl Romeo and Juliet. (pub. 2019; UK Book Publishing)

*"'Downhill' is endearing and scary, sweet and disturbing, all at the same time. [...]we get to love the characters and wish their lives wouldn't take certain directions. To me, only a well written and powerful book can do that."*

**Matt Ferraz,** Author. *(Five-star review)*

Will Elaine ever be able to lay the Castle Ridge ghosts to rest? Or will she always be followed by her dark shadows?

The heart-rending and dramatic sequel to *Downhill*. (pub. 2022; UK Book Publishing)

*"The author's 3rd book in her own 'spooky' style, this is a good drama that I enjoyed and had me questioning the whole way through."*

**Mark Fearn,** "Book Mark" online reviewer. *(Five-star review)*

"*Even if she be not harmed, her heart may fail her in so much and so many horrors; and hereafter she may suffer–both in waking, from her nerves, and in sleep, from her dreams.*"

– Bram Stoker, Dracula

# Prologue

## Dark Dreams

*"Are you my mummy?"*

*"No."*

*"Oh,"* said the mind-voice. *"But you're so nice. Will you be my mummy?"*

*"No. I can't be your mummy."*

*"Why not?"*

*"Because you're dead..."* Rose's eyes rolled behind her closed eyelids, her REM continuing to disturb her sleep. Mind-images; dark, light, floating, coming close, moving away, a faceless mouth speaking to her, and she speaking back.

*"It's my birthday today,"* said the voice.

*"That's nice. How old are you?"* she asked the floating dream-image.

*"That depends. I could be one, or I could be three."*

*"I don't understand what you mean – how can you be one or three?"* asked Rose, perplexed.

*"Maybe not now, but one day you will understand. I'll make sure of it."*

*"Stop! You're scaring me..."*

*"Scaring you? But I'm only a baby – I can't walk or talk yet."*

1

*"But you're talking to me now…"*
*"I know. But that's because I'm inside your head. I can do whatever I want when I'm inside your head."*

# Part One

# Chapter 1

## Too Close for Comfort

### *1976*

'Will you two turn down that infernal racket!'

The muffled, insistent bangs and cursing permeated through Kate's bedroom floor, her mother obviously unhappy with the music and out-of-tune singing coming from Kate and Maggie. Undeterred, the two girls carried on miming into their hairbrush-microphones, determined to do justice to David Essex.

Bang, bang, bang.

'I won't bloody tell you again. If you don't turn it down, there'll be no *Top of the Pops* this week!'

The magic words had been spoken. Kate rolled her hazel-green eyes in teen-protest, then hastily went over to her record player to turn down the volume before flopping onto her bed, the tired, old springs creaking in protest.

Still gripping her loaned hairbrush mic, Maggie flopped down beside Kate then began gently brushing out her friend's copper-blonde curls into a wavy, golden halo.

*Soft, golden hair. So soft.*

Kate giggled at being bounced around, then tucked her hands behind her head, seemingly unaware that she'd messed up Maggie's halo-handiwork. She studied the posters on her bedroom ceiling.

'Look at David Essex's eyes – they just follow you, don't they.' Kate meant it more as a star-struck statement than a question. 'If only he would, you know, hold me close...' She wrapped her arms around herself, then continued, 'like in one of his songs.' A peachy colour rose in her cheeks to blend with the cluster of freckles across her nose, followed by a girly giggle. Her attention moved to her other prized ceiling posters – David Cassidy, and the Bay City Rollers. 'Wow, their girlfriends are soooo lucky!' After a moment of wistful daydreaming, Kate craned her neck to look at the poster above her headboard. Two guys, one blonde, one dark, smiled by the side of their cop car. 'Starsky or Hutch? Which is your favourite? Hutch is mine.'

Maggie mused for a moment. 'Probably Starsky, but only 'cause I like his big, woolly cardigan.'

Kate looked at her friend like she'd just dropped in from another planet. She paused before cautiously asking, 'Have you ever let a boy kiss you, or, you know, touch you?' She studied Maggie's delicate, elfin face and spiky pixie haircut while waiting for a reply.

Now it was Maggie's turn to flush. 'No! Have you?'

'No, not yet. But I would like to...' She mimicked kissing on her forearm before breaking out into giggles again.

Maggie studied the posters of Blondie and Suzi Quatro. Her crystal-blue eyes traced the lines of Debbie Harry's pout and pose, then visually caressed the contours of Suzi Q's hips, tightly clad in black leather trousers. She levered herself onto her side to face Kate, then reached out to stroke her friend's face before allowing her fingers to gently trail down her body, seemingly unaware of her actions, trance-like.

'Have you ever wondered what it's like to kiss a girl, or touch a girl, you know, down there...?' She nodded her head towards Kate's crotch, as her hand continued downwards.

Kate slapped hard at Maggie's hand before flying up and off the bed, her eyes wide.

'What the hell do you think you're doing!' her voice rising in tone. 'Get off me. What are you – some kind of lesbo!'

Suddenly aware of her unable-to-retract actions, Maggie sat up and pulled her knees up tight below her chin, enveloping her arms around her legs in defence.

'I...I...I'm sorry. I just thought, you know, we've been friends for so long. We do so much together...'

Kate's voice spat in the direction of Maggie, her words taut. 'Yes, but not *that* kind of friend! Good God...'

Seconds ticked by, each girl with their own reasons for holding their silence. Maggie stole a glance at Kate before speaking, her voice barely audible. 'I'm sorry, Kate.' She paused briefly, trying to find the right words. 'It's just...I don't know how to explain it, but...I just don't feel anything for boys. Not in *that* way.'

Kate looked at her friend. Her brows furrowed, causing her eyes to appear malicious.

'What do you mean, in *that* way? You mean you don't want a boyfriend, or let a boy kiss you, or do things to you?'

'That's exactly what I mean. Maybe I'm just not ready, I don't know.' Maggie tried to defend what she really knew to be true. She sighed before continuing. 'It's hard to explain, but I *feel* something deeper towards girls. I want to share myself with another girl. I want to touch and be touched by soft hands. I thought you might feel the same...' She looked at Kate from under her dark lashes in the hope for some glimmer of understanding. Kate's face remained puzzled, stony looking.

'Well, you got that fuckin' wrong, didn't you!' Kate's words came out sharp, venomous.

Feeling an unwelcome rush of adrenaline surge through her veins, Maggie eased herself off the bed. 'I think I'd better go...'

Kate folded her arms as if defending her body against further female intrusion. 'Yes, I think you better had. And, Maggie...I think we can safely say that this friendship is over. How could you even think about trying to touch me?'

'Sorry...'

With slow, measured footsteps, Maggie tentatively made her way past Kate, out of the bedroom and down the stairs, away into the chilly late-April evening air, omitting to shout her usual cheery "Ta-ra, Mrs Gould," to Kate's mum.

# Chapter 2

## Broken

'C'mon, love, eat up your toast while it's still hot.' Liz Braithwaite clucked and fussed around Maggie, while she made a fresh pot of tea. 'Or would you prefer some porridge, or cornflakes?'

Maggie flicked away at a few burnt toast crumbs on her plate, her face deadpan and emotionless.

'...Not really hungry.'

'Maggie, love, you can't go to school on an empty stomach. You've got exams soon, your 'O' levels. You've got to feed the brain.'

'Ugh, don't remind me. Exams, exams, exams – it's all I seem to hear these days!' Maggie's voice began to rise in frustration, as she attempted to get up from her chair without touching her breakfast.

'Sit down and eat, my girl. Please...' Her mum softened her tone, and continued. 'I don't know – you seem to be well out of sorts since you and Kate fell out. You two never used to fall out for long when you were little. One minute a battle, the next minute best friends. Been best friends since the first day at infants school. I don't know what–'

Maggie interrupted her mother's tirade. 'Just leave it, will you, Mum. *Please.*' Seeing the crestfallen look on her mother's face, Maggie similarly softened her voice. 'Look, we just fell out. Something big. It's making things a bit tricky in school, that's all.' She picked up the slice of toast as she headed for the kitchen door. 'Anyway, I'd better go or I'll miss the bus. I'll see you later, yeah. And, Mum…I love you. Sorry for being so grumpy, just got a lot on my plate, what with the exams and stuff. I'll see you later.'

Liz looked at her daughter, her eyes moist.

'I love you, too. And I'm sorry for being an old grump. It's a mum-thing – I worry, that's all. Try to have a good day in school – just ignore her. And take your brolly, showers are forecast for later.'

Maggie nodded and did her best to put on a reassuring smile as she headed through the kitchen door, closing it behind her. She leaned against the wall near the coat hooks and looked upwards, forcing her eyes closed in order to squeeze back unshed tears.

*Yet another day of torture to face. Another day of kids sniggering behind my back. Of kids pointing, laughing, teasing. Another day of kids shouting, "Look, there she goes…Maggie Minge-Muncher… Maggie Minge-Muncher…Maggie…"*

A tear escaped. She couldn't hold it back. *I hope you burn in Hell, Kate Gould!*

Grateful for having heeded her mother's perceptive weather-advice, Maggie sheltered under her umbrella as she waited at the bus-stop; her mind absently counting down the days to the end of the school year, and to the end of the hurtful teasing. All in all, it had not been a good day. Again. A predictable replay of name-calling.

'Ay-up, Mags. Wanna ride home?'

A familiar voice broke through Maggie's jumbled thoughts. She peered from under her umbrella to see Kate's older brother, Jimmy, pulling up to the edge of the pavement in his beloved MkIII Cortina. Jimmy was blessed with the same copper-coloured curly hair as his sister, putting no shadow of doubt over the family lineage – the Goulds with the golden hair. He and the car were rarely separated. Maggie noticed how even the raindrops barely dared to touch the hallowed paintwork; the colour of tomato soup, waxed and polished to perfection.

'Long time, no see,' he continued. 'So, are you gonna jump in, or should I just leave you here to get wet?' He grinned, and proffered the front passenger seat to Maggie.

She returned his grin with a cautious half-smile, and tentatively stepped towards the car. Maybe Kate hadn't said anything to him about their fall out?

More to the point, she hoped that Kate hadn't said anything to him about the *reason* for their fall out.

She rather hoped not.

As she got into the car, she became acutely aware that two of Jimmy's mates, Mick and Jason, were sitting in the back seat – a couple of no-gooders from the local council estate who liked to hang out with Jimmy on account of his fancy car. At least that's what Kate had once told her. The hair began to prickle on the back of her neck. She looked at Jimmy in an effort to deflect her nervousness away from the goons.

'Thanks for the lift, it's kind of you.' Maggie frantically searched her mind for something with which to make small-talk. 'You still working at Halfords?'

'Yep. Suits me fine – plenty of perks. Look at this new car-stereo player.' He directed his finger towards his newest point of pride, then cranked up the volume to allow *Queen* more ear-splitting space and sound in the car.

Maggie winced as Brian May unleashed a guitar-assault on her ears.

'Sorry, Mags.' Jimmy reached over to turn down the volume before surreptitiously glancing over his shoulder to wink at the goons in the back. He resumed his conversation back towards Maggie; his tone loaded. 'Haven't seen you round at our place for a few weeks. Our Kate tells me that you two have had a big fall-out...' He let his words hang a little before continuing. 'Kate told me what you did...' Jimmy turned full-face and stared at Maggie, then began lewdly flicking his tongue and wetting his lips, causing her to hang her head. Her cheeks burned with heat.

Maggie could feel her heart hammering in her chest and the blood rushing through her ears.

He reached over to stroke her thigh. She flinched, then froze.

Suddenly becoming more interested in what was happening in the front rather than murdering harmonies and guitar riffs to "Brighton Rock", the goons in the back stopped their air-guitaring. Mick leaned forward to join in.

'Oh, yeah...Is this the dyke that munches minge? The one you wuz telling us about?'

Maggie recoiled as she smelled the full force of his cigarette-breath.

Encouraged by Maggie's show of disgust, he elbowed his back-seat partner, then began making lewd slurping noises. The rising tension and ease by which they were making Maggie feel uncomfortable only served to fuel Mick's ego and increase his berating.

'You know what we need to do, lads? We need to introduce this young lady to some cock. What do you think, Maggie? Wouldn't you like that better than minge?' He tried to stroke her shoulder.

Maggie's whole being refused to cooperate; her breathing, heart-rate and gut-feeling all rolled out of sync. Only her brain functioned, hitting the big, red panic button. She looked across at Jimmy in the hope that the brother of her former friend – this guy that she had known almost all her life – would step in.

He did.

But not to help Maggie.

Jimmy eased the car towards the edge of town and headed in the direction of the ancient woodland, towards the old, abandoned Miller's Cottage and derelict mill. Over the years, local kids had scared each other with stories about this place – about how the old miller had lain dead for weeks before anyone had found him; his eyes pecked out by crows, his corpse nothing but a maggot infested cadaver...

A scream began to rise in Maggie, but wouldn't come out. It stayed inside, choking her breathing, choking her reasoning and life-preserving functions. She clung to her old leather satchel in the hope that it would miraculously offer protection; a talisman to ward off evil, a shield to defend her honour.

It didn't.

The two goons quickly clambered out of the rear of the Cortina then roughly dragged Maggie out of the front seat towards the old stone cottage, the overgrown foliage snagging on their legs as they pushed their way through. Jimmy went ahead to kick away the "Keep Out – Danger!" boards which were barring the doorway.

With the exception of par-for-the-course vandalism, the old kitchen looked like a time-capsule, frozen in the exact moment that the occupant had dropped dead and left this world behind. The old electric stove still had a saucepan and kettle atop, and plates were jammed into the small, porcelain sink. A wing-backed armchair lay on its side in front of the fireplace, as though it had simply rolled over and died with the owner and with the cottage. The once highly-polished brass coal scuttle had presumably been kicked around by those brave enough to enter; its once-curved body now dented, its black contents strewn about the floor.

The door was closed...

Jimmy roughly pushed Maggie backwards onto the dusty kitchen table, knocking off an old china mug in the process, where it smashed on the grimy linoleum floor. Ignoring the broken pieces under his feet, he shoved her school skirt over her hips before ripping off her knickers. His partners in crime held Maggie by the arms so that she couldn't wriggle free.

She didn't try.

Her mind and body knew what was about to happen, and knew that she was defeated. She shut her eyes, and shut her mind while the ultimate invasion of privacy took place. Her ears caught snippets of their jibes...

'Hey, Maggie, how does cock feel...?'

'Tight little sixteen year old, never been fucked...'

'I got the cherry, look there's blood on my dick...'

Laughter. Laughter. Laughter.

'My turn, move over so that she can feel a *real* man...'
Laughter. Laughter. Laughter.
'See, told ya that cock's better than minge...'
'You wanna have a go, Jase? We've opened her up for ya!'
The sound of another zip...

Realising that she was shivering and that the cottage was now quiet, Maggie dared to open her eyes. Her arms felt light as she lifted them to shield her eyes while they adjusted to the gloom.

She was alone.

She was no longer whole.

Maggie slowly inched forward to the edge of the table – the altar on which she had been defiled – until her feet touched the filthy floor. She allowed herself a few moments of reorientation while her awareness returned. In her awareness, she felt sticky wetness oozing down her inner thighs. Not wishing to touch what was there, she cautiously made her way to the corner of the kitchen to squat down and pee. The heat and cleansing qualities of the urine stung her damaged skin, causing her to bite her bottom lip. Involuntary tears began welling in her eyes, while her stomach lurched, causing the rise of acid bile to prickle the back of her throat and make her gag. She squeezed her pelvic muscles and waited, expelling as much of their liquid detritus as possible. Not wishing to look at or touch the point of invasion, Maggie eased herself up and began searching for her knickers. They lay by the side of the kitchen table – she could just make out the picture on the front: a red heart with Happy Friday. She gingerly stepped into them, feeling dampness as skin met cotton. The stinging feeling remained, and her arms felt stiff and sore from where they had held her down. Pain accompanied every step as she slowly moved towards the doorway. Her foot kicked something solid and sent it scudding across the floor – her school satchel; the shield that didn't protect her. But where was her umbrella? Her mind fought and twisted as she tried to remember the moments before...before...

In the dim light, the old furniture began morphing into crouching monsters...

She was late home.

Mum would be worried.

The walk home was painfully slow, and painfully raw. Maggie willed her mind to shut out what had just gone before; willed her mind to shut out the fact that her defilers were most likely sitting around drinking beer and laughing, reflecting on their conquest. She mentally prepared some plausible excuses for her lateness and the missing umbrella – possibly still in Jimmy's car, or dropped at the cottage. She couldn't be sure. "I must have left it on the bus" was as good a lie as any.

Maggie wiped the mud from her shoes on the rough fibres of the front doormat before going in.

'Only me, Mum. Sorry I'm late...'

She entered the front hallway and listened for a brief moment, quickly determining that her mother was in the sitting room watching TV. She could hear her beginning to move around at the cue-sound of Maggie's voice. The sitting room door opened just as Maggie reached the bottom of the stairs.

'Is that you, Maggie? You're late – I was starting to get worried. There are all kinds of bad people out there, you know. Girls getting attacked or murdered – there was another one only last week...'

'Mum! Besides, that's up in Yorkshire, in the Leeds area. That's miles away from here. I decided to go to the library to get in some extra study time, what with the 'O' levels coming up,' she lied. 'Sorry, I should have called to let you know.'

Masking her pain through gritted teeth, Maggie scurried her way upstairs, her satchel clanking by her hip.

'What about your tea? Are you going to come down for something to eat?' Liz's voice held its usual "tinged with worry" tone.

'Nah, I'm just gonna jump in the bath and then get an early night. I don't feel so good – I've got a headache. Think I overdid the studying.'

Her mum looked at the clock on the hallway wall and frowned. 'But it's only half-six. Surely you must be hungry. Come and have a bite to eat after your bath. Got to feed the brain–'

'Yeah, yeah, so you keep saying...'

'I was going to get us fish and chips with it being Friday. But what with this damned cod-war still going on with Iceland... Anyway, I cooked instead. It's your favourite, shepherd's pie with Yorkshire puddings.

Maggie sighed. As much as she could understand her mother's over-protective ways there were times when it could be so cloying.

'Okay, you win. I'll be down after my bath.'

Maggie dumped her satchel on the floor by her dressing table before sitting down as gently as possible on her bed, grateful for the softness of her bedspread. Every fibre of her being felt defiled, violated. She glanced over to her bedside table and picked up the photograph of her and her dad, Joseph – the last photo ever taken of the two of them together before he'd been cruelly snatched away by a drunk driver.

*How life can change in the blink of an eye...*

She recalled the night when Kate's dad, Sergeant Gould, had come round to their house to break the news – seeing the police car pull up outside, and him getting out accompanied by a WPC. Sergeant Gould was on duty when the station got the call about the accident, and he knew he was the only one who could deliver the news. Removing his hat, head bowed low when her mum opened the door; the look on his face. No words were needed.

*It's a pity that he'd never spoken to his son about the laws on rape.*

Would she have told her dad what Jimmy and his mates had done to her? He'd always said that if any boy hurt his princess, then he would cut off their tackle with a rusty old blade.

*Oh, to see the look on their faces if my dad had been around to keep his promise...as he systematically cut off their balls, one by one – Jimmy. Mick. Jason. And as for Kate, the bitch – this is all her fault... I would have gladly made her watch while my dad ripped off her brother's balls.*

After selecting her comfiest jim-jams and "Bay City Rollers" tartan robe, Maggie crept along the landing to lock herself in the sanctuary of the bathroom. She turned on the bath taps, then let her fingers walk along what she and her mum called their "Avon shelf", full of lotions, potions, creams and bubble bath. Keen to sanitise every inch of her body, she selected one of the more highly scented bubble baths and tipped almost the whole bottle under the running taps. Froth and fragrance began to rise from the hot water, inviting Maggie to sink into its depths. As she removed her school uniform, she noticed bruises already visible on her arms where the boys had held her down, and bruising and smears of blood and...and...traces of them, between her thighs. Though the hot water and perfumed bubble-bath stung her wounded skin, she felt grateful for the cleansing feeling that it gave. Maggie felt equally grateful that it was Friday evening – the weekend lay ahead. It would be easy to make excuses to stay in her room and study, or watch her portable TV. And tomorrow was *Jackie* magazine day; perhaps her mum would pick one up for her.

Safely enveloped under the soapy water, Maggie closed her eyes and allowed her mind to drift towards the distant future. Only a few weeks remained of school and exams before the long summer holidays. She was now, more than ever, determined to return for Sixth Form and 'A' levels, with a view to Art School or University – anything to get away from the limitations and prejudice of small-town life. At least all the bullies, scumbags and teasing bitches from her year would soon be out of the school doors, on their way to careers in the local factories or down the pit. Perhaps some might go to Technical College to learn a manual trade. She knew that Kate was returning for Sixth Form, but with any luck they could avoid each other.

Maggie rather hoped that would be the case.

# Chapter 3

## Red

Thursday 19th August – the single red circle on the calendar signified the date that the 'O' level results were due. Any day now…

Maggie's stomach lurched in anticipation – in spite of *recent events*, she felt reasonably confident of achieving her much hoped-for high grades.

She fanned herself, and absently began studying the calendar – something didn't quite add up. August was so far devoid of red crosses. There was just the 'exam-date' circle. Her brow furrowed as she flipped back to the previous month – July was similarly unmarked – no crosses. The only marked date was a circle for the last day of school. Maggie searched the recesses of her mind. Had she simply forgotten to mark things up? She went back one more month – June; no crosses, just circles indicating the exam dates. With shaking hands, Maggie flipped back one more page – the last line of three red crosses was in early May. Even though her periods were still teen-irregular, there was usually something to mark on the calendar…

Now she knew what her light-headed, sickly feeling meant. And it had nothing to do with the heatwave.

*Good God, no…*

\*\*\*

Liz Braithwaite dropped a couple of ice-cubes into two glasses before carefully pouring dandelion and burdock over them. She watched the bubbles as they rose and popped, fascinated by their spitting effervescence. She put a glass of the dark, fizzing liquid in front of Maggie, before eyeing over the calendar hanging up beside the kitchen door.

'Well, just a few more days, then the summer holidays will be over. We'd best head into town and get you some new things ready for school.' She looked at Maggie, expecting a response. All she got was a shoulder-shrug by way of a reply.

'What is it, love? You've been right off it all summer. Is it the heat? Is this heatwave getting to you?' She fanned herself with the newspaper. 'It's getting to me, I can tell y–'

Maggie cut her off, her voice low but firm. 'I won't be going back for Sixth Form. I won't be doing my 'A' levels.'

Liz stopped fanning herself, her face taut. 'But... I thought... I thought you were all set?' Her brow furrowed in puzzlement at this unexpected announcement. 'You did so well in your GCEs – you got the grades that you wanted...'

'I'm pregnant. At least, I'm pretty sure that I'm pregnant.'

Liz froze, eyes wide.

'But how? I mean, I know how, but *how*? Who? When? I don't understand...' She grabbed the edge of the sink to rebalance herself before sitting down opposite her daughter. This waif-like girl, with her whole life and career ahead of her, had just dropped the million-pound, stop-dead-in-your-tracks bombshell.

Maggie stared into her glass and held her head low so that her mother couldn't see her eyes.

'It was at the end of the school year. There was this boy – it only happened once. We were experimenting and it got out of hand. I didn't like it, so we stopped. But it was too late, if you know what I mean.' Her head remained downcast.

'Who is this boy? We need to speak to his parents...' Liz could feel the blended heat of anger and embarrassment coursing through her veins.

'Leave it, Mum. It doesn't matter. *He* doesn't matter. There's nothing between us, we were just trying things out.'

Her mother pondered her next line of questioning before asking, 'But how do you know for sure? Did you go to the chemist's to get a pregnancy test?'

Maggie raised her head, her pale blue eyes on the edge of brimming over. She looked at her mother, her face rapt with incredulity. 'A pregnancy test – in this backwater of a town? Don't be stupid. It would be round Millers Common like wildfire! No, I went to the main Family Planning Clinic in Thorpe Haddon. At least no-one knows me there.'

Her mother twizzled with her wedding ring while she contemplated the situation, calculating what to do or say next.

'And you're sure...?'

'Yes, Mum. One hundred per-cent sure. The test was positive.'

'Did the clinic give you an approximate date?'

Maggie nodded. 'Early February. They estimate somewhere around the tenth.'

A deep sigh escaped from Liz – louder and more forcefully than she intended. She looked at Maggie, uncertain of what to say or do next. A strange, heavy silence descended between them, as if time was holding its breath.

Maggie was first to break the silence. 'I want to have the baby – I don't want to take an innocent life.'

'But, Maggie, you're only sixteen. Your future...?' Liz managed to refrain from exposing her true thoughts; "destroy your life at sixteen" was what she really wanted to say. Her gaze was intent, her face set with seriousness. She chewed on her bottom lip before continuing, 'I understand. At least, I'm trying to understand. But... But what about

19

having the baby adopted if you can't face a termination? There are lots of willing couples desperate to have children and adopt.'

Maggie closed her eyes and took a deep breath before letting the flood-gates open. Her tears spilled over, her pent-up fear suddenly finding its release. Liz sprang from her seat to embrace her daughter, her only child.

'Cry all you want, my girl. Let it go. We'll figure this out, don't worry, my love.'

'I'm scared, Mum. I'm so, so scared...'

'Sshh, my love. I can well understand – I'm scared too, and I'm the grown-up here.' Desperate to burst into tears herself, Liz held Maggie even tighter. She smoothed down her daughter's spiky hair, and kissed the top of her head. Her own tears would have to wait – she needed to keep a clear head in order to figure out a way to deal with this embarrassing, inconvenient situation.

*** 

'How the hell are we going to cover up this mess...?' The rustle of the Yellow Pages being frantically turned blended in with Liz's huffed and puffed expletives. She looked up at the sound of Maggie coming into the sitting room. Her brow furrowed at the sight of her daughter before intently resuming her finger-walk through the business directory.

Maggie's voice cut through the noise of rustling pages. 'I'm really sorry, Mum. All this embarrassment I'm causing you.'

Liz looked up from her "no idea what I'm really looking for" search and stared at Maggie. She pondered a moment before answering. 'Yes, it is a little embarrassing, Maggie.' She longed to say "embarrassing, shameful and inconvenient," but thought better of it. She continued, 'But I've been doing a lot of thinking. You're only young, my love – even if you still go through with the birth, I really think the wisest thing would be adoption.'

Maggie held her head low while her fingers picked at imaginary fluff on her top. A sigh expelled as she spoke.

'Yes, you're right. Let's just give away the embarrassment and get on with our lives like nothing has happened.'

'Maggie! Don't you dare talk to me like that! How on earth can we afford to raise a baby? There's only my part-time income from working at the accountants – you know that.' Liz re-composed herself and lowered her voice. 'When I was younger, there used to be special homes run by nuns for girls who unexpectedly found themselves in the family way. There was one over in Woodcliffe, if I remember rightly. They took care of everything. Thank goodness there's a bit of rainy-day money tucked away from your dad's insurance.'

Maggie looked up at the mention of her dad, her eyes meeting her mother's. She knew *exactly* what her mother was going to say next.

'And thank goodness your dad isn't here to see this. I'm quite sure he would have...have... Well, I don't know, but he wouldn't have been very happy!'

In her heart of hearts, Maggie knew that her mother was right – giving up the baby for adoption meant that she wouldn't have to face a daily reminder of her private ordeal. But it wasn't the child's fault – he or she was just an innocent player in all this.

*No need to punish the innocent...*

'Ah, here it is, under "Private Nursing Homes".' Liz marked the page while she went to get a notepad and pen to write down the details.

The blood began pounding in Maggie's head and she could feel her palms becoming moist with nervous energy. There was so much more that she needed to off-load, so much more that was chewing away at her soul. Should she live her life full of secrets and lies? Honesty had always been the very backbone of her upbringing.

Liz came back into the sitting room and sat down while she wrote out the information for "Woodcliffe Grange – Sisters of St Mary; Home for the Welfare & Care of Young Ladies". She tapped the pen on the notepad, her composure having almost returned to her usual efficient-secretary mode.

'There, I'll give them a call and see what they've got to say.' She came and sat by Maggie and put a reassuring arm around her daughter. 'I'm sorry, my love. But the shock of your news just knocked me sideways.' She squeezed Maggie, who remained tense in spite of the hug. 'We can always tell people that you decided to go away, to art college or something, instead of doing your 'A' levels. No shame in that.'

*Honesty...honesty is the best policy* – 'Mum...'

'Yes, love.'

Maggie kept her head low as she spoke. *Okay, maybe just a half-truth, not the whole truth...* 'There's something I want to tell you. There was a reason why I was experimenting with this boy...I...I–'

'Maggie – we all experiment and try things out.'

'I know that. But, I don't... I don't know how to explain... I don't–'

Liz patted Maggie on the knee and stood up, grabbing the Yellow Pages and notepad as she headed towards the sitting room door. 'Life is full of experiments – that's how we learn from our mistakes, my girl.'

Maggie, mouth open, stared wordlessly at the back of her mother's head as she vanished into the hallway to the telephone.

*I wanted to tell you that I don't feel anything for boys – I wanted to tell you that I'm a lesbian. But if I was really brave enough to tell you the whole truth, the real truth, I would tell you that it wasn't really an experiment, it was rape...*

But they were words that remained in her mind and unspoken.

Words that never reached her mother's ears.

# Chapter 4

## Hidden Away

The ornate wrought-iron gates swung open to allow the taxi entry into the grounds of St Mary's at Woodcliffe Grange. Beautifully tended and manicured gardens were bounded by a high red brick wall, and framed with gnarled old oak trees and tall, elegant silver birch, elm and maple. The flower beds were in their last breath of early autumn colour and splendour before expiring into their winter sleep. Central to the gardens, the old Grange stood on a slightly raised mound, its arched Gothic-windowed eyes maintaining a watchful presence over the grounds, while its pointed roof-line reached heavenwards. To the side of the Grange stood a small, private church – the beating heart to the Sisters at St Mary's.

Alerted by the arrival of the taxi, one of the young novices was already waiting on the doorstep to greet Maggie and her mother. The simple event of seeing the Sister come out of the large doorway caused Maggie to smile, being reminiscent of a figure popping out of a cuckoo-clock doorway. She half expected her to be on a spring and pop back in again. If nothing else, it relieved a little of the tension that had been plaguing Maggie prior to their arrival.

Sister Alice greeted mother and daughter warmly, before leading them across the expansive hallway to the Reverend Mother's office. The

Sister's soft shoes squeaked on the highly polished wooden floor as she walked ahead of them, causing Liz to playfully glare at her daughter and shake her head, as if to say *"don't you dare laugh..."*.

'Ah, Margaret, Mrs Braithwaite, welcome to Woodcliffe Grange.' The Reverend Mother extended her hand, her shake firm and authoritative. 'Sister Alice, perhaps you would bring a tray of tea for our guests. Thank you, dear.' She sat behind her desk, and indicated to Maggie and Liz to sit in the armchairs opposite. Late afternoon sunlight filtered through the tall, stained glass windows, framing the Reverend Mother with a jewel-like, ethereal glow.

After Sister Alice had delivered the tray of tea and plain biscuits, Reverend Mother began explaining the routine that would become Maggie's daily life at Woodcliffe Grange until the baby was born and signed over for adoption.

'Your day will begin at 7:00 am with prayers and quiet contemplation, before breakfast at 7:30. After you have helped to clear away and clean up, you will attend school until lunchtime. We feel that it's important for you to maintain your education – you're about to go through one of the biggest emotional challenges that you will ever face, so you need to build your resolve and maturity. Our study programme will help you with this.'

Liz nodded her approval, as the Reverend Mother continued. 'After lunch, you will again be expected to help with kitchen duties, then there will be a rotation of different recreational activities over the week.'

'Such as?' asked Liz.

'I was just coming to that,' replied the Reverend Mother, rather stiffly. Maggie and Liz unconsciously adjusted their sitting positions to bolt-upright in the armchairs, an auto-response to the Reverend Mother's chastisement.

'As you can see, the Grange has extensive, beautifully tended gardens, so the resident girls help out with light gardening duties. There are also home economics classes, art, sewing, reading, and relaxation classes, as well as guidance on what to expect as the due date draws near.' She paused for a moment to allow the list to sink in. 'Dinner is at six o'clock sharp, then once all the kitchen chores have been completed, evening prayers are at seven. The daily routines, lessons and prayers are overseen by the Sisters of St Mary's. The girls are then allowed a little evening recreational time from seven-thirty until lights-out at ten. And finally, you will be allowed two fifteen minute telephone calls per week, and can write and send two letters per week. This is all included in the expenses that you pay, of course. Any questions?'

Maggie and Liz looked at each other then shrugged their shoulders with an absence of what to say next.

'I...I think that you've, erm, given us a good overview of everything, thanks, Reverend Mother,' Liz replied. 'What do you think, Maggie?'

Maggie nodded, her mind blank; overwhelmed with the still-to-be-absorbed information.

'Good. That just leaves us with the formality of the paperwork. We need to go over that, and all here present to sign. When is the baby due, by the way? Did the Family Planning Clinic give you an estimated date?'

Liz interjected without giving Maggie the chance to speak. 'Yes, they gave her a due date of February 10th.'

The Reverend Mother popped her half-moon spectacles onto the end of her nose while she wrote down notes pertaining to the approximate birth date. She took a deep breath before carefully going over the different sections of documentation, her voice formal: Duties and Maternity Care, Midwifery Care, Postnatal Care, and Adoption. Every now and again she would look over the rim of her glasses to make sure that her audience was following along.

Liz squeezed Maggie's hand, the hand of her bewildered little girl. The little girl who was pregnant by an unknown boy, and this was the best solution.

It was time to sign.

After completion of the paperwork, the Reverend Mother rose from her seat then rang a little bell. 'Wonderful. Then I'll hand you over to Sister Theresa – she will show you to your room and help you get settled in.' The old nun extended her hand, the handshake signalling that their conference was over. And as if on cue, the sunlight which had been filtering through the stained glass windows suddenly became blocked out by clouds, effectively turning off the colourful aura from around the Reverend Mother.

A silent Sister Theresa had already slipped into the office ready to take Maggie and her mother to what would become Maggie's home for the next few months. A place of sanctuary; a place where she would be hidden from view until the embarrassment had been dealt with.

Maggie picked up her suitcase and dutifully followed Sister Theresa and her mum.

*Damn you to hell, Kate Gould...*

*Damn you to hell...*

# Chapter 5

## Bohemian Anarchy

The meagre supplies rolled around the wire supermarket basket, testimony that Liz was no longer doing the weekly shop for a family. Or even for two. But for one. One lonely person.

Though it had only been a few weeks since Maggie had gone away, Liz could already feel the adverse effects that it was having on her own well-being. She was hardly cooking for herself, preparing only the simplest of meals, and then when she ate, her stomach could barely hold down the food she was trying to nourish herself with.

*Is this what guilt feels like? Is this what refusal to accept Maggie's predicament feels like?*

But it was for the best, of that she was sure. It wasn't right for the poor girl to be burdened with the results of an *experiment*; not when there were willing, childless couples who were desperate to adopt.

She moved down the aisle, selecting a small can of baked beans. Or was it better value to buy a large one and split it for two meals? The word "experiment" came to her mind again – it had been haunting her since, well, since Maggie first mentioned it. What did Maggie mean by *experimenting* with boys? Experimenting with sex? She really must ask Maggie when next they spoke on the telephone.

'Oh, hello, Liz. How are you? I haven't seen you in ages.'

Liz's train of thought was interrupted by a familiar voice. Kate's mum, Barbara, pulled alongside her; her shopping trolley loaded to the brim with the "feeding the five thousand" look. Liz couldn't help but notice the packets of chocolate biscuits, bottles of fizzy drinks, and bottles of wine and beer. She smiled, and nodded towards the trolley.

'Looks like someone's having a party...'

Barbara Gould waved her hand dismissively, 'Oh, this little lot. Just the usual Saturday trolley load, feeding the hungry locusts. They eat me out of house and home, they do.' She laughed lightly, and shook her head. 'Anyway, how are you? I hear from our Katie that your Maggie didn't go back to school for her 'A' levels. Gone to some art school instead.'

Liz knew the day would come when she would have to start fending off invasive questions, yet she still felt cornered, particularly with Kate's mum. They had been friends, well, acquaintances, for as long as their daughters had been friends. Lying didn't feel right, but it was her only option.

'Yes, that's right. Decided that art was more her thing rather than academics. Much happier with a paintbrush and pencil than an ink pen.' She nodded and shrugged, her eyes looking everywhere except at Barbara in a bid to cover her dishonesty.

Barbara either didn't, or wouldn't, take the body-language message that Liz was trying her best to convey, and pressed on with her mild interrogation and investigations. Her voice took on a nasal tone.

'Well, I suppose art college is more for those of a bohemian nature. Which one did she go to?'

'Erm, she's gone to the one over in Chesterfield. A two-year foundation course. Staying in student digs,' came Liz's quick, rehearsed and researched reply. 'And if all goes well, she'll probably go to Salford University for her degree.' She knew Barbara was bound to check out the validity of this information. Then again, her husband was a police sergeant – investigations were standard practice.

'Hmm, the Art College in Chesterfield, you say. Yes, these arty types...anything goes. Should suit Maggie perfectly.'

Liz could feel that Barbara's tone of conversation was leading somewhere. She began picking up tins and adding them to her shopping basket as a diversion, regardless of whether she needed tuna, or sweetcorn, or peas. But Barbara remained firmly parked beside her, the shopping trolley a physical barrier blocking Liz's escape.

'You know what Maggie did to our Katie, don't you?'

The direct question stopped Liz dead in her tracks, catching her off-guard. She looked at Barbara, her brow furrowed in puzzlement, her mouth open ready to speak.

Barbara cut in first.

'Your Maggie touched her, you know, in *that* kind of way, in places where girls shouldn't touch each other. And she tried to kiss her. Our Katie was in shock, obviously. Well, that was that as far as our Kate was concerned. Doesn't want anything to do with a weirdo. So, like I say, art school, with its arty-farty bohemian types, should be right up her alley.'

Liz immediately sprang to her daughter's defence. 'Did you just call my daughter a "weirdo"?'

Barbara took on a snooty air. 'Well, no, not me. But our Katie did. Well, it is a bit weird, isn't it? It's not natural... I'm not having any of that kind of hanky-panky in my house.'

That was the limit for Liz. She rammed the wire basket into Barbara, forcefully pushing her out of the way. Then she let her anger fly.

'You and your family think that you're so high and mighty. Mr and Mrs Perfect and their perfect kids. Well, let me tell you – your daughter made Maggie's life hell at school. Now I know why she didn't want to go back. So, if you'll excuse me...'

Supported by a wave of adrenaline, Liz pushed her way past Barbara, holding her head as high and as proud as she could. Not sure how long the adrenaline would hold her legs, she quickly headed for the exit, dumping her basket of shopping near the check-out. She needed fresh air.

But at least she had now figured out the mystery of why Maggie had been experimenting with a boy. She was trying to find her true self.

*Oh, Maggie, Maggie, Maggie – I'm so sorry for not listening to you...*

\*\*\*

Eager to divulge her newly acquired gossip, Barbara Gould had prepared the family's favourite meal of meat and potato pie, followed by apple crumble and custard – an evening meal which was bound to draw everyone to the dining table. Her lips curled with a sly tilt – time to dish out the news as an accompaniment to the food.

'Guess who I saw in Sainsbury's today? Maggie's mother.'

The clatter of knives and forks lessened as the family tuned in their attentions to Barbara.

'Yes. She looked a little bit surprised to see me. Anyway, it turns out that Maggie has gone to the big art college in Chesterfield.'

Kate rolled her eyes feigning disinterest, yet eager to know more. She pushed her plate towards her mother for a little more pie, and an extra portion of information.

Playing to her audience, Barbara continued. 'Well, I said to her, art college is perfect for these bohemian types. And let's face it, Maggie is a bit weird like that, with her punky hair – all anarchy and loud music.' Her verbal diatribe had been unleashed, and would not be curtailed until she'd expunged all her prejudice. 'Arty-farty hippies, all kaftans and communes. Think the world owes them a living. Harks back to the sixties. Anyway, I told her that I wasn't having any of that lesbian stuff in my house.'

Kate's eyes went wide-eyed with shock.

'Mum! Surely you didn't say anything to her mother about that. It's embarrassing!'

'Well, of course I did. She has a right to know what her daughter's been up to.'

Jimmy blanched then spluttered, as flakes of pastry got stuck in his throat. He quickly took a gulp of water to clear his airway. Just how much had Maggie told her mother? He rallied to his own defence, just in case. 'These lesbians get what's coming to 'em, if you ask me...'

Mr Gould interjected, surprised by Jimmy's outburst. 'Well, nobody's asking you. And what do you mean by that?'

'Nothing! Just a bit weird, that's all.'

Drawing on his years of having been exposed to every aspect of human nature, Mr Gould took a more open stance. 'Leave the poor girl alone – it takes all sorts to make a world. Maybe she's just going through an experimental phase? Or maybe that's just the way she is. Love is love, in all its forms... Now, let's change the subject.'

Eyes downcast, the family knew that Mr Gould had retained a defensive soft-spot for Maggie ever since he'd had to convey the news that her father had been killed by a drunk driver.

Case closed.

# Chapter 6

## Sunday Confessional

It had been a long day. A long, long, boring Sunday filled with mundane, time-killing jobs. Anything to pass the time until Maggie's Sunday evening phone call. Sundays and Wednesdays – they were Maggie's assigned times, after evening prayers.

Liz closed her eyes as she sat by the phone waiting for it to ring; *willing* for it to ring. Though it had only been a few days since she'd last spoken to Maggie, she felt such a strong pull to speak with her daughter. Yesterday's chance meeting with Kate's mother in the supermarket had thrown a completely different light (or was it cast a shadow?), over the whole sordid affair of Maggie's pregnancy. Liz could feel her adrenaline beginning to surge and pulse quicken as she recalled Barbara's accusations.

She tapped the telephone receiver as if to encourage a connection. The clock showed just a few minutes after seven-thirty.

*Calm down, Liz. Give the poor girl a chance to get from the church to the office...*

Before the telephone had even announced the incoming call with half a dingle, Liz snatched up the receiver.

'Maggie? Is that you, love?'

'Yes, Mum, it's me. Hi. Wow, that was a quick pick-up...'

Liz could hear her daughter giggle at her mother's speedy response, but sensed that it was guarding tension.

'Just eager to hear from you, and hear all your news...'

'Mum – I'm stuck in a convent. I eat, I sleep, I do chores, I pray. Or, at least, I pretend to pray... There's not really much in the way of news.' Maggie paused for a moment, then laughed, 'Having said that, Reverend Mother ripped off her habit this morning, and ran naked through the convent...'

'Maggie!'

'Okay, okay, sorry. But no, nothing much is happening. The baby is really beginning to move and roll around now, and I've got a little bump showing. The Sisters have given me some hideous maternity clothes to wear – I can barely fit into any of my own stuff now. That's about it really...' Maggie turned the conversation towards her mother. 'What about you? What's been happening in the world beyond the high walls? I'm sure life in Millers Common must be full of excitement.'

Liz seized the moment. 'Erm... Well, I saw Katie's mum in Sainsbury's yesterday.' She could feel the hair beginning to rise on her arms in anticipation of the impending news that she was about to divulge. 'She told me why Kate had fallen out with you. That you'd tried to touch her, you know, *like that*, and that it had freaked her out...'

Maggie could feel her heartbeat beginning to quicken. 'Oh... What else did she say?'

'She said that you were one of those lesbians, and a weirdo. And that's why Kate didn't want to be your friend anymore. Is it true, Maggie?' Liz paused to give Maggie time to reply. She could hear Maggie's breathing, heavy, tense.

'I've been wanting to tell you. I keep trying to tell you. But it's just so difficult – I don't know where or how to begin. But yes, Mum. I just feel – I don't even know how to describe it – but I just feel cold around boys. I look at boys, and, well – I don't know. There's just nothing there.'

'I don't really understand what you're trying to explain, Maggie. What about talking to one of the Sisters, or to a doctor?' Liz waved her free hand around, as if in a face-to-face conversation.

'Mum, you can't just wave a magic wand and make it go away. Or take tablets for it. It doesn't work like that. It's how I feel deep within. It isn't something that I can turn on or off like a switch. You have to understand that.'

'I'm trying to understand, Maggie, but–'

Maggie's voice began rising in pitch. 'There are no "buts", Mum. This is me. This is who I am. What I am.' She heard a shuffle the other side of the office door, a reminder that Sister Theresa was within ear-shot. She lowered her voice. 'Please try and understand, Mum.'

'Have you tried *it*, you know, with a girl? How do you know for sure?'

'Oh, come on, Mum. It isn't something you shout about, and certainly not in our town – I found out the hard way, remember? Look at all the problems that it caused at school – all the bullying and teasing, just because I told my best friend. My life was made hell.' Maggie could feel the heat rising in her eyes as she fought back tears.

'Is that why you experimented with this boy? To see what you really felt?' Liz still felt like she could convince Maggie that it was all in her head.

'Yes, I suppose so, if that's what you want me to say.' Maggie paused, her eyes catching sight of the crucifix behind the desk. Despite his obvious pain, Jesus was smiling at her; benevolent, understanding. Her pain was his pain. She shifted uncomfortably in the armchair.

*Honesty, Maggie. Honesty...*

She took a deep breath before continuing, 'Mum, I... Well, it was... The boys – they... It's hard for me to talk about, very hard, but they–'

Sister Theresa knocked gently on the office door then entered, gesturing on her watch to signal that Maggie's fifteen minutes were over.

'Look, Mum, I've got to go. My time's up. I'll call you again on Wednesday, yeah. Love you, Mum...'

A silence hung between the two of them. A silence that held a thousand unspoken words and a seething mass of caged emotions.

'I love you too, Maggie. Take care...'

The line buzzed, disconnected.

The defensive nature of Maggie's replies ignited Liz's instinct – that innate instinct which tells a mother when her child is withholding information. She returned the telephone receiver to its cradle and closed her eyes. October rain lashed against the front door, and she could feel a draught blowing through the letter-box. Liz's mind fixated on one statement –

*Maggie said "The boys – they". "They" is a plural pronoun...*

# Chapter 7

## Quiet Contemplation

Sister Theresa turned off the office light then locked the heavy wooden door, the key turning with a rusty, scraping reluctance. Maggie dutifully waited, sitting on one of the hard, wooden chairs which were positioned two either side of the door.

'There, all locked and safe. Shall I walk with you to the sitting room? Perhaps we could play a board game together, or watch some television?'

Maggie shrugged noncommittally, her eyes downcast.

The young Sister looked at her charge, her head slightly tilted.

'You look troubled, Margaret. Would you like to talk?'

Maggie shrugged again, then nodded. She looked up at Sister Theresa, her eyes full to the brim with unshed tears.

'Oh, you poor girl.' Sister Theresa reached out her hand towards Maggie and gently led her towards the empty sitting room. The wall lights and single table lamp offered a calming glow to the heavily wood-panelled room. She placed Maggie in one of the armchairs beside the fire, and sat opposite in the other armchair.

'There, that's better. Was it a difficult phone call? I'm guessing that you called your mother?'

The flood-gate of tears opened, wetting Maggie's cheeks. She nodded, and accepted a handful of tissues from the Sister, wiping her face dry before replying.

'Yes, it was a difficult call. I confessed something to my mum that she didn't seem willing to accept. Something about me.' She paused to gather her thoughts. 'But I was always brought up to be honest, and that's what I was trying to be – honest with myself and honest with others...'

'Well, maybe she just needs a little time to let it sink in. I'm sure she'll come round and accept what you say, whatever it is.' The young nun patted a reassuring hand on Maggie's knee. 'I know these fifteen-minute phone calls don't allow much time, especially when you need to talk about deep or difficult issues.'

Maggie nodded. Her hands fidgeted with the damp, crumpled tissues.

'There's just so much that I need to tell her, but I find it really difficult to say the words, or explain things. To explain how I feel, and what's going on in my head.'

Sister Theresa pondered a moment. 'Well, you say that it's difficult to *say* the words, but what about if you try writing them? Put all your thoughts down on paper? You can take all the time that you need to write, but it gives you a chance to say all the things that you want to say. Why don't you try writing a letter instead?'

The cloud that had been hanging over Maggie appeared to have been lifted. She looked up and smiled at Sister Theresa.

'Thank you, Sister. Yes, I think that would help.' She eased herself out of the armchair, fuelled with new purpose.

'Happy to help, Margaret. Tell you what, why don't you go and make yourself a cup of tea and take it up to your room. There's some writing paper in the desk drawer.'

'Yes. Yes, I will. And thanks again, Sister Theresa. Thanks for the talk.'

Maggie screwed up the third attempt at her letter and launched it into the wastepaper basket. She drained the last of her tea, her pen tapping on the writing pad as if to draw out her thoughts.

Tap-tap-tap.

Tap-tap-tap...

Sun. 17th October, 1976.

Dear Mum,

I know I keep saying it, but I can't apologise enough for the mess, shame and embarrassment that I've brought to the both of us. I'm so, so sorry!

I had so much that I wanted to say to you on the phone tonight, but it's really difficult for me to find the words, or to explain things. I hope that you can accept me for who I am and what I am. I have accepted it. This is me.

There is one thing that I really want to tell you. That I really NEED to tell you. I didn't end up pregnant because I was trying things out with a boy. This is going to be really difficult to explain, and will come as a shock to you, of that I'm sure. But I'm pregnant because I was raped. Yes, that's what I said — raped. Three boys took me against my will and they did these horrible things to me. Remember that day when I was late home from school? I'm really sorry, I should have told you, but I just didn't know what to say. I hoped that it would all just go away — I never expected it to come to this. They drove me to the old Miller's Cottage on the edge of the town. I'm sorry, I couldn't stop them. One of the boys was Katie Gould's brother, Jimmy. I'm not sure of the names of the other boys — it's those two thugs that he hangs around with. They did it because Katie told them that I'd touched her and all that stuff.

Please don't go to the police about it. I just want this all to be over. I just want to have the baby and move on. Please, Mum. Promise me that you won't go to the police!!! I can't face all the public humiliation and shame. This is bad enough. But I at least owe you some kind of explanation and reasons for this situation.

I love you, Mum, and I never meant to hurt you.

Thank you for everything.

Maggie xxx

With shaking hands, Maggie re-read the letter, her confessional. Seeing the words on paper somehow made the whole sordid ordeal even more official – in black and white for all eternity. Could she trust her mother not to say anything? Not to go to the police? It was, after all, a very serious crime that had taken place. She began tapping the pen again.

Tap-tap-tap.

Tap-tap-tap.

'Bastards!' She took the sheets of vellum and screwed them up into a ball before launching them into the waste bin.

Defeated, Maggie lay on her bed. The last thing that she saw before she fell asleep was the picture hanging above her desk. Jesus, with arms outstretched, was smiling benevolently at her once again.

When Maggie awoke to the alarm clock the next morning, she was still on top of the bed. Cold and stiff, she was sorely tempted to wriggle under the blankets to thaw out her chilled muscles and joints. Realising that it would soon be breakfast and prayers, she slowly began flexing her fingers and toes in order to get the blood flowing again.

Jesus was still smiling at her.

'Oh, fuck off! Sorry, I don't mean to be rude, but there's really nothing to smile about…'

After her warming stretches, she lay for a moment, allowing her senses to return and her mind to fully awaken.

*Another day of...what? Solitude. Shame. Shame. And even more shame. My cross to bear.*

She smiled at her religious analogy.

The letter that she'd written to her mother came to her mind. She padded across the cold bedroom floor to the waste bin and retrieved the letter from its depths. The crumpled confessional. She placed the sheets of vellum on the desk and began smoothing out the creases. Words that needed to be said. But...

Maggie carefully folded the letter and placed it inside her Bible. She looked at the picture of smiling Jesus above her desk.

*Our secret – for now...*

# Chapter 8

## Unholy Thoughts

Maggie looked at the Nativity display; *Mother Mary, the virgin who gave birth to a child in a barn. What did Joseph really think? He seemed very accepting of the situation. Mary was having another man's child...*

She touched her bump and felt her unborn child move.

*"No room at the inn. No room at the inn."* Wasn't that how the *story went? Moved on. Push the burden somewhere else. Hide it away.*

The cold stone of the church floor struck up through her central core, causing her to shiver. She could feel the end of her nose tingle with the frigid air. A childhood memory invaded her thoughts; her dad always said that she looked like a little elf in the winter, with her rosy cheeks and bright pink nose – like one of Santa's little helpers.

Santa.

Christmas. The time of goodwill to all men.

*What would Christmas be like in the convent?*

If she hung her stocking on the end of the bed, would Santa come?

*No.*

He'd already checked his list. Checked it twice.

She'd definitely been naughty.

Not nice.

# Chapter 9

## It's Time

The midwife examined Maggie in-between her contractions.

'You're doing well. You're almost there, my dear. I can feel the top of the baby's head beginning to crown.' She massaged Maggie's bump as if to encourage the baby to quicken its exit.

Another contraction tightened around Maggie's abdomen, causing her to cry out and grip the cold flannel that she was holding.

'I'm so hot...' Tears of frustration joined the sweat rolling down her forehead. She put the cloth over her face to try and dissipate some of the heat. 'Where's my mum?'

'She's on her way, Margaret. The Reverend Mother called her once your labour was well established. I'm sure she'll be here any mo–'

'Maggie, my love. I got here as quickly as I could.' Liz blustered into the delivery room, gowned and ready to support her daughter. Seeing her in distress, she cradled Maggie, then took the cloth to run it under the cold tap.

As if reading Liz's mind, the midwife began updating her with Maggie's current status, just as Maggie heaved herself up onto her knees into a squat, feeling the overwhelming urge to start pushing. The midwife checked, feeling the baby's head breaching, ready.

Assisted by the midwife and her mother, Maggie pushed, panted and screamed her way through the delivery, straining with every fibre of her bloated body. She almost looked too small for the purpose of carrying a child.

Too small.

Too young.

Too innocent.

All stripped and taken away from her prematurely, thrusting her into the very different world of adulthood.

In the calm moment that descends after birth, Maggie swaddled her tiny son close to her body. His inky blue newborn eyes looked around, bewildered; suddenly thrust from darkness into the light. His tiny fists flailed; the movements jerky and uncontrolled. She gazed in wonderment, finally getting to meet the innocent passenger that she'd been carrying.

The midwife interrupted her quiet moment of contemplation.

'Well, he's only little; 6lb 2oz, but otherwise he seems fine.' She smiled. 'Saturday's child – how does the rhyme go? Saturday's child...?

'Isn't it, "works hard for a living"?' Liz answered.

'Yes, I think that's it – "Saturday's child works hard for a living". There you go, Margaret – his little hands are already busy working.' She laughed lightly, and nodded towards the baby, who now had his hand gripped tightly around Maggie's little finger.

She finished writing up her notes, speaking as she wrote. 'Date: Saturday 12th February, 1977. Weight: 6lb 2oz. Father: Unknown...'

Hearing the midwife make an official note of the child's unknown paternity, Maggie blushed. She looked down at the now sleeping newborn. The fair, slightly copper-coloured fuzz crowning the child's peachy head was a prime indicator as to who had spawned him.

'Do you have a name for the child yet?'

Maggie nodded. 'Ben – Benjamin Braithwaite. I'm going to call him Benjamin in honour of my grandad.'

Liz looked at Maggie and smiled at the mention of her father's name. The old renegade had always been a hero in Maggie's eyes – both he and Maggie's grandmother. The "Gallivanting Glovers" as they used to be known, were nomads and adventurers who used to go everywhere together on their motorcycle and sidecar combo, until they retired to Matlock Bath. Just because they were too infirm to ride motorbikes didn't mean that their biker-passion had lessened. Walking the Parade to admire the bikes had become their Sunday afternoon ritual to replace their own cruising.

The midwife made a note of his given name, then commented, 'It's perhaps not for me to say, but you realise there's every likelihood that his adoptive parents will change his name.'

With tear-loaded eyes, Maggie nodded and shrugged. Her hormones and newly acquired maternal instincts kicked in. She held the child to her; protective, defensive.

'Right then, you're all sorted, my love. Everything went well. Just a couple of stitches from where I had to cut you, but otherwise, the delivery was fine. Well done, Margaret.' The midwife came and gave Maggie a hug before shaking Liz's hand. 'I'll go and get one of the porters to come and wheel you up to the ward. Right, I'll leave you two ladies for the moment.'

'Thanks for your help,' acknowledged Liz.

'No problem, Mrs Braithwaite. I have the best job in the world...' She smiled at Maggie, who seemed to be deep in thought while gazing at little Ben.

She was indeed deep in thought –

*Here's your bastard, Jimmy Gould. And one day you're going to pay for this...*

# Chapter 10

## Burning Bridges

'Are you quite sure about this, Margaret? It's a huge decision and commitment that you're contemplating.' The Reverend Mother looked over her spectacles at Maggie, looking for signs of weakness or ambivalence.

Maggie nodded. 'Yes, Reverend Mother, I'm very sure.'

'And what does your mother say about this?'

'I haven't talked to her about it. It's my decision.'

The heavy, rhythmic clunk-clunk of the old grandfather clock marked the length of silence between the Reverend Mother and Maggie.

The elderly nun changed to a more sympathetic tone. 'You do realise that parenting isn't a decision to be taken lightly? And you'll endure an awful lot of judgment beyond these walls, Margaret. There's a lot of negativity and stigma attached to being a young, single mother, you know.'

'Yes, I realise that...'

A deep-seated concern plagued the old woman – she was not giving up easily on her teen charge, and fought hard with her wise words of counsel. 'Why don't you give yourself a few more days to think about it, Margaret? Your hormones are putting you in a very vulnerable position.'

Maggie cradled Ben closely to her, his copper-blonde fuzz poking through the top of his crocheted baby blanket. After returning to the Grange since the birth, the past few days of convalescence had only served to strengthen the bond that she felt with the innocent child. Though only she knew the truth behind Ben's conception she had never wanted to terminate the pregnancy, as scared as she was at the time.

'Like I said, Reverend Mother – yes, I'm very sure that I want to keep Ben. We'll make it work.'

'Very well, Margaret. But I need you to sign a disclaimer which reneges on your adoption agreement. This is quite irregular, you know. Most of our young girls are usually relieved to hand over their illegitimate children.' She placed a kindly hand on Maggie's as she reached for the pen to counter-sign the paperwork.

'Then may God go with you, and keep you safe on life's journey, Margaret. God bless you both. I'll make the necessary arrangements for your departure.'

\*\*\*

'You did what...!'

Maggie held the telephone handset away from her ear, the screech in her mother's voice posing a risk to her ear-drum.

'I reneged on the adoption agreement. I'm going to keep Ben.'

'And the Reverend Mother let you?'

'Yes, she was very sympathetic towards my decision. I reassured her that I'd thought it through.'

'How could you, Maggie? After all that you've been through. After all that WE'VE been through. And how am I going to explain this to people, eh? Won't I look a fool after all the lies that I've been spinning on your behalf!'

'But, Mum...I--'

'But nothing, my girl. Have you really thought this through, eh? How on earth are we going to manage?' Liz was struggling to catch her breath, her head in a spin of confusion. 'This is all just too much...too much! And what about all this lesbian stuff – has that changed now that you've had a baby?'

Liz's question caught Maggie off-guard. 'Mum, just because I've had a baby doesn't change the way that I feel, or the way that I am. That has nothing to do with this discussion.' She could hear her mother's "hrmph..." at the other end of the phone line. Maggie tried a more reassuring take, giving her voice a more assertive edge. 'Honestly, you don't need to worry about anything, Mum. The convent has a contract with a private landlord. They will help set me up with a little refuge home. It's basic, but it's furnished. They'll put me in touch with the right people in the social services. Besides, the Sisters have a "Care of Duty in the Community", or something, so they will come for regular fortnightly visits. We'll be fine, Mum. Really.'

'You'll be fine – is that what you really think? Do you really think that it's going to be so easy, Maggie?'

'Oh, come on, Mum. The Reverend Mother told me that the door will always be open at the convent if I ever need any spiritual guidance. She told me that Jesus is always happy to welcome stray lambs back to the fold.' Maggie began chewing on her bottom lip, her composure on the verge of crumbling.

'And since when did you get a dose of religion?' snarled Liz.

'I didn't – nothing's changed there! I just took the Reverend Mother's words metaphorically – she meant that she wouldn't see me forsaken or abandoned.'

Liz closed her eyes and tried to even out her breathing while she thought of her next line. 'Well girl, you've made your bed, you can lie in it...'

'So, what are you saying exactly, Mum?'

'Maggie – I never wanted you to have this child in the first place. That stay at the convent cost me a fortune, and now they've gone and brainwashed you that everything will be okay because Jesus says so. Well, you're on your own with this ridiculous decision.'

'You mean you're cutting me off?' The disbelief in Maggie's voice was evident, her voice suddenly small. She looked at the receiver, eyes wide, before blinking away the threat of tears.

But the conviction in Liz's voice told Maggie that she meant every word as she repeated them.

'Yes, Maggie. That's exactly what I'm saying. I never wanted any part of this, and I still don't.'

The connection on the telephone line went as dead as Liz's relationship with her daughter.

# Chapter 11

## All Grown Up

'Here we are – home sweet home, Margaret.' Sister Alice slowed the Morris Traveller to a stop at the kerb-side, outside of what was to be Maggie's new home.

Maggie wiped the condensation from the car's side window then craned her neck to take a preliminary look at 23 Woodland Row; a neat little mid-terraced house with a tiny garden, fronted by a low brick wall. Steps led up to the front door.

Sister Alice jumped out then flipped the front passenger seat forward to allow Maggie and baby Ben to struggle their way out of the back into the grey, late-February fog.

Ben grizzled, nonplussed at being handled in such an ungainly manner. With breath-clouds leading the way, Maggie followed the Sister up the little front path then waited at the bottom step while the door was unlocked.

'You two go on in and take a look around, while I fetch your bags and Ben's pram. Oh yes, and there's a little box of food to help get you started. It's what people donate, so that we can make food parcels for the needy.'

Maggie smiled, and nodded her acknowledgement.

*So, is that what I've been reduced to – a "needy" case...?*

She snuggled Ben close to her body as she glanced around the sitting room – there was an old bamboo two-seater sofa plus two armchairs, with a matching circular glass-topped bamboo coffee table. At least there was a portable TV, even if the little TV stand was missing a strip of teak veneer. The wall unit on the back wall was in a similar flaky condition, resplendent with circular hot-cup marks. Maggie noticed that the room had a homely-looking rustic brick fireplace with open-fire grate, but there was no radiator to be seen. A Persian-style hearth-rug framed the front of the fireplace and added a splash of colour to the otherwise neutral décor; the swirling, decorative pattern cleverly hiding any evidence of burn marks from stray embers. Having only ever been acquainted with a gas fire and central heating at her mother's house, the knotted tassel fringes of the rug seemed as tangled as the knots that were starting to form in Maggie's stomach.

She wandered through to the dining kitchen, and was again greeted with basic but functional furniture. A length of work-surface with a little fridge and twin-tub washing machine below were under the window, at the side of the sink unit, and an old, four-ring electric cooker stood in the chimney-breast alcove.

*Oh, God, no! Not another open fire!*

There was a multi-storage unit with sliding glass doors and a blue drop-down frontage positioned along the back wall. In the middle of the dining kitchen stood a square, teak-veneered table, again cup-stained, which was complemented with three matching chairs. There was even a pantry under the stairs – the door having been traded out for a hippie-looking beaded curtain. Maggie noticed that though the rooms were sparsely yet sufficiently furnished, clean and functional, everything carried a second-hand look to it – again, donated for the "needy". She chastised herself for her snide, ungrateful thoughts, replacing them with ones of gratefulness. At least people were kind enough to give, and to help.

*What was the saying? "One man's junk is another man's treasure," or something to that effect…*

Once she had brought in Maggie's belongings, Sister Alice joined her in the dining kitchen, placing the box of food on the little table.

'It's just a few basics to get you started – but there's bread, milk, cornflakes, eggs, teabags, instant coffee, baked beans, corned beef, and things like that. There's also a little starter pack for Ben, with some terry-cloth nappies, zinc cream, and a few clothes. There should be some washing-up liquid and wash-powder under the sink. Look, there's even a little twin-tub washing machine. Do you know how to use one, Margaret?'

'This is all new to me, Sister Alice. But I'm sure it can't be that difficult. All part of growing up, and the learning process, eh.'

The Sister smiled at Maggie. 'That's true. We never stop learning, as long as we live. Oh, and while I remember – the electricity is on a meter, so you just feed it with coins. It's better to pay for it as you go along, rather than have a big bill each quarter.'

Maggie nodded, then gave a wan smile before asking, 'I see that there are only open fires. What do I burn?'

'Ah, yes. I'd better explain about that, too. There's a coal-shed down at the bottom of the garden, and there's still some coal kindly left over by the previous tenants. They didn't need it, as they moved to a house with gas central heating. You just make little coal fires to keep warm, plus you can burn all your rubbish. I think they're great – an open fire makes a room feel so cosy!' The young nun rubbed her hands together, as if warming them. 'I'll help you to make a fire before I go. Oh, and this fireplace here in the kitchen has a back boiler for your hot water.'

'Which means what?' asked Maggie, shrugging her shoulders.

'It means that the heat from this fire goes through to the boiler behind, which then heats up the water. The hot water is stored in a cylinder tank upstairs. This fire will give you all the hot water that you need.' Sister Alice waved her hands around, trying to describe her meaning.

Maggie's face looked perplexed. 'So, I won't have any hot water without a fire?'

'There's also an electric immersion heater which you can use for instant hot water, but they're quite costly to run. Come on, I'll show you. It's upstairs in the airing cupboard.'

Like a faithful little puppy, Maggie dutifully followed Sister Alice as she showed her the upstairs rooms; a good sized front bedroom overlooking the street, a small rear bedroom which overlooked the gardens and beyond, and a compact but clean bathroom which also housed the hot water cylinder and immersion heater.

'As you can see, we've prepared the front bedroom for you, Margaret. There's a single bed, and an old wardrobe – sorry, it's rather shabby. And we managed to get a little cot for Ben, so he can be in the same room as you. Probably much easier while he's still so tiny and having night-feeds.'

Maggie noticed that there was another small Persian-style rug at the side of the bed, similar to the one downstairs. This one seemed to be covering a threadbare patch in the nylon bedroom carpet. 'You seem to have thought of everything. Thank you, Sister Alice – you've all been very supportive. I'm really going to miss all of you.' She smiled at the young novice, her smile one of genuine warmth.

'Well, we're only a phone call away if you need anything. There isn't a phone in the house, but there's a telephone box at the top of the road, near the corner shop. All very close and convenient for you.'

As Maggie looked out of the front window, she noticed an elderly lady walk past the front wall and up the path to the next house, pulling a shopping trolley on wheels.

'What are the neighbours like?' she asked.

Sister Alice came to join her at the window. 'Ah, they're a retired couple at No 25, and then there's a single lady at the other side, in No 21. I think she's a primary school teacher, if I remember rightly. I don't think the neighbours will give you much bother. More likely to be helpful, if you need it. You should get yourself acquainted with them.' She looked at her watch. 'Right then, I'd better show you how to get a fire going. I have to head back to the convent shortly, as I've still got a few chores to finish before dinner.'

While Sister Alice went down to the coal-shed to get some coal, Maggie busied herself with setting some firelighters and scrunched-up newspaper in each of the fire-grates, as per the Sister's instructions. Cobbles of coal would then be carefully placed on top before lighting the paper to make a fire. Maggie wrinkled her nose at the paraffin smell of the firelighters as she broke off a couple of pieces.

'Here we go. I brought two buckets of coal, one for each room. This plastic one can go here in the kitchen, but look what I found in the old outside toilet... Isn't it pretty?' Sister Alice proudly showed off the brass coal scuttle. A wave of nausea rose in Maggie's throat as she recalled the last time that she'd seen such a coal scuttle – on the floor in Miller's Cottage, when... when...

'Margaret... Margaret...'

Maggie felt her cheek being tapped lightly as Sister Alice sat beside her on the floor. She opened her eyes and blinked.

'Wow, you gave me quite a scare! Are you okay? One minute you were laying the fire, the next you just seemed to faint clean away.'

'Ye...yes, I'm fine. What happened? Did I faint?' Her eyes caught sight of the brass coal scuttle, thrown down in haste as Sister Alice had gone to Maggie's aid. Cobbles of coal and coal-dust were scattered all around.

The Sister looked at Maggie, her brow furrowed in puzzlement. 'You look as though you've seen the Holy Ghost, Margaret. You're as white as a sheet.'

'No, it's the coal thingy – it just reminded me of... It just reminded me of something, that's all.' Maggie quickly racked her brains for a feasible excuse. 'My grandfather used to have one. Seeing this one simply brought back a lot of childhood memories, that's all. Wow, it had quite some effect, eh!'

'It most certainly did, Margaret! You gave me quite a scare. Are you sure you're okay?'

Maggie nodded.

'Right then, let's finish making these fires and get the house all warm and cosy. Then I'd better be off.' Sister Alice resumed her task of coaching Maggie in the art of lighting a fire by setting a few cobbles on top of the paper before setting light to it. Acrid grey and white smoke curled around the coal and slowly vented up the chimney, before bursting into flame and catching hold.

'Just one thing, before you go, Sister – can we get rid of the coal scuttle?'

There was something about Maggie's eyes which Sister Alice read as fear rather than nostalgia, but the look told her that it would be best to comply with the poor girl's request.

After Sister Alice had gone, Maggie lay the blissfully sleeping Ben in his pram in the front sitting room before going into the dining kitchen to make herself a cup of tea. Her first cup of tea in her very own home.

While she waited for the kettle to boil, she began unpacking the donated items – hers to place in cupboards and arrange on shelves as she wished. Maggie smiled to herself as she remembered "playing house" when she was much younger. Except now it was all very real. The responsibility was hers – cooking, cleaning, shopping, looking after herself, and looking after Ben... She shuddered as the realisation hit home – she had somehow imagined that it would feel...what? Simpler? That she would have magically matured? After all, she now had a baby to take care of.

She found a little purse at the bottom of the cardboard box. There were a few coins inside with a note "For the electricity meter. To help you get started until your social security money comes through". She smiled – the kind Sisters seemed to have thought of everything.

Thank goodness...

"Ma-ggie...Ma-ggie... Where are you? Come out, come out, where-ever you are..."

"We're going to find you, Maggie, and when we get you, we're gonna...we're gonna do things to you..."

"Boys and girls come out to play, but Maggie won't play 'cos she's funny that way..."

"You can run, but you can't hide."

"Ma-ggie..."

"Ma-ggie..."

"Ma-ggie..."

Maggie twisted in her sleep, her mind frantic, desperately trying to get away from her pursuers. She could see three shapes – dark shapes moving closer; filthy hands grabbing, reaching out, touching, feeling, cold...

"Maggie, we don't want to hurt you..."

"We just want to play with you."

"Don't you want to play with us?"

"Ma-ggie... Ma-ggie..."

Faces came closer to her, heads with the hands, touching her, licking her. She moved her head this way and that, twisting to avoid their tongues and fetid breath.

"You can run, but you can't hide, Maggie. We'll always find you..."

Running through trees.

Running. Running. Running.

Hiding.

A door closing, shut in a room. A dark, dark room. Dirty. Smelly. Putrid, like a rotting corpse.

"Let me go! Let me go!"

Hands. Strong hands, holding her down, pinning her down. The faceless heads began licking her again, trying to kiss her; their tongues drooling, slavering.

"Let us kiss you, Maggie."

"Let us show you what it's like to be with a man."

*"Is it hard, Maggie?"*

*"Does it hurt, Maggie? Good!"*

*"We'll always be here for you, Maggie. Anytime that you need some cock..."*

Her head filled with their manic laughter...

Her head filled with the sounds of her own crying, her own screams...

Her head filled with the sounds of crying; anxious, desperate crying...

She mentally tried to identify the voice.

'Ben!'

Disorientated, Maggie sat up in bed, allowing herself a few moments for her heart-rate to settle. The orange glow from the street light outside helped her senses to quickly re-balance; her eyes to quickly re-adjust in the dimness. She looked around the bedroom – the bedroom of her new house where she was attempting to be all grown up...

'Okay, mister, I'm coming. Mummy's coming...'

She shivered as her feet stepped off the rug and onto the thin nylon carpet, neither giving any comfort or warmth while she padded the short distance to lift Ben from his cot. The coldness of the bedroom prompted a quick turnaround, jumping back into the warmth of her bed with Ben while she fed him and attended to his needs. She was grateful for having had the forethought to bring his nappy-changing paraphernalia upstairs with her and putting it by the side of the bed.

Tears began to build, but Maggie swallowed hard, refusing to let them fall.

*I can do this! I'm almost seventeen...*

But her mother's words somehow crept into her head, invading her confidence...

*You made your bed, Maggie Braithwaite...now you can lie in it–*

# Chapter 12

## The Swan Theory

Signs of spring moving into summer were a welcome signal to Maggie's inner psyche that the grey days were almost over. She looked down over the garden as she absent-mindedly washed the dishes, her eyes focused on the uplifting changes; trying her best to embrace the changing seasons as an aid to her wellbeing. The purple, golden and white crocuses in the flower borders had given way to the bright green leaf buds and daffodils of spring. Even the gnarled old apple tree was taking its turn in giving thanks for the late May sunshine, with an uplifting display of soft pink blossom.

Although Maggie was still struggling with the reality of her immature decisions, enduring day by grey day, week by long week, and month by lonely month, had finally pushed her to explore the wider locale as the mood and weather allowed. And though Woodcliffe was miles away from Millers Common, she remained vigilant, careful to avoid people with sandy coloured hair. Seeing them in her dreams was bad enough, but to see them again face to face...

She had found the corner shop to be the font of all knowledge, whether it was postcard adverts on the notice board, gossip from Mrs Bryson (the lady behind the counter), or just listening-in on conversations between shoppers. All the "who, what, where, when and why" could be gleaned from within those four walls. The corner shop had steered her in the direction of the church's "Mother and Toddler" group (boring and asked too many questions), the local library (interesting and cost-effective entertainment), and the gold-mine of all places – the local Oxfam shop. Having overcome her ingrained stigma of feeling like a needy "charity case", she found the shop to be a veritable treasure trove overflowing with more affordable versions of life's little comforts, whether it be clothes and toys for Ben, or clothes and treats for herself. Ironically, Maggie's purchases had even given her a modicum of cold comfort, knowing that she was helping others less fortunate than herself.

Her greatest and most recent purchase had been a portable record player, complete with a small collection of vinyl LPs. And there, among the Classical albums (not too bad), the Country and Western albums (questionable), and Motown (again, not too bad) was one album which caught her attention. It was a strange album to be mixed in among the others – and maybe it had been thrown out by mistake – but if that was the case, it was very much to Maggie's advantage. *Horses* spoke of a chaotic world – a world that had tainted Maggie; a world that had pushed Maggie into the dark corner of survival. Consequently, the album had become Maggie's greatest ally and sanctuary from the turmoil beyond the confines of Woodland Row. The raw emotion of Patti Smith's voice drew Maggie in. The lyrics spoke to her – they understood her, and she understood them. Moral support on vinyl; poetic food for the damaged soul.

Surviving on a meagre budget was one area in which she was becoming quite adept, particularly in making cheap but filling meals. Perhaps not necessarily the most nourishing, but at least she wasn't going hungry. If it could be put "on toast", then it would do. Anything that could be considered healthy, or a treat, usually came via the little food parcels from the nuns.

The hardest part of survival was the cold. She could well understand the landlord's reluctance to install gas fires and a gas boiler, but coal wasn't cheap, it wasn't instant, and it was very messy. She hated it with a passion. There had been times when it had been too cold to sleep upstairs, preferring instead the discomfort of the sofa over freezing to death. Even sitting on the toilet was a challenge while shivering with the cold, despite leaving the airing cupboard door open to take the chill off the bathroom.

But despite Maggie's best efforts, loneliness had become her biggest enemy. Sure, the Sisters visited every other week, having reduced their initial visits from weekly. They had even been sweet enough to bring a cake for Maggie when it had been her birthday in March – the only card on the mantelpiece being from them. No cards from anyone else… But then again, no-one else knew where she was, and she was *persona-non-grata* in her mother's eyes. Shit to be wiped from her shoes. A disgrace to the good name of the family.

Yet why did she feel the need to avoid human contact when she so desperately craved it? The old lady next door had often waved, or tried to spark up a conversation if she saw Maggie out in the garden while hanging out the washing. Maggie's eyes narrowed as she looked at Ben, who was grizzling away in his second-hand bouncy chair; his cheeks as pink as the apple blossom outside, his copper coloured hair a constant reminder of…

The lurch in her stomach identified the real reason for avoiding contact, and therefore conversation – it was a self-protection mechanism. Self-protection from inadvertently saying the wrong thing – from inadvertently revealing her innermost feelings. Asking for help – from anywhere or anyone – would be admitting defeat. Her decision had become her cross to bear.

One by one, the faces of her tormentors swam before her eyes – a rogue's gallery of sick individuals who had brought her to this… She squeezed her eyes closed and gripped the edge of the kitchen sink, her balance wavering.

But one image wouldn't go away, no matter how hard she squeezed. She could see Kate's face.

She could hear Kate's mocking voice.

She could hear her vicious laugh...

*You've made a big mistake, Maggie! And now YOU'RE paying for it...*

# Chapter 13

## Silent Night

The last embers of the branches glowed in the firegrate; the small pile of wood having been scavenged from the back garden, before being cleverly put together to maximise heat and burn-time.

Careful not to let the sleeves of her sweater get too close to the fire, Maggie cupped her hands around the little pile of sticks. After warming them for as long as she could bear, she put her palms onto her face to thaw her cheeks before slipping them under her sweater to warm her frail body. She repeated the process over the fading embers, this time rubbing some heat back into her icy cold feet and numb toes.

Maggie pulled the woolly tartan blanket over her head and around her shoulders in an effort to trap in some heat. She tried not to shiver – past experiences had taught her that once she started shivering, she had difficulty in stopping it – almost to the point of breathlessness.

And here she was, on the threshold of Christmas, freezing and alone. Well, apart from Ben… She absently recalled being in the cold church at St Mary's and pondering the Nativity scene, celebrating the birth of an innocent little boy. Was it really only a year ago? So much had changed…

The red of the tartan blanket seeped into her suppressed memory-bank, igniting a vision of cropped jeans trimmed with red plaid. Dark memories which she'd managed to suppress for almost eighteen long months suddenly began mind-morphing...

Of the Bay City Rollers.

Of singing along to their songs... "Shang-A-Lang"... "Bye, Bye, Baby"...

Of hanging out in Kate's bedroom, singing, dancing, chatting.

Of Kate.

*Maggie Minge-Muncher...*

Maggie could feel the blood starting to push through her veins and pound in her temples as her heart rate increased. Her focus moved to her heartbeat, to the pounding rhythm.

*Maggie Minge-Muncher...*

Blood pounding... Pounding... Pounding...

Kate, all sweetness and light, safely tucked away from *Maggie Minge-Muncher...*

Kate, all sweetness and light, preparing for 'A' levels; preparing for university.

*Maggie Minge-Muncher...*

Heart pounding... Pounding... Pounding...

Snuffles and movement from the well-wrapped bundle in the carry-cot beside her told her that Ben was beginning to wake. Maggie could feel her eyes tearing up, the warmth and wetness building, ready to spill over. She had one clean terry-nappy left for Ben, and barely any milk-formula. Ben's movements became more noticeable – any moment n–

Right on cue.

His little lungs belied how much capacity they could provide for life-force and volume in spite of the fact that he had a wheezing cold. Maggie allowed her own flood-gates to open – mother and child simultaneously releasing their emotions, their desperation, their need for assistance, comfort and succour.

The Sisters from St Mary's had been very kind, stopping by regularly with little care-parcels of soup and bread for Maggie and basic provisions for Ben. But benefits were meagre, so taking hand-outs had become the best means of supplementing her existence, particularly since her mother's rejection of them both. Maggie closed her tear-laden eyes and swallowed hard, pushing her damaged pride deep within. An overwhelming urge to scream brewed in her chest, causing her breathing to become tight and shallow. Surely there had to be some way of finding relief from this emotional torture? The cries from her tiny son cut through her self-pitying thoughts.

Maggie lifted Ben from under his snug refuge then huddled him under the warmth of her blanket while she went through to the dining kitchen to prepare his feed. Wispy clouds of breath-vapour led the way. She could feel the tip of her nose beginning to tingle with the cold, and her cheeks felt chilled from the damp residue of her tears.

A box of mushroom Cup-a-Soup stood by the kettle, two sachets remaining. Maggie ripped one open with her teeth, shaking some of the dried soup-powder into a mug, the rest spilling either side. She could barely hold her hand steady. She made a similar mess with the baby-formula as she tried to scoop it into Ben's feeding bottle, cursing herself for wasting the precious milk powder. Caught in a financial and maternal catch-22, her undernourished body could barely sustain her own needs, let alone that of a parasitic infant – free breast-milk having long since dried up.

The steam rising from the boiling kettle matched that of her breath, hot vapour meeting cold air. Her stomach grumbled in protest, an eager recipient for the warming soup. Ben's stomach was equally grateful for his feed, as he noisily drank the milky offerings.

After patting his back to release trapped wind, and changing him into his last nappy, Maggie lay the contented child back in the snug warmth of his carry-cot. She resumed her position in front of the rustic brick fireplace, the fire now reduced to a pile of cold, grey ashes, offering no warmth or solace.

A shuffle on the front doorstep alerted Maggie to external activity. Surely it couldn't be the good Sisters visiting at this time of night? The shuffling was accompanied by muffled giggles and the voices of children before they broke out into song, their voices beautiful, harmonious and heart-wrenching with their rendition of "Silent Night". Maggie listened as they sang; she didn't feel blessed like the Virgin Mary – she felt alone and confused. Cold. At least Mary knew that her child had been borne out of love. She looked at the sandy coloured fuzz atop Ben's head. There was no doubting that he had been spawned by the evil of Jimmy, and not by the love of God.

The carol singers knocked on the glass pane of the front door to claim their reward for singing.

Maggie remained silent. Embarrassed. Humbled. Here were a couple of kids out in the cold, singing their hearts out to bring joy to others – as well as earn a little pocket money for Christmas – but it brought her no joy.

They knocked again. She heard their footsteps shuffle and retreat as they shouted a deflated "...And a Merry Christmas to you, too..."

Maggie now added guilt to her current emotional state. It was not the season to be jolly. Not for her.

She closed her eyes to block out her life, but all she could see was Jimmy's face; hear the laughter of the boys as they violated her. Her breathing began taking on a purposeful, deep rhythmic pattern. She opened her eyes and let them fall onto Ben.

Did her mother ever suspect who the child belonged to? She'd never said as much, but it was clear to see that Ben was a Gould. The offspring of an unlawful act. An unlawful act for which Maggie was paying the price.

Not Jimmy, the bastard...

He would be in the warmth of his car.

Or in the warmth of the pub.

Or in the warmth of someone's bed.

He would have money. He would be well fed.

*He – would – have – a – life...*

Her fingers were stiffening once again from the cold, and she began shivering uncontrollably.

*Maggie Minge-Muncher...*

She looked at Ben, his innocent little face becoming that of Jimmy's.

*Maggie Minge-Muncher...*

The coldness crept beyond her fingers, crept through her veins, crept up her spine to numb her primitive brain. It crept through to her heart. The coldness enveloped it, turning it hard, icy.

*Maggie Minge-Muncher...*

A cold, cold heart.

The cold-hearted person that was no longer Maggie – that was no longer in control – slipped the little pillow from under Ben's head and gently placed it over the now-sleeping child's face.

*Maggie Minge-Muncher...*

She watched herself from beyond her detached, icy-cold mind – holding the pillow, forcing it down, blocking off air; smothering the sleeping child until it slept no more.

*Maggie Minge-Muncher...*

Her adoption plan was now fulfilled. Ben had been taken into care by the Christmas angels and was sleeping in heavenly peace.

# Chapter 14

## The Homecoming

As Maggie walked along her old road, familiar childhood feelings and memories stirred within. She saw that the Smiths at No. 12 still put their three-legged Rudolph in the front garden, and the Barkers over the road still had the gaudiest of flashing lights in the sitting room window, adding a touch of garish cheer to the late afternoon gloom. She caught the faint strains of carol singers somewhere in the street, causing the hair on her scalp to tingle and her body to flush with guilt. True to tradition, she could see that her mother had already decorated the house for the festive season. The Christmas wreath hung on the front door, a welcoming ring of plastic holly, ivy and pine cones, bedecked with a faux-velvet red ribbon, and she could just make out the dark, triangular shape of the Christmas tree and twinkling, coloured fairy lights through the net curtains in the bay window. Most likely the same artificial tree that had graced the bay window for as long as she could remember. The Christmas spirit looked to be in full swing, at least for some.

What kind of welcome would she receive from her mother? The Prodigal Child being welcomed home with the fatted turkey? Or as the returning intrusion – the one with a shameful secret to hide?

The train journey from Woodcliffe to Thorpe Haddon, then bus ride from Thorpe Haddon to Millers Common had provided Maggie with a few hours of thinking time. Watching her own reflection in the glass pane was like watching someone else, someone she barely recognised. She knew that past memories and their consequential actions couldn't be erased, but they could be blocked.

Of being held down and raped. Blocked.

Of holding a pillow over her son's face. Blocked.

Of swaddling his tiny, lifeless body in a cotton pram-sheet before cocooning it in his white, crocheted blanket. Blocked.

Of setting the mummy – for that's what it looked like – inside his white plastic baby bath. Of tucking his favourite squashy toy caterpillar alongside his body. Of covering him over with a final layer. Blocked. Blocked. Blocked.

She chewed on the rough edges of her fingernails, effectively cleaning the last residues of dirt and dust from the underside.

Of setting him in his final resting place before covering him over for all eternity, to be adopted by the angels. Blocked.

And though she no longer associated herself as the person who had carried out those acts, she had somehow maintained a clear rationale with which to cover her tracks. Write a note – "Gone Away". No other explanation needed. She had packed a few clothes together with the barest minimum of personal belongings and essentials for herself in a holdall, and clothes for Ben in a separate bag. Her Bible – the guardian of her secret letter and a few photos of Ben – was safely hidden in her handbag. Under the cover of early morning darkness, Maggie had vacated the house with the pram, complete with a fake baby made from a rolled up blanket, their bags on the wire tray below. She had even made sure that her journey went via the convent en-route to the railway station, just in case anyone caught sight of her leaving. The pram and baby clothes had been surreptitiously dismantled and abandoned at the local rubbish tip, well hidden among the other junk. She had devised a cover story that Ben had been taken to St Mary's to be given up for adoption, so the trail would end there. Simple but believable.

Yet despite her external calmness, her inner psyche raged with conflicting emotions. Her body felt free of Ben but still imprisoned by Jimmy. Her mind felt free of responsibilities but was now imprisoned by guilt. Her soul – well, that would be going to Hell, the worthless husk that it had now become.

Maggie stood at the front door and dropped her holdall bag, unsure of her next move. Should she ring the bell and wait for her mother to answer, or just walk straight in? How is it possible that your home doesn't feel like home anymore? It wasn't as though she had gone away as a girl and come back as a woman. It felt more truthful to say that she'd gone away as damaged goods and returned even more damaged.

She lifted her finger to the doorbell and pressed, the chimes reverberating within the hallway with muffled metallic notes. She heard her mother's sing-song reply of "com-ing" and could envisage her wiping her hands on her apron as she strode up the hallway. Maggie steeled herself, her body language humble in its presentation; head hung low, shoulders stooped.

The two women faced each other – wide-eyed gaze met with wide-eyed gaze.

Maggie staggered across the threshold into her mother's arms, her small body racked with sobs.

'Can I come home...please?'

Overcome by involuntary maternal instinct, Liz held her tightly. 'Oh my God! Maggie, love – you look awful! Come in, come in. Here, let me take your bag...' Liz reached down to grab Maggie's holdall as she ushered her daughter inside, into the welcoming warmth. The spicy aroma of freshly baked mince pies permeated the air.

'Why didn't you let me know you were coming. Where's Ben?'

Maggie looked at her mother, red-eyed and deflated. She shook her head.

'I just couldn't go on. You were right...' She bit her lip before continuing, the illusion that she had created in her mind having now replaced the reality. 'I gave him back to the Sisters to be placed for adoption. They have couples on their waiting list. They were sure of finding a new home quite quickly.'

Liz put her hands on her hips, her voice aghast. 'Good God, Maggie – it's not like giving some puppy back to the RSPCA! You make it sound like they're re-homing a puppy!'

'Don't you think that I've thought long and hard before taking the decision!' She began to cry; her tired body, her weary soul, crumpled to the floor, arms wrapped around her knees, feeling small. It was as though her mind had put on a life-preserver of disassociation. 'I just couldn't do it anymore. Don't make me feel worse than I already do. Please...'

Seeing her daughter's evident distress, Liz changed her tone. 'I can see that. I'm sorry for judging you so harshly, Maggie. I'm sure your decision wasn't taken lightly. C'mon, I'll put the kettle on. And Maggie – welcome home, love.'

✻✻✻

*The train rushed through the dark avenue of twisted, ancient trees; their branches reaching out – blackened skeletal arms, grabbing, touching. Like a giant metal millipede, the train ploughed through the cottage door before being swallowed down the throat of the tunnel, as it went on its journey deep into the cold, damp earth.*

*Clickety-clack; from light into dark.*

*Clickety-clack; entering Hell.*

*Clickety-clack – 'Cause that's where you're going, Maggie...to Hell!*

*Clickety-clack...*

*Down. Down. Down.*

*Darker. Deeper.*

*Clickety-clack, clickety-clack.*

*She looked around at the other passengers, putrid rotting flesh hanging from their bones. Empty eye-sockets, maggots; a raven feasting.*

*Clickety-clack, clickety-clack.*

*The swish-swoosh of the connecting carriage door opened. She looked up as she heard a familiar voice...*

*"Tickets please. Tickets please."*

*It was Kate – pristine, clean, glowing. She looked at Maggie's proffered ticket. "You have the wrong ticket, madam. This train isn't going to Thorpe Haddon – it's going to Hell..." The glowing image of Kate began laughing and laughing. Manic laughter, until her head fell off.*

*Down. Down. Down.*

*Darker. Deeper.*

*Clickety-clack, clickety-clack.*

*Kate's face morphed into Jimmy's. Laughing, laughing, as he drove the train deeper into the tunnel: "Maggie Minge-Muncher, Maggie Minge-Muncher...Maggie..."*

*She saw movement near Jimmy. A little clone of Jimmy – Ben – was sitting next to him at the controls. "Daddy, where are we going? Where's my mummy? Where's my mummy?"*

*Down. Down. Down.*

*Darker. Deeper.*

*Clickety-clack, clickety-clack.*

*Down. Down. Down.*

*Darker. Deeper.*

*Clickety-clack, clickety-clack.*

*She tried to get off the train...hit the emergency button.*

*"Let me off, let me off, let me off..."*

*The train to Hell came to a shuddering, screeching, twisted-metal halt...*

Gentle rapping on her bedroom door cut through Maggie's hazy waking phase, igniting her senses to resume their daily functioning. Her body felt damp and clammy.

'Maggie, love. Are you awake?'

Maggie opened her eyes, slowly focusing on the sights and sounds of her surroundings. The gentle rapping came again.

'Yeah, yeah, I'm awake.' She yawned. 'Morning, Mum. I'll be down in a mo.'

'Okay, love. I'll put the kettle on...'

Maggie levered herself up and plumped her pillows behind her back, allowing herself a few minutes of re-orientation. Insipid winter sunlight was being held back from entering her room, curtains drawn against the outside world. Shutting out the manic world beyond...

Apart from fresh bedding and general cleaning, her bedroom was just as she'd left it almost fifteen months previously. The room of a sixteen year old.

Her stack of albums, cassettes and books were still neatly arranged on her book-case; albeit now with the addition of a Bible hidden away on its shelves. Her desk shared space with her art equipment and a record player. The teen-wardrobe unit was the tall guardian of clothes that no longer fit, save for the few that she had brought with her. Even her prized peacock-back cane chair looked worse for wear. Posters above her desk – Bay City Rollers, Slade, Rod Stewart, Blondie – were testimony to the girl she once was.

The innocent girl.

The innocent girl before her innocence was stolen from her.

A lot had changed since confessing her secret to Kate.

Grabbing her now-too-small tartan robe from the back of her bedroom door, she headed into the bathroom. She studied her reflection in the mirror. It was not the Maggie she remembered from those innocent days. The Maggie back then had spiky, black hair, had strong eye-liner, had strong opinions. A mask to hide the confused inner-self. An inner-self that she had revealed, only to be taken away in the cruellest way possible. The Maggie that looked back at her now was gaunt, her eyes sunken and dark-rimmed, lifeless; her hair still semi-spiky, but a natural dark-brown.

A Maggie she no longer recognised.

A Maggie that was forced upon her.

The Maggie she didn't want to be.

'Here's your cup o'tea, love. Did you sleep well?' Maggie's mum fussed around, loading up the kitchen table with almost every breakfast option available: toast, cereal, boiled eggs, marmalade.

'Thanks, Mum. It was good to be back in my old bed. I think the hot bath and Horlicks helped.' She began buttering some toast, desperately hungry while at the same time not sure if she could stomach large quantities of food. Goose-bumps rose on her arms as her unconscious mind trawled through the bad dream; her train journey to Hell. 'It's a little bit weird, seeing my bedroom again, just as I left it.'

'Aye, a lot of water has passed under the bridge, so to speak, since you were last here. But I think you've done the right thing, love. It's a brave decision, and a tough one, but I'm sure that Ben will be placed with loving parents.' Her mother began buttering a slice of toast for herself. 'Anyway, I have to go into work soon, so you just take it easy today, yeah. Then how about we go into Thorpe Haddon tomorrow, with it being Saturday? Spend some time together, and do a bit of Christmas shopping? Maybe get you some new clothes and stuff. You didn't bring much back with you.'

Maggie thought back to the image that had faced her in the bathroom mirror. The defeated image. She felt a sudden wave of empowerment, like she was being given a second chance. It was time to put her "Maggie the Invincible" mask back on. The mask that would tell the world to "Fuck off!".

'Sounds great. Think I'll get a cut and colour too, if that's okay?' She mussed with her hair, running her fingers through the top in a vain attempt to get it to stand up.

'Yes, love, of course. There's one of those drop-in salons on the high street, you could pop in there. In fact, I think I'll join you! That's sorted, then.' Liz smiled at her daughter, then patted her hand. 'And if we see anybody we know, we'll just tell them that the Art College in Chesterfield didn't work out for you...'

*The Prodigal Child has returned; she gets the fatted turkey, and ta-da – mother has already found a way to cover her embarrassment. Wow – it really was that simple...*

# Chapter 15

## Metamorphosis

True to her promise, Liz took Maggie into town, and by way of recompense for the remorse that she felt for pushing Maggie into a corner over the pregnancy, she opened the purse of guilt. They sat side-by-side in the hairdressers – she getting a shampoo and set, and Maggie receiving the full cut, colour and styling. They went in and out of clothes shops, Maggie trawled the latest in LPs in the record shop, and was let loose on the Boots 17 counter. Liz was even persuaded into the Wimpy Bar so that Maggie could have a much-needed cheeseburger and fries. An essential day of rebonding for mother and daughter.

But beyond all the purchases was the affirmation that Maggie was no longer going to be one of life's victims, but rather one of life's rebels. After pushing her way through a bunch of giggling schoolgirls in the magazine section of WH Smith's, she realised that she had long-since outgrown Jackie magazine and teen-hood. She yearned for a new kind of reading energy. She espied a picture of The Clash on a copy of the previous week's NME, and some arty looking rock band gracing this week's cover. Maggie had found her replacement Saturday holy-grail – alternative, poetic, anarchic. She bought both copies. Since leaving home and becoming more independent, she'd noticed that her taste in music had become less mainstream, finding herself drawn to more assertive bands, such as The Clash, Sex Pistols, and the like. The lyrics to their songs were an anthem to the feelings that many of today's youth wanted to convey to society, so suited Maggie's slanted view of the world. But her greatest discovery, both musically and spiritually, was coming across the work of Patti Smith. Her lyrics and life reached out to Maggie in a way like no other artist had. How many times had she played *Horses* album? She'd lost count...

Loaded down with their bags, they linked arms and strolled along the High Street, the fading daylight bringing the Christmas lights and decorations into a whole new twinkling perspective. Maggie relished the gentle breeze blowing through her newly styled hair. It somehow made her feel taller, more empowered – a bold statement to the Christmas shoppers of Thorpe Haddon.

Liz stopped to rub her calves. 'Ooh, my legs are really starting to ache, Mags – I guess we should be heading for the bus. I think we can safely say that we've shopped 'til we dropped! I'm ready for a sit-down.'

'Me too. Thanks for a lovely day, Mum. It really is good to be home. Quick, the green man has come on for the crossing...' Maggie took her mother by the hand and began leading her over the pedestrian crossing, rather like pulling on a reluctant five-year old. From out of the corner of her eye, she caught sight of a red car waiting on the stop-line for them to cross. A certain highly polished red car, with black vinyl roof and chrome bumpers. Her eyes narrowed, then locked and loaded with Jimmy Gould. Buoyed by a rush of rebellious bravado, she dropped hands with her mother's and gave Jimmy the "V" sign and mouthed a very clear "Fuck you". The occupant in the passenger seat gave a jaw-drop in response to Maggie's actions. This gave Maggie all the ammunition she needed to repeat the action, her eyes narrowing to slits as they met with Katie Gould's. She gave her the same, satisfying "V" and "Fuck you, too" gestures. Jimmy revved the engine, causing the other pedestrians to scuttle over the crossing, raking into Liz and Maggie.

Catching sight of Maggie's brazen behaviour, Liz chastised her daughter with a head-shake and tut-tuts, before curiosity got the better of her. 'Who was that, anyway?'

'Just those shysters, Kate and Jimmy Gould. No-one important.'

Liz's eyes widened, then she grinned. 'Okay, I'll allow you that one!'

A familiar face among the throng of shoppers caught Jimmy's attention as he waited at the stop-line of the pedestrian crossing. He could feel his heart beginning to race once he realised who was under the crown of spiky black hair, causing him to tighten his grip around the leather steering wheel. His eyes connected with Maggie's as she crossed.

'Fuck – what's she doing here?' he snarled.

Kate looked up from admiring her freshly polished nails. 'Who?'

'Your old friend – Maggie bloody Braithwaite, that's who…'

'That weirdo! She's no friend of mine. Anyway, why should it bother you – you're not exactly her type, are you?' sneered Kate. 'Besides, she's probably home for the Christmas holidays.'

Jimmy scowled, unable to answer his sister, his throat constricted and dry by the rush of adrenaline.

As they waited for the crowd of shoppers to go over the crossing, Kate witnessed Maggie give her brother the "V" sign and mouth a very clear "Fuck you". Her jaw dropped open. Kate's eyes followed the perpetrator, only to receive the same offensive gesture from Maggie.

'Oh! Oh! Did you see that! Mum was right about her turning all weird and boho since she went to Art College.'

As a sign of defiance, Jimmy revved the throttle, the growl from the engine matching the growl deep in his throat.

'Fuck you too, Maggie Braithwaite…'

*\*\**

Maggie tore up the pile of posters that she'd taken down from her bedroom walls and tossed them into the bin, the flip lid swinging back and forth.

Disturbed by the noise, Liz looked up from peeling carrots at the kitchen table, a proper Sunday lunch being back on the menu.

'What's all that lot?' she asked.

'Just chucking out my old posters. Been having a bit of a clear-out in my room – time to move on from being a kid. After all, I'll be eighteen in a few months' time. Wow, eighteen... Anyway, ta-da! What do you think?' Maggie twirled around in the kitchen, modelling some of the previous day's purchases.

'Is that tee-shirt supposed to be three sizes too big?' asked Liz, puzzled.

'It's about standing out from the crowd – especially when you're my size!' She laughed at her own joke, and it felt good. 'Do you still have any of Dad's old shirts?

Liz frowned. 'I'm not sure. I'll have to take a look. I think I gave most of your dad's stuff to the old people's home. They're usually grateful for extra clothes. Why do you ask?'

'I think that a white shirt would look great over this, don't you?' Maggie model-posed again. 'See my nails...' She held out her hands to show her mother the black nail polish – garish, noticeable.

'Is that what the fashion is all about these days? I keep seeing the older kids in town with this punky, spiky look. Scares the hell out of the old folk.' Liz shook her head then broke out into a smile. 'And I dare say that your make-up will scare the old folk too – black eye-shadow and ruby red lipstick. It looks really creepy, especially with your pale blue eyes.'

Maggie clawed her fingers and snarled, jumping towards her mother in mock-animal style. 'Little old me, scaring the old folks!'

She pulled up a chair and joined her mother at the kitchen table. The teapot felt hot, so she poured herself a cup of tea to accompany the mince pie that she blatantly stole from her mother's plate. She closed her eyes, savouring the fruity flavours and sweet pastry, allowing herself a brief moment of reminiscence. Back to the days of child-like innocent wonder; excited by unwrapping presents left by Santa the night before because she'd been good, new socks for Christmas Day, the compulsory nuts, mandarin and Quality Street in her stocking... Memories which seemed an eon away.

Still relishing her days-gone-by moment, she idly asked, 'I presume that we'll be having a turkey with all the trimmings for Christmas dinner?'

'Of course,' affirmed Liz. 'I've ordered a fresh one from the farm shop. I asked for a nice little fat one, just big enough for the two of us, plus a few leftovers. Don't want to be eating it until the New Year!'

Maggie nodded and smiled to acknowledge her deep approval.

*See, the Prodigal Child gets the fatted turkey...*

# Chapter 16

## 1978

'Quick, quick, quick – it's almost midnight. Here, top up your glass.' Liz poured a splash of Pomagne into Maggie's glass causing it to fizz over, before topping up her own. 'Here we go...five, four, three, two, one – Happy New Year, my love!' She hugged Maggie warmly, almost spilling both their drinks in the process.

The television programme resonated with the audience singing "Auld Lang Syne", accompanied with the cracks of fireworks and the chiming of Big Ben.

'Happy New Year, Mum.' Maggie reciprocated her mum's hug. 'Let's hope that 1978's going to be a better year for us, eh. I think we're due some good luck.'

'Agreed!'

Mother and daughter, united by the mutual wish for consigning the past couple of years to the memory-cupboard marked "Do Not Open", clinked their glasses together.

'So, do you have a New Year's Resolution?' Liz asked. 'What do you wish for?'

Maggie pondered a moment, her smile belying the truth of her dark thoughts. 'Oh, just to be happy. For life to move on, and have a more positive year. What about you, Mum?'

Giddy with the sparkling cider, Liz once again clinked her glass with Maggie's. 'Same here! Let's have a happy, positive year together... Woohoo!'

'Mum! You're drunk!'

Liz giggled. 'Me? Well, maybe a little tipsy. But it's only once a year. Hey, do you know what – I almost bought Blue Nun Liebfraumilch instead of Pomagne, but then thought better of it! I didn't think that you'd want to be reminded of nuns!' She laughed at her own joke.

Maggie shook her head and quipped, 'You're so right, Mum. I don't think I'll be able to watch "The Sound of Music" ever again.'

The adverts intercut the New Year programme; the advertisers choosing this moment to tempt the nation with their usual irritating array of January sales, and summer holiday promotions. That vulnerable time when the country was deep in the middle of winter and people were constricted by seasonal debt.

'Hey, how about we take a little holiday together? Maybe book a little cottage in the Cotswolds, or one of those nice forested areas down south? It's supposed to be very pretty down there. What do you think, Maggie?' Liz asked.

Maggie felt her head beginning to pound, maybe from the intrusion of alcohol, or maybe from the memory that now encroached into her mind.

*Bad things happen in remote cottages in the woods...*

'Sounds great – but how about we book into a guesthouse or hotel? Let someone else do the cooking and washing-up, eh?'

'Do you know what, Maggie, I like the sound of that even better! Yes, let's treat ourselves. I'll pick up some holiday brochures while I'm in town next week, and see what we can find.' Warm and fuzzy from the effects of the sparkling cider, Liz stretched and yawned. 'Well, I'm going to turn in for the night.' She kissed Maggie on the head as she stood up from the sofa. 'Nighty night, my love. And Happy New Year again.'

'Yeah, I think I'll do the same. Happy New Year to you too, Mum. Love you.'

*The red car revved its engine, tyres screeching as they burned rubber, kicking up gravel and spewing out acrid smoke. Maggie could see the occupants of the car, laughing. They were laughing at her, and pointing. The car revved again. She could see Jimmy and Kate, and little Ben was sitting on Jimmy's knee, helping him to drive the car straight towards her. She ran from left to right, zig-zagging, but still the car followed her every move. "We're coming to get you...we're coming to get you..."*

*She could feel their breath hot on the back of her neck and hear their voices in her head. They were in the car, but still she could feel them, she could still hear them. Breathing, shouting...their breath hot, putrid, rotten.*

*Hands began grabbing at her. "Come back, Maggie."*

*"Come back, Mummy...there's no escape."*

*She tripped and fell on the pedestrian crossing, falling, falling, backwards.*

*Down, down, down, into the blackness.*

Maggie jumped involuntarily in her sleep, the strange sensation of falling having wrenched her into wakefulness. She lay still for a few moments, allowing her mind and body to re-orientate itself. The green glow from her bedside clock showed 03:27. Faint night sounds filled the street below – a party was still happening somewhere locally, muffled voices and scuffling, a dog barking, music.

She padded over to the window and blew on it, her hot breath clearing a peep-hole through the pretty jack-frost swirls on the glass. Lights were still on over the road, silhouetted movements behind the curtains. Someone clattered out of the front door and slipped down the front step. Another joined, their drunken laughter filling the night void. Pounding music filtered out through the open doorway.

A car cruised by then stopped, before reversing and pulling up in front of her house.

Maggie tensed at the sight of the two policemen as they got out, her muscles only relaxing once she saw them go over the road. Icy fingers crawled through her mind, icy voices taunted her –

*Happy New Year, Maggie Braithwaite. Never stop looking over your shoulder...*

# Chapter 17

## The Devil Makes Work...

The forceful, melodic rock strains of Foreigner seeped into Maggie's consciousness as her radio-alarm clock burst into morning life; their vocals telling her that she was as *Cold as Ice*. She blinked and looked at the green digital numbers – 09:10.

*Maybe just another ten minutes – finish listening to the song and a bit of morning banter from Noel Edmonds...*

No longer tied by the constraints of school or the demands of baby Ben, restless nights had simultaneously produced groggy, late starts to Maggie's day.

She padded into the kitchen, yawning, her slippers making a shuffling sound on the linoleum flooring. As usual, her mother had left her a note on the table – the daily note which listed a few chores to be done, and was always rounded off with a few kisses and a heart. A reasonable trade-off for rent-free living. Today's chores were the vacuuming and dusting. Not too difficult. The worst chore to appear on the list so far had been cleaning the bathroom and toilet. Which conversely was Maggie's pet hate – as much as she hated *cleaning* the bathroom and toilet, she hated *seeing* a dirty bathroom and toilet. And white toilet paper – another pet hate. White toilet paper, in Maggie's mind, meant that you couldn't afford coloured paper. Coloured toilet paper was posh. White toilet paper was for cheapskates.

After flicking the switch on the kettle, she flicked the switch on the radio – a house devoid of sounds allowed too much empty head-space. And an empty head allowed bad thoughts to creep in uninvited. But then again, bad thoughts were never really invited. Nor were bad dreams, but still they kept coming. She sighed and stretched, pulling her head from side to side to release the tension in her shoulders and neck. Well, some of it. Tension seemed to be a constant companion these days. The jolly voice of Noel Edmonds tapped into her psyche when he announced the next song and helped to shift her mood up a gear – Blondie had released a single, *Denis*, from their latest album. Debbie Harry was a goddess. Oblivious as to whether her neighbours were home or not, Maggie cranked up the volume and danced around the kitchen like no-one was watching – *now* her day could begin!

Once showered, and hiding behind a mask of fresh make-up, Maggie took on her alter-ego persona of life's-victor, rather than that of life's-victim. The vacuum cleaner became her weapon of choice as she attacked the carpets with a vigorous, determined purpose – the main purpose being that of mind-blocking. All the dark corners, all the recesses, all the hidden dross – the dust of life – could be sucked up and tipped away. One by one, she carefully wiped over the photographs on the sideboard: a family holiday to Bridlington, two photos from her parents' wedding day, one of Maggie as a joyful toddler, and one of her maternal grandparents, Benjamin and Violet, standing beside their beloved motorcycle and sidecar combo. Rebels and travellers, they were; always off somewhere new on their Silver Bullet, as they affectionately called their Honda rig, until arthritis and hip replacements had slowed them down. Captured moments of innocence and family joy, before life played its bitchy, cruel tricks. A squirt of Pledge and an invigorating wipe with the duster added the final polish to any tarnish, to any lies, and to slipped halos.

Maggie absently recalled a couple of her most recent lies and highly-polished cover-ups. One was a phone call from the Reverend Mother – the old nun had called, following up on Maggie's sudden exit from Woodland Row. Being the smooth liar that she had become, Maggie had reassured the Reverend Mother that both she and baby Ben had been welcomed back with open arms to her mother's. After realising that "going it alone" was more difficult than she anticipated, she had thought it was wisest to return home. It was remiss of her not to have let them know. Yes, all was well, and yes, she would pass on the Reverend Mother's best regards. Naturally she gave a different version of the nun's phone call to her mother – a version which said that Ben had been successfully placed with adoptive parents and that the Reverend Mother sent her best wishes.

Her other prize-winning lie was only yesterday – what would have been Ben's first birthday. She had beautifully and convincingly feigned the role of a young, innocent mother who had loved and lost a child, and hoped that his adoptive parents were giving him a special first-birthday party, where-ever he was.

And in reality, she had loved and lost a child.

Just not in the way that she had told her mother.

What was it her dad used to say? "If you tell lies, Maggie, your nose will grow bigger, like Pinocchio's. Remember what happened to him!" She smiled and touched her nose to see if it had grown any bigger. Nope – just the same as it was, a little button nose.

*Maggie Braithwaite, you're such a silver-tongued liar...*

Satisfied that her efforts had been completed to her mother's exacting standards, Maggie put away the cleaning materials before heading to the sanctuary of her bedroom.

Always happy to listen to Patti Smith, she placed *Horses* onto the turntable of her little record player. It was the one album that she had allotted space for in her escape baggage. Her index finger traced along the bookshelves to find something to read; a book into which she could fall and escape for a few hours. Title after title, all read before, numerous times. The finger hovered over her Bible then tapped the top of the spine, agitated. Maggie knew exactly what was in there, and knew what feelings it would ignite if she opened the cover. Undeterred, she snatched up the book before sitting at her desk. Pictures of Ben swam before her eyes, causing a sharp intake of breath.

Ben, the innocent.

Ben, the child that was no more.

Ben, the result of...

Maggie closed her eyes and endeavoured to steady her breathing. She opened the folded letter and smoothed out the creases. Her eyes scanned over the words that she had written and never sent. Words that begged her mother not to go to the police. What was she afraid of? Didn't Jimmy and his mates deserve to be brought to justice? Surely there could be no shame on her part? But it was too late – if she rocked the boat now, it could lead to *other things* being discovered.

*Well, Maggie – you made your bed, girl...*

She carefully folded the letter and hid it inside the Bible with the photos, before slipping it back onto her bookshelf. Invited by the comfy look of her bed, she flopped back onto the mattress and tucked her hands behind her head, allowing the words to invade her mind; to ignite her rebellious side.

Lyrical medicine for her tortured soul.

The downside to feeling rebellious, as Maggie had so often found, was that it permitted her mind to open up to a darker side. The side that wanted to rip out Kate's throat; the side that wanted to rip off Jimmy's balls, the side which had betrayed those who she loved. Those whom she was meant to care for.

Feelings of guilt.

They weighed so, so heavy.

She closed her eyes – what would Patti do? What would Patti say about the matter? Maggie listened intently to the vocals for inspiration and guidance.

An epiphany slowly dawned on her, creeping in with the icy fingers that so often wrapped themselves around her mind.

How much longer could she stay in this one-horse town without bumping into the people she would prefer to avoid?

How much longer could she invent plausible answers in order to deflect awkward questions?

How much longer could she go on living a lie?

Staying in Millers Common would be the fast-track to her insanity.

Leaving Millers Common would be the only way of regaining control of her life without the constant need to look over her shoulder. And her upcoming birthday trip next month with her mother would be the perfect exit. She would be eighteen, the small inheritance from her dad would become accessible, and she would be in a place where she could make a fresh start.

*Who am I?*

*Why the fuck am I living this small-town illusion?*

*Regrets? Many.*

*Remorse? Yes, of course.*

*Surely there must be others out there just like me? Kindred spirits.*

*Re-invent myself – the new and improved Maggie Braithwaite.*

There was no reason to stay.

# Chapter 18

## Following the Ancients

The circle of Neolithic stones towered before them; testimony to an ancient civilisation, a conundrum to archaeologists, and an awe-inspiring wonder to the common man. A place that generated more questions than it gave answers.

Maggie hugged her mother. 'Thanks for bringing me. This is the best birthday present ever.'

'Oh, you're welcome, my love.' Liz returned her daughter's hug, before returning her attention back to the stones. 'I know it sounds a bit "hippie", but there is something magical about Stonehenge. Something energising. I can understand why people come here.'

Maggie looked at her mum and laughed, shaking her head. 'Wow, I *NEVER* thought that I'd *EVER* hear you say something like that. You're usually so black and white about life.'

'I know – but these stones are just, well... I mean, how did they get them here? They're so big – they must be at least, what, twelve feet high, if not more? And who got them here? Why?' She waved her arms in homage towards the standing stones.

'Hmm, I know of someone who had the answer – *Stig of the Dump*! He watched them raise a few stones on the summer solstice. He and his tribe had a magical party there. Remember that book, Mum?'

'Of course – it was always one of your favourites. Didn't you do a book study on it at school?' Liz broke into a wistful smile as she remembered helping Maggie with her book-study homework. 'The boy, what was his name? Barney, yes, that's it – Barney found a caveman living at the bottom of his granny's garden, in the chalk pit. Stig the caveman.'

'That's right! Well remembered. And do you recall that my class went on a field-trip afterwards, to the Nine Ladies Stone Circle in the Peak District, and then to that other place nearby with a henge? Oh, what was it called? Arbor Low, that's the place. All very interesting, but nothing on the scale of this.' Maggie began laughing. 'Guess what – I re-read *Stig of the Dump* before we came here this weekend, to get in the mood for Stonehenge and this area!'

'You did? Well, it's the first time that I've been here, but I have to say it's a wonderful place,' acknowledged Liz.

Maggie couldn't resist the opportunity to tease her mother a little. 'There is a world beyond Derbyshire, you know...'

'Hmm, if you say so,' Liz retorted, her voice loaded with sarcastic humour. 'Anyway, this drizzle is starting to run down the back of my neck – how about we head back to the hotel to get dried off and cleaned up before dinner? It's almost five o'clock.'

The visit to nearby Stonehenge had infected Maggie with a welcome burst of positive energy. She could feel the physical charge within herself. Even the fellow tourists didn't irritate her, as they made their way here and there around Barrowfeld. A sudden realisation dawned on her as they strolled back to the hotel, her arm linked with her mother's.

'Hey, it's Saturday! I'm just going to pop into the newsagents to see if they have the new NME, Mum. I won't be long.'

'Okay. You take your time, love,' replied Liz. 'I'm going back to the hotel to soak my feet and give them a rest before dinner. We must've walked ten miles or more today.'

Maggie slipped her arm out of her mother's, before crossing over the road towards the newsagents, waving as she went.

The newsagents reminded Maggie of the one in Woodcliffe – shelf after shelf of cigarettes, row upon row of newspapers and magazines, together with the seemingly unlimited choice of chocolate bars and sweeties. The only addition to this establishment being the well-stocked shelves of touristy bric-a-brac and booklets. And as with all good newsagents, it had amply stocked aisles of local gossip.

As Maggie browsed for her music newspaper, she tapped into a heated discussion that was happening near the knitting and cookery magazines. Her ears pricked up when she heard a local music festival coming under their negatively opinionated scrutiny.

*"Bloody music festival... Summer Solstice... Stonehenge... Brings all those New Age travelling hippies and tinkers... Good for nothing... Churning up the land... Steal anything that's not bolted down... Our Freda says that there's one o'them festivals close to them too, near Knebworth in June... Same problem there... Travellers... Druggies on wheels, that's what they are..."*

Bingo!

Fuelled by this new-found, eavesdropped knowledge, a plan began formulating in Maggie's mind. Okay, it was only the middle of March, but if she hung around long enough – oh, the freedom to just drift...

After paying for her NME, she allowed herself some time to browse the advertising postcards on display in the shop doorway. A few of them grabbed her attention:

*"Part-time help required at The Willows Coffee Shop. Must be clean, punctual, and friendly. Hours: 2pm to 6pm, Mon-Fri. Occasional weekend work. Apply directly to Mrs Green at the café."*

*"Bar-work and restaurant service at The Druid Inn. Thurs & Fri evenings, and weekends – 7-11pm. Must be 18+. Apply to Mr Chambers."*

*"Rooms to let over café. Over 18s only. Non-smoker. Reasonable rates. Apply Mrs Green at Willows Coffee Shop."*

Double bingo!

Maggie returned to the counter. 'Could I borrow a pen and some writing paper, please?'

Liz was sitting on the edge of her bed drying off her now-refreshed feet when Maggie returned to the hotel.

'Did you get what you wanted, love?' she inquired, wiggling her toes.

Maggie waved the NME, and grinned. 'Yep. And...' She waved the piece of notepaper, 'I found a list of jobs and rooms to rent in the area...'

Liz froze, then looked up at Maggie, her eyes quizzical. 'Meaning?'

Maggie came and sat on the bed beside her mother, her head hung low. 'Meaning that I'm tired of looking over my shoulder every time that I go out in Millers Common. I'm sick of feeling like I've let everyone down. Sick of always being on my guard when I have to give lame excuses rather than honest answers. I've been thinking about moving away for a while, and this just seems like the perfect opportunity. Stay here, and make a fresh start.'

The room went quiet, save for muffled, external activity permeating the walls, while Liz considered her reply.

She sighed before speaking, then took Maggie's hand in hers. 'Then I give you my blessing, Maggie, if that's what you want. I can well understand how you feel. It's the same for me, if I'm honest. I feel like people are talking about us behind our backs. I can barely remember what lies and excuses I've woven... I think it could be the best solution – for both of us.'

Maggie could feel tears welling; her whole being tingled with a mixture of confusion and elation. This could well be the turning point that she so desperately wanted, so desperately needed.

Liz's mothering instinct kicked in. 'How will you manage? Don't you blow all your inheritance in one go! Dad wouldn't have wanted that – you know how sensible he was with money, down to the last penny...'

'Here, look.' Maggie smoothed out the sheet of paper. 'Here are two part-time jobs – one at a nearby café, and one at a pub, plus rooms to rent. If I get the job at the coffee shop, surely there'll be free meals from leftovers, right?' She reassuringly nudged and winked at her mother. 'Plus, I'll be eighteen tomorrow, which means that I'll be eligible for the job in the pub.'

Tears were now welling in Liz's eyes. 'When are you thinking of making the move?'

'No time like the present, Mum. I might as well just stay here and start asking around. I can start by asking at these places tomorrow – if that's okay with you?'

Liz nodded. Her daughter would be eighteen tomorrow – what could she do to stop her, anyway? 'Of course. Just promise that you'll stay in touch – please… Give me a call from time to time, and let me know what's happening.'

Maggie gave her mother a reassuring hug. 'I promise. Anyway, you'll still be here for a couple more days – I'll try and find something before you leave, if that makes you feel better. And if there's nothing around here, then Salisbury's just down the road, so to speak. There's bound to be something in a tourist area such as this. You know me, Mum – I'm a survivor.' She squeezed her mother's hand. 'But I need to live my life the way that I want to live it. Life in Millers Common just isn't working for me – it holds too many bad memories. I feel like I'm living a lie. Like I said earlier, I need a fresh start.'

*Evolve or die.*

'Well, if that's what you need to do, my love, then go with my blessing. You're right – it's been a tough few years for us, what with one thing and another. Go and live your life, my girl.' Liz nudged her daughter playfully, then remarked, 'I think that you should tone down your make-up before you go asking around for jobs – you look like a Halloween ghoul. It'll put the customers off their cream tea!' she laughed.

'But then I'm not being "me", am I?' questioned Maggie.

'It doesn't change who you are on the inside, my love. You will always be Maggie Braithwaite, no matter how you package yourself. But – you need to tone it down a bit, especially for the coffee shop. Probably fine for the pub, though. You look tough – no-one will mess with you!'

'Thanks for understanding, Mum. That means a lot to me.' Maggie kissed the back of her mother's hand, before breaking out into a fit of giggles at the onset of a gurgling stomach-rumble. 'And on that note, shall we go and get something to eat? I'm starving!'

# Chapter 19

## The North-South Divide

"*Bing-bong-bing – The train now approaching Platform 2 is the 17:21... changing at Basingstoke...Sheffield...*"

The crackling, metallic intercom voice alerted the throng of evening commuters at Salisbury Railway Station of the approaching train. Liz could feel her stomach roll over as she took Maggie's hand.

'Now, are you sure that you'll be alright...?'

'Yes, Mum, I'll be fine. I've left home before, remember? Now go on, otherwise you'll miss your train. And you have to change once, remember, at Basingstoke, to get to Sheffield.'

Liz laughed, her brow furrowed. 'Hey, who's looking after whom here! Yes, and then it's just a taxi ride from Sheffield to Millers Common. Stop worrying, Maggie – I'll be just fine. I have a book for the journey, and some sandwiches. And now it's my turn to fuss – don't miss the coach back to Barrowfeld. And good luck with the jobs, I'm proud of you, Mags.' She hugged Maggie tightly, reluctant to let her go. 'One last hug...'

'There, you've been hugged – now get on the train!' Maggie gave her mother a gentle shove in the direction of the train doors, watching and waiting until she was seated.

Separated by a whistle, and a final wave, mother and daughter each breathed a sigh of relief, and each for their own reasons.

Maggie drew the curtains then sat on the sofa. As a little joke to herself, she pinched her arm, just to make sure that she wasn't dreaming. The sting to her skin felt real – she was sat on the sofa in her new bed-sit above the coffee shop. Okay, so it wasn't huge; just a living kitchen, a poky little bedroom with barely any walk-around space, and a tiny bathroom in which she could almost reach from side to side. But it was hers. And it wasn't in Millers Common or Woodcliffe. It was miles and miles away from anyone who knew her – the fresh start that she so desperately wanted, and needed. She smiled to herself, then heaved her legs up onto the sofa. Tomorrow would be her first afternoon at the coffee shop below –

*How convenient was that – roll out of bed and into work! And then start at the pub on Thursday evening. Who said that plans can't always come together, to be in the right place at the right time?*

*No more men. No more babies. Turn the page and start a new chapter.*

*Free to be me – whoever "me" is...*

Maggie plumped the single cushion behind her head, wriggling until she found her "comfy", then closed her eyes. It had been a long, eventful weekend.

As she snoozed, her eyelids flickered and twitched – a physical barrier between the relative safety of wakefulness, and the horror that was unfolding behind them. Her fingers moved slightly, a reflex to her mind-visuals.

*Pages...pages of a book, falling into them. Old, yellowing pages. Familiar pages.*

*Pounding, hooves pounding, galloping horses – riding alongside Barney and his sister, Lou, in the lush grass of the Downs. The silver solstice moonlight cast an ethereal glow over the countryside, backlighting the trees into a wavy silhouette of crouching monsters.*

*Pounding, beating hooves, heading straight for the Henge.*

*A movement in the scope of her peripheral vision; dark, hairy, skulking in the tree line. Was it Stig? She'd always wanted to meet Stig. She smiled then waved, before realising that he wouldn't understand her friendly gestures. Stig was a caveman. Was he a real caveman? She recalled the debate in class while they were reading the book.*

*The desperate cries of a baby seeped into her subconscious mind...*

*The horses galloped on, Barney and Lou fading away into the gossamer-fine mist until they were no more. A dream within a dream.*

*Alone...*

*Alone in the swirling mist.*

*Eyes wide with spooked fear, the white horse pounded on with Maggie astride; her fingers entwined in the horse's windswept, flowing mane. Her legs gripped the torso, hard, rhythmic; like other hard, rhythmic body gestures... Like Jimmy. Jimmy the defiler...*

*The baby was still crying, its cries becoming louder, clearer.*

*Shapes loomed ahead in the glowing, swirling mist. Four shapes becoming more defined, framed by the standing stones of the Henge. Like the Four Horsemen of the Apocalypse, they rose before her; one in front, pointing, accusing, with the other three flanked behind. Their faces were nothing more than dark holes, cloaked with long hoods. The first Horseman raised his bony, skeletal hand and pointed it directly towards Maggie, causing her horse to come to a shuddering halt.*

*The golden glow of the solstice sunlight crept over the horizon, its rays kissing the scything blade of the first Horseman, igniting it with hellish flames.*

*Colours began to radiate from under the hood; copper, gold, and red – colours from the sunlight. The colour of Jimmy's hair. The hoods fell away from the Four Horsemen – Jimmy up front, Kate behind, flanked on either side by Jimmy's friends.*

*The baby was still crying, lying on the sacrificial altar. She knew the baby had to be Ben.*

*Still the bony hand pointed towards her.*

*"It was you... It was you, Maggie Braithwaite..."*

*Movement. Dark movement close by the child. She could see Stig gently lifting the child away from the sacrificial altar to safety. Where was he taking Ben? He disappeared, fading into the mist, becoming an angel. Taking Ben away to the angels...*

*The earth began vibrating below her. She could see rocks collapsing; the majesty that was once the Henge crashing all around her, crushing the Horsemen that were Jimmy, Kate and their evil accomplices. As they faded away in the swirling dust, she could hear their voices, laughing, screaming, accusing...*

*"You're no better than us, Maggie Braithwaite – one day you'll join us in the abyss of Hell..."*

*The earth became still. The air silent.*

*As the dust cleared, she could see the Henge still standing, she at its epicentre – stone sentinels protecting her frail humanity.*

*She was safe – for now.*

# Chapter 20

## Apple Pie

Mrs Green slid the door sign to "Closed" before dropping the latch. 'Well done, Maggie. I think that you did a great job on your first day. How about we have little sit-down, with a cuppa and slice of apple pie before we get on with the cleaning up? I think we've earned an end-of-day treat.'

Maggie smiled, relieved to know that she'd done well. 'Thanks, that'd be great, Mrs Green. I really enjoyed my day – everyone was so friendly.'

'And curious. You can be sure that the local crowd was checkin' you out.' She busied herself with pouring out tea and plating two slices of apple pie while Maggie cleared the last of the dishes to the counter before taking a seat.

'There you go, my dear. I hope you like it,' said Mrs Green. 'You can take the last of the soup upstairs with you, and those last two slices of quiche. Saves 'em going to waste.'

'Wow, thanks. That's really kind of you.' Maggie tucked into the apple pie like she hadn't eaten all day. 'Mmm, that's the best apple pie that I've ever tasted,' she exclaimed. 'Does it have a hint of cinnamon in it?'

Mrs Green beamed. 'Yes, it does! It's my Charley's favourite.'

'Is Charley your son?'

'Daughter. Short for Charlotte, but she thought that was too prissy and girlie, so shortened it to Charley. She spells it with an –ey rather than –ie. Anything to be different, that girl!' Mrs Green shook her head as she laughed.

'Does she help you here at the coffee shop?' Maggie asked, finger-mopping her plate for the pastry crumbs.

'No, love. I've no idea where she is. She went on the road a couple of years ago, just after she'd turned eighteen. She joined the circus, as I call it. Just her and her guitar in her camper van. One of those VW camper things. She stopped by last June for apple pie when the circus rolled in again, then off she went. We have this understanding, you see – no news is good news. Stops me from worrying. I just trust that she'll call me if there's a problem. So, providing neither she nor the police call me, then I assume all is well. She's twenty, she's smart, she's independent. What more can I wish for?' Her gaze turned wistful, then she smiled at Maggie.

Prickled by curiosity, Maggie asked, 'Do you have any other children, or is Charley like me, an only child?'

'No, I have a son too – Michael. He's at uni, studying history. I guess you can't live in a place like this without having an interest in history. He did a gap-year touring historical sites, then got his head down for his studies. He's the nerdy one. Charley's the butterfly of the two. So you're an only-child, then?'

Maggie nodded. 'Mum couldn't have any more after me. She had a really bad pregnancy which affected things, so that was that.'

Mrs Green patted Maggie's hand. 'Aye, it's hard for us mums when we have to let you kids go. But you have your own lives to live. Make your own way in the world.'

'So, what's this circus that you talk of? Did Charley join the circus? What does she do?' asked Maggie, with mind-visions of Charley in a clown costume.

Mrs Green wrinkled her nose and rolled her eyes before laughing. 'Oh no, sorry! By "circus", I mean when the convoys of pop fans and travellers arrive in June, for the big music festival near the stones. Can be quite a nuisance, some of them. Mostly it's all good spirited, but there are those who get a bit wild. Too much to drink and take all kinds of drugs. It's just so colourful, so that's why I call it a circus. Then when the festival is over, they just move on to the next one. Travel wherever they want, whenever they want.'

'I see,' acknowledged Maggie. 'But how do they live, or make money, these travellers? How do they survive?'

'Well, I don't know about the others, but our Charley sings around the local pubs with her guitar. She has a beautiful voice. It earns her meals, and a few pounds for fuel. She busks here and there, too.'

'It sounds like fun.' Maggie was already picturing the freedom of life on the road...

'Oh, I'm sure you'd love it, my dear. Our festival goes on for days, come rain or shine. Mostly rain!' she chortled. 'The locals are divided on their opinions about the festival – it makes money for some and leaves a big mess for others. Perhaps our Charley could take you along for a few days, if she stops by. You'll have to work it off, mind. Make up for any lost time.'

A flush of excited anticipation surged through Maggie. 'Agreed!' She offered her hand to Mrs Green to shake on the deal before she changed her mind.

'Right then, let's get this place cleaned up and ready for tomorrow morning. And don't forget to take that soup and quiche up with you.'

'I won't, Mrs Green. And thanks again – for everything.'

# Chapter 21

## A Sense of Pride

Maggie piled the coins onto the top of the payphone. She had been away for one whole week, and as promised, was going to call and update her mother. It had been a good week; one of new beginnings, new friends and new routines. After dialling the number, she poised the first coin ready.

'Hey, Mum, it's me. How are you?'

'Maggie! So lovely to hear from you!'

Maggie couldn't help but smile at her mother's over-exuberance, sensing that Liz had been sat by the telephone waiting for her to call. 'I'm fine, Mum. Everyone has been so nice; really friendly, and helpful. Mrs Green at the café has made sure that I've been eating – her apple pie is soooo good! I swear that I've already put on a few pounds.'

'Well, I'm glad to hear it, Maggie.' Liz stopped fiddling with the phone wire, her nervousness slowly easing away.

'We had some French tourists in the café the other day. I got a chance to practise my school-book French. It was quite funny, really. They must have been impressed though, as they gave me a fifty-pence tip! Mrs Green said that it was okay for me to keep it.'

'Fifty pence! Goodness me, these tourists don't seem to know the value of money. Lucky you. And what about the pub – what's that like?' asked Liz.

'Wow, there's been a lot to learn there – all the different drinks and stuff. Plus, you have to add up in your head as you're going along. That's really polished up my mental arithmetic skills. It's mostly pints and shorts, though. The punters don't seem to drink fancy stuff like wine. And they have theme-nights each weekend, so there's always something different happening...'

'Such as?'

'Well, this weekend had a Mexican Night, next weekend will have a Pub Quiz, then a local band will play the weekend after that – those kind of things. I heard them talking about having a Fifties Night soon – that'd be right up your street, Mum, something from the rock and roll era.'

Liz laughed, as she recalled her younger days. 'Oh, your dad certainly looked very handsome in his teddy-boy outfit, and his Brylcreem quiff! And me with my polka-dots and tiny waist. We knew how to jive!'

Interrupted by the beeps, Maggie fed a few more coins into the telephone box. 'The locals keep laughing at my Northern accent – they think it's funny how we pronounce words like "bath" and "grass", rather than "baarth" and "graars". Anyway, what's been happening up in your part of the world?'

'Oh, nothing much. Millers Common is just the same as when you left it. No births, deaths or marriages to report. No gossip. It sounds like you're better off where you are, Maggie. I'm well proud of you for taking the initiative, my love.'

Maggie felt a glow rise in her cheeks. 'Aww, thanks, Mum. That means a lot to me.'

'Well, I'm just relieved to hear that things are working out for you. At least I can sleep a bit easier, as they say.'

'I feel a lot easier too – at least I don't have to worry about that bitch Katie Gould breathing down my neck.'

'Maggie! That's no way to talk about someone. Besides, she'll soon be off to uni. Good riddance to bad rubbish,' sneered Liz.

'Now who's talking badly of someone! Anyway, you've nothing to worry about, Mum. Mrs Green at the coffee shop seems to have taken me under her wing. I think she's grasping at maternal straws since her kids left home,' laughed Maggie. 'She's got two kids, both a little older than me. Charley and Michael. Michael is at university – he's the brainy one; and Charley lives life on the road in a camper van. Can you believe it – just visits Mrs Green once a year when the music festival comes to the area. Charley's the butterfly, flitting from festival to festival, and town to town. Hopefully we'll see each other more often than they do, eh?'

'Oh, I hope so, Maggie. But so long as I know you're okay, then that's fine by me. Maybe I could come for another visit in the summer? Take in some more of the area.'

*It also means that I'm not constantly having people asking about you, and having to make up all kinds of excuses…It's enough to say, "She's working away, down South. Besides, she's eighteen now, and got her own life to lead".*

Maggie looked at the small pile of coins on top of the payphone as she heard the beeps yet again demanding a top-up. 'Anyway, that's me done; all my change is used up,' she lied. 'Love you, Mum. I'll call you next week, yeah…'

'Love you, too, Maggie. I look forward to it…'

# Chapter 22

## The Butterfly

Maggie wrinkled her nose at the smell of stale beer – she hated being down in the cellar among the dark shadows and lurking uncertainty. She dodged the bare light bulb, landing instead in a puddle of beer on the old flagstone floor. She cursed under her breath as the sticky brown liquid splashed up the legs of her jeans.

A voice from above channelled a request down the cellar hatch.

'And can you bring up an extra crate of Newcastle Brown – I'm anticipating an influx of festival goers, and that seems to be quite a favourite with 'em.'

'Will do, Mr Chambers...'

As she emerged from the cellar trapdoor, she plonked the wooden crate down on the floor, clattering the bottles.

'Go steady with the merchandise, Mags – you pay for what you break,' chided Mr Chambers, his tone teasing.

Maggie rolled her eyes and feigned the actions of a subordinate serf, tugging at her forelock. 'So humbly very sorry, Mr Chambers, sir. Beggin' your forgiveness, sir!'

He flicked out at her with the tea-towel, the tip cracking in the air. 'I should think so, too, girl. Behave yourself, or I'll send you back down into the dark hole!'

Maggie could feel her core glowing with a sense of belonging. In the few months that she'd been there, the locals had made her feel welcome, and she had slotted right in with the bar crowd; an eclectic mix of rock music fans, emerging punks, and hippies – mostly local outcasts with a smattering of travelling outsiders, which suited Maggie just fine. Many a drunken punter had found Maggie to be a trustworthy confidante; whether it be listening to their tales of woe, stories about their hedonistic lifestyles, or their frequent brushes with the law as they were moved on from place to place. They treated her well, they had a laugh, and best of all, there was a wooden bar separating them if they got too flirty with her. Plus the punters were big spenders in the jukebox, keeping it constantly fed. It was reputed to be one of the best jukeboxes in the locale, loaded with everything from Foreigner to Status Quo, Janis Joplin to Patti Smith, and Pete Seeger to Bob Seger.

While she scrambled around on the floor behind the bar, restocking the shelves before opening, her ears pricked up when she heard the faint strains of an acoustic guitar being tuned up, then a practice run-through of Lennon's *Working Class Hero*. Maggie felt the hairs rise on her forearms as she absorbed the smooth yet powerful vocals.

From her ground level position, Maggie threw a packet of salted peanuts at Mr Chambers to get his attention. 'Psst – who's that?' She nodded and pointed towards the direction of the voice and the guitar.

He threw the nuts back at Maggie, and grinned. 'It's tonight's singer. I slotted in a Friday act for this weekend. You approve, I take it?'

'Shit, yeah! She sounds amazing. Who is it?' she whispered, not wanting to disturb the tune-up.

'She's some local kid. Well, she was local, but she's one of those travellers now. You know her mum, Mrs Green. It's her daughter, Charley. She played here last year as well, when the travellers stopped by for the festival at the Henge.'

Her shelf-restocking finished, Maggie smoothed her fingers through her hair to make it presentable before emerging from under the bar.

Mr Chambers checked the clock, then went around the bar to turn on the jukebox. 'Five minutes to opening, Maggie. I reckon it's going to be an extra-busy Friday night.'

Maggie gave him a thumbs-up and broad grin of acknowledgement, and took this as her cue to remove the bar towels from the pumps. Unaware that Charley had moved over to the bar area, Maggie jumped at the sound of her voice.

'Hi, I'm Charley.' She extended her hand towards Maggie, her slim fingers offering a firm grasp with her friendly handshake. 'Erm, where can I leave my guitar case seeing as how the changing room seems to have become the stockroom these days?' She laughed.

'Sorry, that's the safest place,' apologised Maggie. 'Most of the acts either shove their stuff in there, or put their boxes and cases back in their car or van.'

'Okay.' She smiled, then headed towards the stockroom sandwiched between the bar and the small, elevated stage area.

Maggie watched her, mesmerised by the intense azure blue of Charley's loose kaftan style top. A matching floral headband crowned her long blonde hair. She lowered her gaze as Charley returned, and began fiddling with pulling-off pints, to make sure that the hand-pumps were primed and ready.

Charley seated herself gently on a barstool at the side of the opening hatch – her perch for the rest of the evening between the performance sets.

'So, you're the girl who's working at my mum's coffee shop, uh? Mum's told me all about you.'

A flush rose to Maggie's cheeks as she stammered to answer. 'Hopefully only nice things!' She laughed, her voice betraying a slightly nervous edge.

'Of course.' Charley fiddled in her little handbag for her lip gloss. 'She says that you're doing a great job. Don't you have the grotty little flat over the coffee shop, too?'

Maggie nodded. 'It isn't so bad. It's all that I need – somewhere to call home. Your mum tells me that you live on the road, in a camper van.'

'Yep, that's right. Just me and my guitar. I decided that village life wasn't for me – at least, not this village. So I bought the van, and went off with the crowd that follows the festivals and stuff. Free to be me...' She smiled at Maggie. 'Have you been to any of the festivals?'

'Not yet. I'd really like to, though. I've read about them in magazines and stuff.' Maggie hoped that Charley had taken the subliminal bait.

'You should come with me to this year's festival at the Henge – I can take you, and introduce you to the rest of the tribe. There's usually six other vehicles in our group, with about fifteen people, give or take. We all travel together. Quite the little community on wheels, we are. Watch out for each other, help each other. Share stuff.'

*Bingo! Bait taken!* 'Thanks, I'd love that. I probably can't get any time off from the pub this weekend, but I could come during the daytime. Your mum said that it would be okay for me to get some time off next week to come with you, if I wanted.'

'It sounds like you and Mum have already been plotting my arrival!' laughed Charley. 'But yes, you can come along.'

After pouring a still-orange for Charley, Maggie slipped into her role as barmaid once the doors were unbolted and the pub magically filled with thirsty, music-hungry punters.

Over the course of the evening, Maggie found her eyes wandering in the direction of Charley – the subtle but decisive way she moved, the controlled yet friendly way that she spoke, the passionate, powerful way that she sang. Here was a girl who had taken control of her life, moved around as she pleased and was doing what made her happy.

Maggie was smitten.

# Chapter 23

## Initiation

Maggie lay in bed looking up at the ceiling and absently let her thoughts drift over the mind-blowing evening at the pub, and her meeting with Charley Green. Her eyes followed the swirls in the Artex; swirls that became waves on an ocean – an ocean on which she floated free. The illusion of the sea-swell rocked Maggie, the image gently soothing. It was just what she needed to calm the sparking neurons. The blue colour of Charley's top filtered into the swirling images, the patterns morphing into a beautiful Mediterranean ocean.

Shimmering.

Mesmerising.

Just like Charley – shimmering, like the blonde of her hair.

Mesmerising, like her voice, her smile, her music...

At the end of the evening, Charley had graciously taken her applause from the crowd, graciously accepted her payment from Mr Chambers, then graciously given Maggie a lift home from the pub to her little flat, before heading to her mum's place for the night. Maggie reflected on her new-found friendship and smiled. Although they hadn't been able to persuade Mr Chambers to give Maggie this coming Saturday and Sunday evening off, he had given in to their begging for the following Thursday and Friday evening as a compromise. Maggie recalled his rosy-cheeked blush as Charley hugged him with thanks, such was the effect that she seemed to have on people. She felt her own cheeks rising with warmth – though she hadn't really had any physical contact with Charley apart from the initial handshake, she had occasionally felt as though she was being observed from a distance, and had sensed that Charley's goodnight-wave and broad smile was one of...something. Maggie couldn't quite put her finger on it, but the gesture seemed subliminally loaded. Maybe it would all seem different in daylight – tonight had been quite a highly-charged, full-on evening in the pub. As for tomorrow – well, that would be her initiation into the world of festivals...

Battling with the weight of her eyelids, Maggie succumbed and closed them, allowing sleep to creep in and claim her. And for the first time in a long time, it would be a dreamless sleep.

Like a kid in the proverbial sweet-shop, Maggie's eyes darted from left to right, her senses having already gone into overdrive as Charley led her by the hand through the throng of festival-goers. None of the "tribe", as Charley called them, was near their encampment, so now began the search for them in the crowd. The slick, muddy earth of the field proved to be challenging yet amusing to walk on, as the two girls slipped and laughed their way through the colourful sea of people. And what people! Clothed. Half-clothed. Unclothed. Singles. Pairs. Groups. Long hair. Short hair. Spiky hair. No hair. But all smiling and happy. Thumping music drifted through the air, intertwined with sweet, mind-intoxicating smells, the pungent smell of wood-smoke and greasy food wagons. The all-encompassing atmosphere of the site penetrated through to Maggie's core and surged through her veins. Utopia had been discovered.

Charley pointed off to the right. 'There they are – see the flag with the sun and rainbow on it? And the girl with blue hair? That's Penny. She's dyed her hair every colour of the rainbow – I'm surprised that she's got any hair left, she's coloured it so often! C'mon...'

By the time Maggie returned to the pub that Saturday evening, she had learned more about life in a few hours than she had ever imagined possible. An alternative life – the kind that she'd only ever seen on news stories, or heard grown-ups tut-tut about. The kind of lifestyle that she craved. The group had made her feel welcome, and she could sense the community spirit that threaded between them – each member was either running away from something or had some skeleton in their family cupboard, yet they provided freely given moral support for their own. Nothing was asked of each other, but everyone played a role in the success of the group.

*Kindred spirits.*

\*\*\*

The aroma of freshly baked tea-cakes wafted through the air as Mrs Green lifted the baking tray out of the oven. She set the tray down beside the wire racks loaded with cooling sausage rolls and scones before going to open the little window over the coffee shop door. It was a sales trick that she'd learned over the years of running the café – first, allow the tempting smells to build up within, then open a window to allow them out into the street just before the ten o'clock opening. After all, who can resist the smell of freshly baked goods? She looked up as the door marked "Private" opened, with Charley exiting first; her gait calm and measured, followed by a broadly grinning Maggie.

'Somebody looks excited,' she teased.

'Oh, I am!' Maggie's voice gushed with a release of bottled-up eagerness. 'Thanks for letting me take this week off work, Mrs Green.' She hugged the coffee shop owner almost as if it were her own mother. 'It's really kind of you.'

'Oh, you've earned it, Maggie, my love. You've worked up the time, just as promised. Now – you just make sure that you enjoy yourself.' Mrs Green then turned to Charley to give her a goodbye hug. 'Make sure that you look after Maggie, do you hear?'

'I will, Mum. Don't worry – I'll take good care of her.' Charley gave her mother a knowing wink and wry smile without Maggie seeing. Mrs Green narrowed her eyes as if to question Charley's intentions.

Deflecting any further eye contact with her mother, Charley grabbed Maggie's hand. 'Right then, we've got a festival to go to – are you ready? Got your bag, and toothbrush, and everything?'

Maggie nodded, a little dazed and overwhelmed with excitement, her grin almost childlike.

'We'll see you at the end of the week, Mum. I'll stop by before heading off to the next festival. I think Knebworth is next.'

Mrs Green unlocked the door to the coffee shop, and gave the girls one last hug each as they left. 'Be good! And if you can't be good, at least be careful!'

The crowds had already swelled in numbers by the time Charley and Maggie returned to the site, making negotiating the drive back to the camping area a tricky one. A light drizzle had begun to fall, adding to the greasiness of the grass and mud.

Charley laughed when she saw the "Reserved for Hovis" sign hammered on a stake in the ground by their encampment.

'Who's Hovis?' asked Maggie.

'The VW,' replied Charley, laughing.

Maggie looked puzzled. 'Okay – explain!'

'Well, if you look at the shape of the camper, it's shaped like a loaf of bread, right?'

'Right – and...?'

'Well, because of their shape, they're affectionately called "bread" or "loaf" in the camper-world. And because this one is a beige colour, I gave it the nickname of "Hovis",' Charley clarified, grinning.

Maggie began howling with laughter. 'So I'm going to be living in a loaf of brown bread for the next few days! That's so cool.'

'Anyway, here we are.' Charley pulled on the handbrake, then smiled at Maggie. 'Be prepared to get very wet and muddy. It looks like the weather's going to be its usual poxy self. Oh, for a festival without mud and rain!' she laughed. 'Grab your coat, and let's go find the others. It's time to rock and roll!'

Irritated by an afternoon of intermittent drizzle, rain and sparse sunshine, the tribe headed back to their encampment to seek some much needed warmth and respite, their youthful exuberance having fallen victim to the spirit-deflating elements of persistent shitty weather. As a seasoned group of travellers, they had learned to position their camp in such a way that all tent flaps, rear van doors, or side camper doors opened out onto a central point, encircling their camp-fire. And by parking two of their vehicles side by side, tarpaulin sheets could be lashed between them, top and back, to create an enclosed communal area. All safe, all equal.

After warming up and drying off, they all gravitated towards their communal area armed with instruments, cider and camping chairs.

As Maggie looked around the group, she could see that she was the youngest – their ages spanning from smooth-skinned like Charley, to quite a bit older and careworn. Society's victims, taking strength in their comradeship. Some were in couples, others were single, but all had chosen to step out of the conventional lifestyle for something much less constraining. Yet they were still classed as outcasts, victimised for being on the fringes of society; for not paying their way in life's daily white-collar grind. It was a life that outsiders – the white-collar, bricks-and-mortar communities – didn't understand, nor did they try to. But the travellers *did* pay their way; maybe not with money, but they would exchange farm labour for food, or a field in which to camp. With the landowner's permission, they cleared wooded areas of broken trees for firewood. They scoured rubbish tips for useful equipment that would otherwise become toxic landfill. They knew how to live at one with the earth, and at one with each other, yet they were shunned as weirdos and frequently moved on from place to place.

Charley tuned up her guitar, while the blue-haired girl, Penny, took up her penny whistle. One of the older guys, Bingo, gave his bodhrán a quick tap-around in order to loosen up his wrist. Maggie was intrigued with the array of appropriate character nicknames with which they had given themselves, having (probably) long since forgotten the names that they were baptised with. Penny's was obvious, because of her instrument. Bingo was apparently so called because he was always fiddling with his balls. There was an older guy with unkempt hair and tatty beard whom they called Catweazle; an affectionate homage to the old wizard from a children's television programme. He appeared to be in charge of the tambourine. Others within the tribe bore nicknames such as Bones, Rolo, Queenie, and Fred and Wilma. The twin sisters within the group had earned the monikers of Pinky and Perky (on account of their rosy-cheeked, piggy-faced appearance), but they had taken their alternative appellations in good humour. Maggie briefly wondered how long it would take her to learn all of their names. Only Charley seemed to have retained her own name, but even then, it had been shortened away from Charlotte. She fleetingly pondered what name they might give her...

*Maggie Minge-Muncher...*

*Maggie Minge-Muncher...*

Kate Gould's face swam involuntarily through Maggie's mind. She closed her eyes and squeezed them tight, trying to crush away the image of Kate.

*Not now – why now? Please, Kate, just fuck off, and leave me alone!*

The sound of Charley's voice disrupted Maggie's moment of mental distress, unwittingly helping to dissolve the unwelcome image of Kate.

'Right then,' said Charley, 'time for a little sing-song. Let's show our guest what polished performers we are...' She gave a nod to Penny to lead them into Jethro Tull's *Living in the Past*, accompanied by Bingo and herself, while Catweazle proved himself to be a great vocalist; his movement and expressions perfectly emulating those of Ian Anderson.

Maggie found herself in open-mouthed awe as this tangled tribe of outcasts became a unified tribe of musicians and singers, morphing from song to song on the briefest of musical cues from each other.

As the evening wore on, the grey clouds moved to one side to allow the golden rays of the setting sun to reach out and touch the damp earth, creating a blanket of swampy warmth over the festival site. One by one, Charley's tribe stood and stretched then turned towards the fading light, like meerkats soaking up the final dregs of warmth ready to take them through the coolness of the night.

Charley disappeared inside her camper to put away the guitar, while others busied themselves with piss-breaks, replenishing cider stocks, stoking the fire, and bringing food. Like ants in a colony, each seemed to know what was needed before the evening could continue.

'Time for a little *Space Ritual*, methinks...' muttered Bingo, as he started his van so that he could turn on his cassette player and sound system.

Once the tribe reconvened, not only had the atmosphere changed to one of something edgier and more electronic, but the air had changed into a smoky, sweet-smelling fug. Maggie hadn't really noticed anyone smoking before, but could see that quite a few of them were now smoking hand-rolled cigarettes. Her naiveté slowly began to peel away once she realised what the cigarettes contained. She could feel her pulse quicken, nervous of being offered a toke – she'd never even tried a regular cigarette, let alone anything like this.

The electronic musical wizardry of Hawkwind cut through the speakers of Bingo's van; circulating, reverberating, back and forth. The sound waves cut through Maggie's consciousness and tickled her mind. She closed her eyes, but this only made the experience more intense, more focused. When she opened her eyes, she noticed Bingo watching her.

'Are you okay, young lady?' he asked.

She shook her head, not quite sure. 'Wow! Who is this band?'

'Ah, you mustn't panic, Maggie, for this is Hawkwind – the gods of electronic sound are merely launching a sonic attack on the mind...' He clapped his hands over his ears, his head swaying from side to side, then suddenly made a gesture like his head had exploded. 'Boom!'

Some of the others giggled at his implied musical reference from the lyrics, which, of course, went right over Maggie's head. Her brow furrowed with the realisation that some of the tribe were having a little giggle at her new-kid expense.

'Ah, ignore this old stoner, Maggie. Listening to Hawkwind has cooked his brain!' defended Penny. 'So, what kind of music do you like?' she asked.

'Mostly punk and new wave – basically anything that that's anti-establishment and tells the world to "Fuck off",' she laughed, feeling a little more emboldened. 'My absolute favourite though, is Patti Smith. I just love her stuff. Her music really talks to me...'

'Hey, she's playing at the Reading Festival later this summer. You should come with us. That's okay, isn't it, Charley? Maggie could travel with you, couldn't she?'

Maggie's eyes lit up at the prospect of actually seeing Patti Smith in concert. Not only that, but she'd been semi-invited to join them on the road. She looked at Charley for some glimmer of hope and acceptance.

Charley cocked her head to one side and scowled at Penny with fake admonishment. 'Well, it isn't just my decision,' she teased. 'All those in favour of Maggie joining the tribe say "Aye".'

A group chorus of "Aye" was returned.

'It looks like you're in!' Charley clapped Maggie on the back. 'Welcome to the tribe.'

'Anyway, I think it's time for a few more ciders and a game of Truth or Dare,' initiated Penny. 'Do you know how to play it?'

Maggie shrugged and shook her head. 'I'm sure I'll soon pick it up,' she replied, a little unsure about what she was getting herself into.

As the game progressed, she realised that for each "Truth" or "Dare" that was not acted upon, the person had to take a good swig of cider. And it would soon be coming to her turn. She swallowed hard, trying to decide which option she should go for.

'Right then, young Maggie,' bellowed Bingo, his voice now well and truly lubricated with cider, 'Truth or Dare?'

'Truth,' she replied.

Bingo thought for a moment. 'Have you ever...hmm... pissed your pants?'

'Yes, actually. When I was six years old, at Infants School. I was so engrossed in story-time that I peed myself. The teacher was cross with me because she had to clean up the puddle.' She laughed, now feeling a little more confident.

Bingo scratched his chin while he considered her reply. 'Aye, okay, it sounds genuine. Now it's your turn to ask.'

She turned to Charley, following the game format to question the person on the right. 'Truth or Dare?' she asked.

'Truth.'

Maggie pondered what question to present to her new friend without fear of offence or retribution. 'Have you ever been arrested by the pol...by the pigs?' She quickly amended her terminology to sound a little more anti-social.

'Yep, I once got nicked for speeding – and yes, my van can go fast enough, before any of you dispute the fact!'

'What do you think, Maggie? Do you think she's telling the truth?' asked Penny.

'Yeah, I think so...'

Charley smiled at Maggie, catching something deep in her eyes. Maggie felt her heart flutter and stomach roll over, unsure of how to read Charley's subliminal message, if indeed, that's what it was.

By the third round of the game, the loosening effects of the cider and grass was becoming evident on some of the older players, making the questions more obscure, random and dubiously personal. And although Maggie was only drinking not smoking, she could feel her throat beginning to constrict and head-space tighten. She took a swig of cider to try and ease her nervousness. Bingo readied himself to ask Maggie.

'Truth,' she replied.

He grinned, his mouth wet with cider residue. 'Have you ever had a threesome?'

Maggie felt the bile rise up from her stomach without control, throwing up a belly-full of warm cider all over the grass in front of her, splashing her Doc Martens and jeans.

Bingo bellowed with laughter. 'Well, I'm not sure how to take that reply, young Maggie.' He waved his hand dismissively. 'Let's move the game on. I'll ask Charley while our young friend here sorts herself out. Charley – Truth or Dare?'

Feeling a little bolder, Charley answered, 'Dare.'

'I dare you to kiss Maggie now that she's just thrown up.'

Ripples ran through the tribe, some erring on the side of disgust, others egging on the dare.

Charley looked at Maggie and gently wiped her face and mouth with the corner of her shawl. 'Sorry about this,' she whispered, before closing her eyes and gently kissing Maggie on the lips. The mutual feeling of softness, of warmth, of something igniting, cursed through Maggie, and she returned the kiss with involuntary tenderness.

The world stopped.

Suddenly aware that they were being observed, and were still part of a drinking game quickly brought them back into the moment.

But it had been their moment.

A moment that had brought a shift in their friendship.

'Well, I think we can safely say that Charley won the dare. Anyway, my lovelies, this old man is getting ready for some shut-eye. Big day tomorrow, solstice and all that.' Bingo saluted the tribe and stood up, his body swaying with the loosening effects of the alcohol and weed.

A murmured ripple of agreement went through the group, as they followed suit, and headed for their respective sleeping accommodation.

Charley held out her hand to Maggie, who was by now quite unsteady on her feet. 'C'mon you – bedtime...'

# Chapter 24

## You Can Run...

Charley drew the curtains, then fiddled around in the camper to pull out the table and make up the bed. Maggie tried her best to help, but could still feel a bucket-load of uncertainty sloshing about in her stomach.

'How are you feeling?' asked Charley, her concern sounding genuine.

'Like shit...'

'Here, come and jump onto the bed. Don't worry, I don't bite,' she laughed, patting the mattress.

Maggie sat on the edge of the bed and cautiously began unlacing her Doc Martens before trying to wriggle out of her jeans and socks. The front of her boots and the shins of her jeans were wet with sour smelling puke splashes, causing her stomach to lurch as her fingers touched the damp fabric. She could feel a blush rising to her neck and cheeks at the thought of taking off any more clothes.

As if by instinct, Charley shook her head. 'It's okay; you can sleep in your clothes if you feel more comfortable.

Maggie gave a nod of shy thanks and wriggled under her blanket, making sure that she tucked it under her feet and legs.

Charley turned off the main camper light, then squirmed into her sleeping bag beside Maggie. Before switching off the little reading lamp above their heads, Charley looked over at Maggie, who was lying prone and staring at the ceiling.

'What a day, eh! Welcome to festival-life and life with the tribe.'

Maggie turned her head towards Charley and smiled. 'Thanks. It's certainly been interesting. Is it like this all the time?'

'Only at festivals – we tend to get a bit carried away with the atmosphere. We're not like this with day-to-day living. Then we just get on with the routine business of survival. Anyway, like Bingo said, tomorrow's a big day, so let's get some sleep. Night, Mags.'

'Night night, Charley. And thanks for everything.'

*The bright glare of the stage lights intensified, burning into Maggie's eyes.*

*They began flashing...*

*Red, yellow, green, blue.*

*Red, yellow, green, blue.*

*Beams of light, all pointing at Maggie, putting her under the spotlight.*

*Red, yellow, green, blue.*

*Red, yellow, green, blue.*

*She put her hands over her eyes to shield them, to protect her retinas, but the translucent skin on her hands offered no defence against their glaring power.*

*Red, yellow, green, blue.*

*Red, yellow, green, blue.*

*Changing to:*

*Blue, blue, blue, blue – four blue lights, swirling.*

*Morphing into:*

*Police lights, swirling.*

*A sonic noise; sirens. Piercing, shrieking.*

*Chasing, chasing, chasing.*

*The police car moved up a gear.*

*A metallic voice came over the police radio...*

*"We're coming for you, Maggie Braithwaite..."*

*The sides of her body burst outwards as she sprouted another set of arms and hands, and used these to cover her ears, to protect them from the wailing, sonic screech of the sirens.*

*The four bright, flashing lights of the police car burned through the paper-thin skin of her hands, offering no protection for her eyes. Her second set of hands offered no defence to her ears. She could feel blood running through her fingers as her eyes and ears imploded with the intensity of the audio-visual attack.*

*Blood began to run down the back of her throat causing her to gag and vomit. Her sides ruptured once more, to give birth to a third set of arms and hands – hands to cover her mouth. To hold back the spewing blood.*

*The voice came again, louder and clearer...*

*"Vishnu cannot protect you, Maggie."*

*The voice became a chant –*

*"Hear no evil, Maggie. Hear nothing.*

*See no evil, Maggie. See nothing.*

*Speak no evil, Maggie. Say nothing.*

*SAY NOTHING, Maggie.*

*SAY NOTHING, Maggie."*

*The four police lights evolved into the head of her four tormentors: Kate, Jimmy and his two accomplices.*

*Four grotesque heads; spinning, spinning, spinning, spinning.*

*She could just make out baby Ben driving the police car as it bore down on her. He was a baby, yet he was a grown-up.*

*"No, Ben! Please... Ben, stop! Tell them to leave me alone!"*

*The crackling, metallic, police-radio voice filled the air, accusing...*

*"You only ever think about yourself, Maggie Braithwaite. You don't care about anyone else. You never want to help anyone else..."*

*"Keep running, Maggie Minge-Muncher."*

*"Keep running."*

'Maggie! Maggie – it's okay! Don't panic, I'm here...' Charley reached over to shake her friend gently, not wishing to frighten her more than she already appeared to be. 'It's okay, stay calm, take a breath...'

Maggie's eyes flickered open before suddenly sitting bolt upright in bed, her right hand clasped over her mouth.

Realising what was happening, Charley grabbed the night-time piss bucket and shoved it under Maggie's chin just as a five-finger spread of puke exploded from her mouth and down her nose. She heaved again, her fingers dripping with the acrid mix of cider and stomach fluids.

Once she was sure that Maggie had finished heaving, Charley took the bucket, then got a glass of water and some tissue for Maggie and helped to clean up her hands and mouth.

'Are you okay now? It sounded like you were having a bad dream.' Charley took the glass and tissue before going to tip the bucket of puke away under the van. She left the door open to allow some fresh air to circulate. After rinsing the bucket, she came and sat beside Maggie, her brow furrowed with genuine concern. 'Did you take anything tonight? Any drugs?'

Maggie shook her head. 'No. Not that I'm aware of, anyway. I've never done drugs before. Do you think one of the tribe could have slipped something in my drink?'

'No – we have clear rules about taking care of our own. They wouldn't do anything like that. We might take the piss out of each other, but we would never risk hurting each other with that kind of thing.' Charley put her hands over Maggie's as if to reassure her.

'Then I think it was just the cider, and the excitement of being here. Guess I was just a bit overwhelmed by it all.' She looked at Charley and smiled. 'Thanks for taking care of me. I didn't get off to a very good start as your guest, did I?' She laughed.

Charley rubbed Maggie on the shoulder, her touch friendly, soothing. 'Hey, no worries. We've all done it, and I'm sure we'll keep on doing it. You did seem to be having quite a bad dream, though. Can I ask you a personal question – and you don't have to answer if you don't want to – but who's Ben? You mentioned his name a couple of times in your dream.'

'I talked in my sleep!' Maggie was horrified. Adrenaline began trickling into the pit of her stomach, setting off a chain reaction through her veins. She held her head downcast so as to avert direct eye contact with Charley. 'I suppose I owe you some kind of explanation as to why I'm here...'

'Only if you want to, Maggie. No pressure.' Charley got back into her sleeping bag and sat up, making herself comfy with cushions and a pillow.

Maggie began picking at her fingernails. 'It all started a couple of years ago. I told my best friend – who, by the way, is no longer my best friend, that I'm a lesbian. Anyway, she spread rumours about me, called me all kinds of names – particularly "Maggie Minge-Muncher", and I got bullied at school because of it.'

Charley frowned, then nodded. 'Go on,' she urged, her voice gentle, non-judgemental.

Maggie took a breath before continuing, knowing that she was about to speak of her worst nightmare. 'Kate must have told her older brother about it, and so one day, when I was on the way home from school, Jimmy and his mates picked me up in his car – it was raining, and I thought he was being kind. Anyway, they took me to an old, derelict cottage and raped me. All three of them. I've never told anyone, though...'

'What! Not even your mum?'

Muted by the painful memory, Maggie shook her head. 'I guess I was scared what her reaction might be. I felt so ashamed, so dirty...'

Even in the low glow from the reading lamp, Charley couldn't hide the shock on her face. 'Poor you! You've carried this secret all this time...'

'Oh, it gets worse. The rape left me pregnant – that's who Ben was – is, I mean. He's my little boy. But I still hadn't told my mum about, you know, being queer; I just told her that I was pregnant because I'd been experimenting with a boy.' Maggie absently smoothed the blanket on her legs before continuing. 'Anyway, cutting a long story short, we decided to keep the pregnancy a secret – I went away to a convent, and eventually gave up Ben for adoption. But at least I got the opportunity to tell Mum about being a lesbian, though I know she still struggles with that. She thinks that it's something a doctor can cure with tablets.' She finally looked up, then raised her hands, giving them a little hallelujah-shake. 'And so here I am. Rather than suffocate to death in our poxy little town, I decided to make a new life for myself – with my mum's blessing of course. It's a win-win for both of us.'

'My, my, aren't we birds of a feather. In case you hadn't figured it out, I'm a lesbian, too. My parents were shocked at first, but they've grown to accept it. That's also the reason why I gave up on village life – too claustrophobic. Maybe it was our destiny to meet, if you believe in all that kind of stuff.'

Maggie looked at Charley, a blush rising in her cheeks. 'Maybe. But in all honesty, I've never been with a girl before. It's just something that I feel inside. It feels right to be sitting here with you, but on the other hand, I haven't a clue what to do.'

'Well, I'm not exactly what you would call experienced. I've only had a few drunken, experimental fumbles,' she chuckled. 'Anyway, let's just get through tonight, and take one day at a time, eh. No pressure. I'm happy to just be your friend, if that's as far as it goes. And, if it goes beyond that, then lucky me...' Charley gave Maggie a coy shove with her body. 'What about your dad? What did he say about all this?'

'My dad was killed a few years ago by a drunk driver. We've had our fair share of bad luck, me and Mum. But despite our differences, we are still friends.' Maggie stopped to take a breath – that sharp intake of breath that preludes the onset of tears brought about by abject despair. 'By the way, you're the only one that knows about the rape – apart from the bastards that did it, of course. Please don't say anything to anyone.' The floodgates opened to release an accumulation of pent-up emotions: of lies, fury, horror, self-loathing and self-pity.

'Wow! Maggie, I had no idea that you'd been through so much. Poor you! I'm honoured that you trust me with your secret. Come here...' Charley reached out to take Maggie in her arms and snuggled her head in the crook of her shoulder. 'Sshh, it's okay. You're safe now. I'll take care of you...' She kissed the top of Maggie's head and held her close, forging an unconditional bond between them. 'C'mon – let's snuggle down and get some sleep. You must be exhausted.'

Framed by streaks of black mascara and eye shadow, Maggie's crystal blue eyes looked up at Charley. She smiled weakly and sighed; one of exhaustion and defeat. 'Sounds good. Thanks for everything, Charley.'

'No probs. We girls have got to stick together, eh. Night, night.' She kissed Maggie's forehead, not wanting to intrude further into her personal space.

'Night, Charley.'

The new day dawned with the gentle tapping of light rain on the camper van roof. Muted sounds of people moving around outside penetrated the thin walls. The solar rays of a lukewarm sun eventually won the battle to push away the showers, backlighting the orange floral curtains, creating a cosy, honeyed glow within.

Charley propped herself up on one elbow and looked at the just-waking Maggie. She smiled and gently ruffled Maggie's hair.

'Look at the state of you, girl – anybody would think that you were partying all night. How are you feeling?'

Maggie stuck out her tongue. 'Ugh. My mouth feels like the bottom of a bird cage, all dry and gritty...' She could feel an involuntary blush rising.

'What you need is a medicinal cup of tea and some toast! I'll put the kettle on.'

While Charley pottered about making tea and breakfast, Maggie eased herself out of bed and put on a change of clothes before stripping down the bed and returning it to the daytime table area. The whistle from the kettle indicated that the water was boiling and ready.

'Wait for it – any minute now,' laughed Charley.

Maggie looked at her, puzzled.

A firm knocking came at the door of the camper.

'Namaste, ladies. Would that be a cup o'tea that you're making? Old Bingo would love a cuppa!'

'He does this every morning – as soon as he hears the whistle from the kettle, he comes knocking.' She went to open the door and let him in.

'Namaste, Bingo. I suppose you want a slice of toast too?' she asked their morning guest.

'Don't mind if I do – that would be lovely.' Bingo smiled, then plonked himself next to Maggie on the bench seat. 'So, are we ready for today?' He rubbed his hands together, and grinned. 'I think the plan is to mooch around and watch a few bands, before heading up to the woods and the stones later. Will you two young ladies be joining us?'

Charley came and joined them at the table, bringing a tray laden with the pot of tea, mugs and toast rack. 'We wouldn't miss it for the world, Bingo. Marmalade?'

Wherever Maggie looked, she could see groups of people engaging in all kinds of partying, the carnival atmosphere setting the stage for the moment leading up to the solstice. She could sense the building excitement rippling through the festival-goers.

As the tribe headed into the wooded glade, they passed a group of naked people holding hands and dancing in a circle around a small clump of trees – their faces were streaked with colour; their only clothing the beads around their necks. They passed couples making love. They passed people talking to the trees. The woodland had become a garden of hedonistic ritual.

The tribe found a suitable old tree around which they could sit and hold hands – this would be the tree that would soak up their hopes for the forthcoming year, its branches delivering their messages out into the cosmos. The iridescent luminosity from the rising moon pierced the dimming sky, its fullness casting an ethereal glow into the woodland. One by one, each tribe member addressed the tree with a serene, quiet reverence as they proclaimed their personal wish, before giving thanks to Mother Earth, the universe and all those who had gone before. Maggie could feel her anti-establishment core being temporarily quashed as she was drawn into the moment, delivering a wish to ask the tree for renewed hope. When it came to Charley's turn, she asked the tree to deliver the unity that would make her whole – to find the Yin to balance her Yang. Maggie felt Charley's hand gently squeeze her own. She smiled inwardly, tentatively returning Charley's squeeze.

After their earth-bound homage to life and the cosmos, the tribe moved to the site of the standing stones, before separating – each needing their personal space in which to honour the solstice.

Charley came and stood behind Maggie then curled the protective wings of her shawled arms around her partner's diminutive frame.

'I can feel your heartbeat,' whispered Maggie, as Charley rested her chin on Maggie's shoulder and snuggled closer to her head.

'Sshh. Take one last look at the full moon then close your eyes and open your senses. Let the moment wash over you. You'll feel cleansed, different somehow. I promise you. Listen to Mother Earth speaking to you.'

The full moon hung like a silver pearl in the wakening sky – kissing the heavens before being extinguished by the rising sun. A low misty haze cloaked the trees and landscape of the serene Wiltshire countryside, soaking up the first rays as they broke free. Maggie did as instructed and closed her eyes, the scene before her now securely imprinted into her mind's-eye.

An eerie silence descended over the crowd as they all experienced their own interpretation of the moment – that soul-cleansing moment when the first flush of solstice sunlight creeps over the horizon to kiss the earth; to kiss all those who are facing towards it in the simplest, most basic form of Earth worship.

Maggie instinctively opened her eyes to witness the spectacle; to absorb the light and life-giving energy of the new dawn. She slowly became aware of sounds returning, as the birds broke the silence and burst into song to herald the birth of a new day. The unified body of mankind slowly began their collective salutation of the moment, soaking up the first energising rays as they mingled among the ancient standing stones of the Henge.

Many faces were wet with involuntary tears; mouths open in awe, or moving in silent prayer. Others lay prone on the ground, allowing the sunlight to wash over them; to cleanse away the dark shadows of their past.

It was a moment that Maggie knew would forever be a part of her psyche – a moment that she hoped would cleanse her of past sins and lead the way to a new light and a new life. New hope.

She gently pulled Charley's arms tighter around her shoulders and snuggled closer. Her mind swam, suddenly invaded by the voice of her lyrical Earth Mother, Patti Smith. The strains of *Because the Night* began weaving into her soul, the powerful voice embracing every fibre; telling the story of lovers. The music rose to a crescendo in her mind. This night would be theirs – the sealing of Charley's wish. To become as one.

When the sun met the moon.

When daytime met the night.

When light met with darkness.

When Yin met Yang.

A brief moment in time woven into their infinity.

# Chapter 25

## Moral and Morale Dilemmas

Charley looked through the window of the VW camper and waved to Bingo to acknowledge that she'd seen him. She could see others in their group hurriedly making their way through the heavy rain to the communal tarpaulin-covered area between Bingo's van and Catweazle's mini-bus.

'C'mon, Mags. Looks like there's a group meeting. Grab your coat and boots...'

Shivering, the girls joined the huddled throng.

Bingo banged his bodhrán to get everyone's attention. 'Right then, my lovelies – the word is out that people are going to move on. Seems like there's not only us getting pissed off with all this rain. Probably best to get off the site before we all get stuck.' A ripple of agreement moved through the group. He held his hand up for quiet. 'Anyways, there's talk of moving over to Knebworth before going to Glastonbury.

'Who's on at Knebworth?' asked Penny.

'Genesis are headlining, I think.'

'All those in favour, say "Aye".'

'Aye.'

'Right then – let's get packed up, and get the fuck outta here!' laughed Bingo.

Charley turned to Maggie. 'Are you going to come with us then?'

'I'd really like to,' Maggie replied. 'But what about your mum – what do you think she'll say if I don't go back to work at the coffee shop?'

'What can she say? It's your decision. Anyway, what about *your* mum – what will she say if you give it all up, and go on the road?'

Maggie hesitated before replying. 'I dunno. Yeah, perhaps I should give her a call and let her know…'

\*\*\*

'Well, would you look at that,' Liz exclaimed to herself, as she picked up the dog-eared copy of *Stig of the Dump* found tucked away under Maggie's pillow – obviously left there prior to their visit to Wiltshire. She recalled Maggie saying that she'd re-read the old classic before they went. Liz carefully unfurled the cover, bending back the corners so that they could once again lie flat. Her smile of reminiscence was soon swept away as the thoughts of her sister's upcoming visit invaded her thoughts.

*Why on earth did I agree to go with our Sandra on this trip to Paris? Just 'cause she's got money to throw around… "Let's go to Paris for our birthdays," she says – "our joint celebration; my fiftieth and your forty-fifth. My treat! You'll love Paris!" Oh, will I? Paris in July – it will be hot and dusty, and stink of garlic and Gauloises cigarettes!*

Liz looked around the bedroom – it would have to suffice; fresh bedding and a quick polish and vacuum.

*After all, she's only my sister, not royalty. Just 'cause we share the same birth-date doesn't mean to say that we share the same ideals. She'll just have to take things as she finds 'em. Let her run her fingers over the surfaces; let her try and find dust! I suppose she has a cleaner… Well, lucky for some.*

Liz stripped off the sheets and threw them out onto the landing before retrieving fresh bedding from the airing cupboard, huffing and puffing as she went about preparing the room for her sister's visit.

*"I've booked us into a lovely hotel – it has a view of the Eiffel Tower,"* she says. *"How about I stop by at your place for a couple of days en-route to Manchester Airport, then we can travel together. Have you ever flown before?" Really! No, Sandra, I don't have the jet-set business life-style that you have… You chose to remain single and chase a career. I chose family life, remember!*

After making the bed, Liz gathered together all the loose odds and ends that Maggie had left lying around. She smiled at Maggie's penchant for sinister looking black make-up and nail polish.

A flash of gold lettering caught her eye as she slotted *Stig of the Dump* back onto the bookshelves.

A Holy Bible.

On Maggie's bookshelves.

What on earth was Maggie doing with a Bible? Of course – her time spent at the convent. It must be a standard issue from the nuns. Strange that she'd brought it home with her, though. Bitten by the curiosity bug, she picked it out from the bookshelf, gasping as Maggie's secretive contents fell out from their hiding place. Liz looked around and flushed as if caught in the act, or on a hidden camera, then quickly bent down to pick up the escaped pieces. She looked at the photos of Ben and sighed.

*How I would have loved to have a little boy – one of each, that's what I'd always wanted. But…well, it was never meant to be. Just grateful to have been blessed with Maggie. It must have been hard for Maggie though, to give up this little chap for adoption.*

As she carefully placed the photos of Ben back inside the cover, Liz felt a pang of guilt sting her through the heart for what she'd forced Maggie to do.

*Well, maybe "encouraged" was a better word than "forced"…*

She noticed some folded pieces of vellum paper among the photographs, and turned them over in her hands. They looked like the pages of a letter. Slowly, slowly, she found herself opening the folds.

Liz noticed that the letter was addressed to her. Written, yet never sent. She sat on the edge of Maggie's bed, and began to read. Why would Maggie write a letter but not send it? As her eyes scanned over the words she could feel her stomach lurch and roll. Her hand shot up to her mouth to stifle a gasp. With her breath now coming in short jags, she picked up the photos of Ben and studied them. The glowing, golden fuzz – surely not...

Exasperated, Mrs Green dusted the flour from her hands before picking up the telephone. It was as if people knew that she would either be elbow deep in flour or lifting something hot from the oven, and chose that particular moment to call.

'Hello, Willow Tree Coffee Shop. Oh, hello, Mrs Braithwaite. –Yes, fine thanks. –Maggie? No, sorry, she isn't here. –No, I mean she's left. –Yes, just a couple of days ago.' Mrs Green held the receiver at a safe distance from her ear, Liz's voice having risen a few octaves at the news of Maggie's sudden departure. 'No, she took a few days off to go to the festival with my Charley. You know – the one here at Stonehenge. Then they stopped by last Friday to pick up all of Maggie's belongings. They've decided to go on the road together and do the summer festivals. Left me in the lurch, it has, until I find somebody else. –Well, no, it's not for me to stop her. She's eighteen... Didn't she call you to let you know? –Oh, I see. –Yes. Yes, of course I'll tell her that you called, next time I hear from Charley. –Yes, lovely to hear from you, too. –Okay. –Yes, bye, Mrs Braithwaite.'

Liz glared at the telephone handset as if it would change the news that she'd just received – Maggie had quit her job at the café, presumably the pub, too – and upped sticks. Gone "on the road" as Mrs Green called it.

Without a word to her own mother.

A mother who'd helped to pick up the pieces when Maggie had announced that she was pregnant.

A mother who'd helped to pick up the pieces when Maggie returned home distraught after finally giving up Ben for adoption.

She toyed with the Holy Bible, careful not to damage the letter and photos. But then again, who could blame Maggie for going on the run? Liz could feel hot tears welling behind her eyes. The torture that Maggie must have been going through, the guilt and shame that she must still be carrying. It would never go away.

*Those Goulds have got a lot to answer for!*

She looked at the photos of Ben. The sandy coloured fuzz was a clear give-away as to his paternal heritage. Without any shadow of a doubt, Jimmy Gould was the father. She'd seen him with his two friends – neither of the other two had a look that could be matched to Ben.

But perhaps it was just as well that she hadn't spoken to her daughter – Maggie would have only accused her of snooping in her room and going through her private business. Of that, she could be sure. But there must have been some reason why Maggie had chosen not to send the letter – Liz could only speculate that shame and guilt must be the root cause. The letter had specifically asked for Liz not to go to the police – that Maggie didn't want the matter to go any further. And who could blame her for not wanting to relive her ordeal in court; to face the people who had ruined her. But at least Maggie had had the courage to write something down, to release the burden to paper.

As sick as the contents made Liz feel, she now had some kind of understanding or explanation for Maggie's behaviour and attitude towards her, and towards life in general.

*And who wouldn't rebel after such an ordeal?*

Liz thought of Barbara Gould and her superior, holier-than-thou persona.

*Well, if only you knew your children!*

But then again, does any parent really know their child? She recalled one of Maggie's updates after she'd first started at the café – even Mrs

Green had said as much – her Charley lived life on the road in a camper van and, how did Maggie put it – "no news is good news". Mrs Green had resigned herself to Charley – or heaven-forbid, the police – only getting in touch if there was a problem. Out of sight, out of mind. And although Liz hated to admit it, she knew that this also meant losing control. Well, hopefully Charley would be taking good care of Maggie.

Liz carefully folded the letter and placed it back inside the Bible with the photos of Ben.

*I truly hope that you find peace and retribution, Maggie. Stay safe, my love.*

She kissed her fingertips and blew the kisses off into the air, hoping that they would find Maggie – wherever she was.

Maggie licked the flap of the envelope to seal it, then flipped it over to write on her mother's name and address, and stick on the stamp. Though she'd only just upped sticks and gone on the road with the tribe, pangs of guilt had already started gnawing at Maggie, despite the tough persona that she was trying to sculpt for herself. She knew in her heart of hearts that her mother would be worried if the weekly Monday phone call didn't come. But she also knew in her heart of hearts that if she tried speaking to her mother, they would only end up arguing about such a flagrant decision. Plus she'd made a promise to Charley that she would let her mother know about their road trip. At least sending a birthday card with a brief note should provide a modicum of explanation – that she was okay, but felt the need to vanish for a while. And not to worry; she was in experienced company with Charley – she promised to be in touch if there was a problem. She also sent a bucket-load of love and kisses with the birthday greeting.

She kissed the envelope before slipping it into the wide mouth of the grinning post box, then checked the collection time – good, there was a Saturday afternoon collection. At least by Monday her mother would get the card rather than a phone call. And, seeing that it was Maggie's handwriting on the envelope, her mother's curious nature would hopefully invite her to open the card early rather than wait until her birthday on Saturday, on 1st July.

At least she had now given the past some kind of closure.

Time to move on.

# Part Two

# Chapter 26

## Our Loss is Their Gain

### *1980*

'Good afternoon, Watkins and Harvey Estate Agents, how may I help you?' With a practised skill, the receptionist jammed the receiver between her shoulder and ear while she reached for the viewings diary and her pen. '–Ah-ha. –Ah-ha, yes. 23 Woodland Row.' She grabbed the blue page-marker ribbon and flicked open the book, while listening intently to the speaker. '–Ah-ha. Yes, it's been for sale for quite some time. –Empty? Yes, it's empty. –Just let me check…' Her finger traced down the time slots. 'How about later this afternoon? – Yes, our sales guy could meet you there around five-thirty on his way home. –Lovely.' The receptionist began writing details into the diary, speaking as she wrote, 'Mrs Bradshaw, Rose. Okay, James will see you there later. Thanks, Mrs Bradshaw. –Yes, five-thirty. Bye.'

At the mention of his name, James looked up from his desk, and then balled up some scrap paper to throw at the receptionist.

'Jeez, I'll be glad once we've sold that place. It gives me the creeps. Why do I have to go?'

The receptionist closed the diary with an efficient flourish and returned it to its precise spot on her neatly arranged reception desk. She threw the ball of paper back at James, narrowly missing his mug of coffee.

'Because you're the guy that shows people around the empty houses.'

James exaggerated a shudder as he walked over to the key cupboard to retrieve the keys to the little terraced house. 'Well, I ain't goin' in. I'll just let her have the keys and I'll wait in the car. It's empty, there's nowt she can nick.' He shuddered again. 'Definitely somethin' creepy about that place.'

The metallic clatter, clatter, clatter, ding of the receptionist's typewriter was a clear indicator to James that the conversation about 23 Woodland Row was over.

After returning the telephone receiver back in its cradle, Rose went through to the kitchen to put the kettle on.

'A cuppa, that's what we need, baby, a lovely cup of tea…' She absently rubbed her swollen baby bump as she conversed with the little person inside. 'What do you think about this one?' she asked, waving the sales details in front of her tummy.

Rose sat down heavily at the kitchen table and kicked off her shoes, giving instant relief to her swollen feet. She wriggled her toes in a bid to get the blood flowing again, then picked up the batch of property sales details which were lying on the table. Like a pack of cards, Rose fanned the details out in front of her, along with the one that she'd shown to her bump, and studied them intently. One by one, she pushed them away.

'Ugh, nope.

Nope.

Nope – too expensive.

Nope – too much work needed.

Nope.'

Her hand hovered over the details for 23 Woodland Row, the one on which she'd just booked the viewing – a shabby, brick terrace with grimy windows and peeling blue paintwork. Tall weeds could be seen peeking above the wall of the little front garden.

'I don't know what it is about this one, baby, but I can picture us living here. I can picture honeysuckle growing around the front door and up the wall. I can imagine cosy nights in front of the fire. Yep, I think this could be the one for us. Do you think Daddy will like it?'

Rose found herself looking across at a framed photograph on the Welsh dresser – she in her big meringue wedding dress, a smart, young fire-fighter by her side, resplendent in his uniform. A young man who could no longer be a fire-fighter on account of his injuries. A young couple with a baby on the way, and soon with nowhere to live.

She absently recalled the moment when she'd taken the phone call from Chris's Watch; the phone call that no service wife ever wants to receive. While attending a fire at a large de-construction site where an old factory was being demolished, scaffolding had collapsed and landed on Chris, leaving him hospitalised and battling for compensation.

When James pulled up at the property, Rose Bradshaw was already on the front steps waiting for him. Her smile broadened when she saw his car, and she gave him an involuntary wave. Switching his persona from cocky arrogant prick to smooth sales guy, he waved back before grabbing the keys to the property and getting out of the car. He extended his hand to meet Rose's outstretched hand, her shake firm and warm. James nodded towards her baby bump and grinned – he always found some client-characteristics that he could pick-up on – be it kids, cars or holiday suntans; something with which he could ease his way into conversation before going into a property. It not only put his prospective clients at ease, but made it easier to recall people when doing the ubiquitous follow-up phone calls.

'Mrs Bradshaw, lovely to meet you and your little passenger!'

Rose giggled, then patted her bump.

After making baby-smalltalk, James went to open up the front door, guiding Rose inside. Although only standing on the threshold, he could already feel the hair on his scalp and arms beginning to stand up and prickle, despite the early autumn warmth.

'You know what, I'm going to let you wander around by yourself. You take all the time you need, Mrs Bradshaw, and I'll just be out here in the car. We can chat afterwards, if you have any questions.' He gave Rose his best "I trust you" smile before handing over the keys, then headed back to the automotive sanctuary of his Morris Marina.

Though the house was devoid of any homely furnishings, Rose immediately felt drawn into the front sitting room of the little terraced house. Placing herself centrally in the room, she stood stock-still and absorbed the feel and energy, as though breathing in the very essence of the house. She felt her baby give a little kick and roll over, which Rose always took as a positive sign. To her, it was the baby's direct line of communication.

Rose smiled, and whispered, 'So, you like it here, too, huh?'

She recalled James telling her that the house had had all manner of short-term tenants, to the point where the landlord had given up and placed it for sale. And here it had stood; empty and uncared for, for the best part of a year. Judging by the graffiti on the bare plaster of the walls, she deduced that the last tenants to reside in the property were pot-smoking hippies or something of the sort. They had obviously sworn their allegiance to Led Zeppelin, having declared that "Jimmy Page is GOD!!!" and "Robert Plant is KING!!" by way of a spray-painted homage. She noticed signs of dampness creeping into the plaster in the corner of the room and under the window. Black soot and smoke stains scarred the length of the chimney breast and the front of the rustic brick fireplace; testimony to all manner of things having been burned on the open fire.

Rose moved through to the dining kitchen, separated from the sitting room by a central staircase. At first glance, the kitchen had fared no better at the hands of the previous occupants, with spray-paint wall decorations and signs of exuberant cooking activities on the blackened and grimy electric cooker. That would have to go. But in Rose's eyes, she could only see the positive; she could visualise the Welsh dresser along the back wall, the matching table centrally located, and the walls painted a sunny yellow. A few units here and there...

Since receiving the notice to quit from their own landlord, Rose and Chris had been on the desperate hunt for a little home. Any condition, cheap and cheerful, on account of Rose's dad being a builder. This place would be ideal. Her dad would be able to whizz through this in a jiffy and make it whole again. And she knew that he had enough negotiating acumen to buy the property for a good cash price. Being a chip off the old builder's block, Rose mentally calculated the extent of the work needed and the approximate turn-around time for purchase and repairs. Yes, that should work out just fine before Chris came out of hospital and the baby was born. At least something good would soon be arriving to sweep away their recent run of bad luck. The baby would be a welcome distraction and positive aid to Chris's healing.

At some point in its life, the under-stairs pantry door had been removed and replaced with a now-hanging-off beaded curtain. Curiosity took hold, unconsciously drawing her in. She patted her bump.

'Shall we take a look, baby? I wonder what's behind the curtain.' Rose could feel the baby rolling around. 'Hey, don't kick so hard!'

The shelves of the pantry were empty, save for one small can of baked beans and a thick layer of dust. An old ironing board was propped up against the flat wall, though she doubted it had ever been used. Rose's foot inadvertently kicked a mouse trap, still fully loaded with the splayed-out remains of a little field mouse. Though only small, the sour, rank smell of its decomposition permeated the air, causing her to cover her nose and mouth. She gagged slightly, grateful nonetheless that the estate agent was taking precautions to ensure the house wouldn't become overrun with mice.

Three rows of brick steps led down to a small floor area and an old-fashioned cold stone slab, presumably once used for keeping food cool before the days of refrigeration. An old, Persian-style rug covered the bottom floor, giving the dark pantry a quaint, homely feel. At least it would give a layer of insulation away from the cold, dank depths.

Rose looked out through the large kitchen window, which had a view over a small lawned garden, currently laid to an unkempt jungle. Crumbling, ivy-clad brick walls divided the garden from the ones either side. A forlorn looking apple tree competed for space with an old rotary dryer, which lay broken and abandoned on its side in the long grass; metal fingers reaching skywards in its final death throw. The washing line itself hung like dried-up, shrivelled veins. There were two outhouses at the bottom of the garden – presumably an old coal-shed and outside toilet, sided with a tangled pile of builder's rubble and weeds in the corner.

Upstairs were two bedrooms, both of which had mercifully escaped the artful treatment of the downstairs. And as with the downstairs area, both bedrooms were devoid of furniture, save for an old, threadbare carpet in the front bedroom, resplendent with all manner of dark stains.

Rose noticed that there was a streetlight directly in front of the house, which pleased her. There was something about the orange glow from a streetlight in winter which made a house feel cosy inside.

The back bedroom had obviously been divided at some point in its history to make way for the inclusion of a bathroom, thus making the bedroom smaller. She tried to imagine what life must have been like for the people who lived there in the old days, having to battle their way to the outside toilet in all weathers just to execute their most basic bodily functions. She shuddered involuntarily at the thought. The view from the rear upstairs window extended over the garden, beyond to allotments, and woodland.

Lost in time and quiet contemplation, Rose soaked up the energy of the house.

*Something, something was...*

Knock, knock, knock, knock–

'Hello, Mrs Bradshaw. Are you okay?' James stood on the threshold, unwilling to go any further inside. Goose-bumps were once again beginning to rise on his forearms despite the early-evening warmth. 'Mrs Bradshaw...'

'Yes. Yes, sorry, I'm coming...' Rose rubbed her eyes, unsure of how long she'd been absorbed by the moment, or indeed how long she'd been in the house.

After locking up, Rose found James leaning against his car.

As she approached him, her broad smile told James that he'd got a sale – he was finally going to be rid of 23 Woodland Row, Woodcliffe from his listing.

And it felt good.

# Chapter 27

## Welcome

*N*ow where did I put those pastry cutters?

Unconsciously driven by the nesting instinct to do some baking, Rose rummaged around in the box marked "kitchen bits & bobs". It had remained unpacked from their recent move into the newly renovated terrace, having been unceremoniously dumped on top of the old cold-stone in the bottom of the pantry in their haste to get settled in before Christmas.

*Ah-ha, there they are! And there's the rolling pin – going to need that...*

In her mind's eye, the pantry floor suddenly began undulating, wave after wave, ripple after ripple, as though the rug was trying to levitate. Rose grabbed onto the stone shelf as a vice-like grip tightened around her stomach. The floor continued to move, shifting, waving, rippling. She could feel hands crawling up her legs, crawling over her skin, crawling inside her. Her head began to swoon as nausea took hold.

*Breathe, slowly, slowly, in through the nose and out through the mouth. And again. And again...*

She eased her grasp on the shelf and rubbed her stomach.

*Shit! Shit! Shit! Not now!*

The floor began moving again, her head swimming and moving in time as the floor ebbed and flowed; ebbed and flowed. Her legs began shaking, jelly-like. She allowed herself to sink to her knees while she endeavoured to regain her composure, grateful for having retained the old rug. The gripping pains returned, stronger, sharper; breathe, slowly, slowly, in through the nose and out through the mouth. And again. And again...

*Chris... Oh, no!*

Sounds began swirling around her head, knocking. The knock came from within, like a wooden stick banging on an old empty skull.

Pop!

Rose slowly eased herself semi-upright, only to be ushered back to the crouching position as another wave of tension gripped her girth. She waited until the moment had passed before trying to stand again, this time with a degree of success.

Fascinated, she continued to watch the strangely undulating rug, suddenly aware that warm liquid was trickling down her leg and wetting her socks. She realised that the crotch and inner thighs of her maternity trousers were also wet, turning from wet-warm to wet-cold, as the material stuck to her legs. Every time she moved another squirt of liquid eased its way from her body. It was funny, but not funny.

*Breathe, slowly, slowly. Pain, pain, go away; come back on another day...*

Hands, little hands, began grabbing inside, pulling, tugging. An unconscious voice... *"Baby come out, baby come out. Come out, come out and play–"*

'Argh...'

In a moment of calm between the contractions, Rose cautiously made her way out of the pantry and across the kitchen to get to the phone, each step causing the release of another squirt of amniotic fluid down her legs. Her trousers flapped, cold and clammy.

'Dad... Dad, can you come over?'

*Breathe, slowly, slowly...*

'No, Dad, it has to be now…the baby's coming. –Chris? No, he's over at his sister's…'

*Breathe, slowly, slowly…*

'He's babysitting while she's gone into town to do some Christmas shopping. Please, Dad, hurry. –Yes, I'll phone the ambulance. –Yes, my bag's packed ready. Okay, see you in a mo…'

'Well, not quite a Christmas baby, but close enough.' Chris snuggled his newborn son, his eyes alight with awe at the little creature in his arms. He kissed Rose, the tenderness saying more than words could. 'So, do you think that he looks like a "Peter" or a "Timothy"? Which name should we go for, then?'

'Oh, I think he looks like a little Timothy. Little Timmy Bradshaw. It's got a nice ring to it, don't you think?' answered Rose.

'Yep, agreed.' He gently kissed the top of the baby's head. 'Welcome to the family, little Timmy Bradshaw…'

Right on cue for seven o'clock visiting, the doors to the maternity ward swung open, allowing the whispering horde of excited visitors to enter. Rose smiled as she saw her dad, Eddie, accompanied by Chris's parents.

True to generous form, her dad was weighed down by an enormous bouquet of flowers in one hand and a huge teddy bear in the other.

'I called your mum, by the way. She sends her love and congratulations, and says sorry that she couldn't come over. She'll try and get over in the New Year, when flights are a bit cheaper.' He bent over to kiss his daughter, then whispered, 'Sorry, love. I offered to buy her a ticket, but I don't think that she wanted to leave the warmth of Spain, or miss out on Christmas with Carlos…'

Rose shrugged in a non-committal way – today was not really the day for raking up family feuds. 'No problem, Dad. She'll come over when she's ready.'

# Chapter 28

## Dark Dreams

"*A*re you my mummy?"

"*No.*"

"*Oh,*" said the mind-voice. "*But you're so nice. Will you be my mummy?*"

"*No. I can't be your mummy.*"

"*Why not?*"

"*Because you're dead...*" Rose's eyes rolled behind her closed eyelids, her REM continuing to disturb her sleep. Mind-images; dark, light, floating, coming close, moving away, a faceless mouth speaking to her, and she speaking back.

"*It's my birthday today,*" said the voice.

"*That's nice. How old are you?*" she asked the floating dream-image.

"*That depends. I could be one, or I could be three.*"

"*I don't understand what you mean – how can you be one or three?*" asked Rose, perplexed.

"*Maybe not now, but one day you will understand. I'll make sure of it.*"

"*Stop! You're scaring me...*"

"*Scaring you? But I'm only a baby – I can't walk or talk yet.*"

*"But you're talking to me now..."*

*"I know. But that's because I'm inside your head. I can do whatever I want when I'm inside your head."*

# Chapter 29

## Jealousy

Disturbed by Timmy's fretful crying, Rose stole a peek at the bedside alarm clock. The green glow showed 02:20 am.

*I'll be glad when you start sleeping through the night, young man!*

She quickly lifted him from his cot so as not to disturb a sleeping Chris, and cuddled him close while she fumbled with the flap of her nursing bra.

'Sshh, sshh, sshh, here you go...'

Timmy eagerly took his night feed, latching on immediately. 'Boy, you're hungry. No wonder you're getting so big and heavy!'

Rose reached behind her to grab her pillow as a comfort-aid to set under Timmy and support his weight. As she lifted the pillow towards the suckling child, she felt a sudden, sharp blow between her shoulder blades, causing her to almost drop Timmy. Momentarily stunned, she turned towards Chris, growling in a low voice,

'What the hell was that fo–'

Even in the dim glow from the streetlight, Rose could see that Chris's eyes were firmly closed and his breathing deep and rhythmic. 'But...' She shook her head, and shivered.

She gently slipped the pillow underneath Timmy, allowing him to take his feed in mutual comfort, and then listened in the darkness. Rose shook her head again, unsure of what she'd just experienced, or indeed, if it had really happened at all. Yet the sting at the top of her back told her that it had been very real.

Having to do the night feeds never bothered Rose – it was as though the stillness of the night amplified all sounds and keened the senses. She listened to the lashing of the hail and sleet, sounding like pebbles being thrown at the window. March was a strange month for weather – no longer winter, but not quite spring; a kind of climatic no-man's-land. The battery-powered drone of the milk float joined the night sounds as it rattled, clanked, and then paused; before resuming its whiny journey down the road. Even the malevolent howling, hissing and spitting of cats fighting had its place in the nocturnal orchestra. And while all was amplified from the outside, the inner sanctum of the house whispered, hummed and ticked away, offering a calming, rhythmic retreat from the world beyond.

Until now.

The pain that had hit Rose between the shoulder blades seemed implausible yet very real. Right from day-one there had been a bond with the house; a strange connection which she could feel but couldn't explain.

She yawned and rolled her now-stiff shoulders, silently swapping Timmy over to the other breast before resuming her eyes-closed feeding meditation. Rose regulated her breathing; in-out, in-out, in-out.

An icy coldness slowly, slowly began creeping up her spine.

Breathing; in-out, in-out, in-out.

The icy coldness crept higher...shoulder blades...neck. Rose felt the icy-cold sensation prickle her scalp, caress her unconscious mind.

Breathing; in-out, in-out, in-out.

A voice, but not a voice –

*'Are you my mummy?'*

Rose's eyes snapped wide open, her sudden body-flinch disturbing Timmy. He quietly grizzled at the momentary interruption.

The mind-voice came again. *'Where's my mummy? I'm looking for my mummy.'*

Unnerved, she forced questions through her thoughts. *'Who are you? Why do you keep coming to me?'*

The icy-cold mind-fingers began melting away, trickling down Rose's body in the reverse order of its arrival. And as the iciness left, it took the faded, distant sound of a crying baby with it.

'Morning, beautiful.' Chris passed the plate of toast to Rose as she sat down at the kitchen table. 'Tea?'

'Huh? Tea? Yes, please.' Rose ran her fingers through her hair then stretched her arms over her head in an effort to loosen her sleep-stiff joints.

'Bad night with Timmy?' He poured a mug of steaming hot tea then pushed the marmalade towards her plate of toast before sitting down to join her for breakfast. He topped up his own mug of tea from the cottage-shaped teapot – a gaudy house-warming gift from his mother.

'No, Timmy was his usual darling-self. Quietly gets on with it, then back to sleep.' A questioning frown began moulding itself on her brow as she buttered her toast. 'Chris, do you sometimes hear a baby crying? Other than Timmy, I mean? Or get a strange feeling, something you can't explain?' She could feel a flush rising to her cheeks, knowing how ridiculous her question sounded – Chris was a down-to-earth ex-fireman...

He grinned and shook his head before replying. 'Did you find some left-over pot from the pot-heads that used to live here? No, sweetie. A house is a house, made from bricks and mortar. You're a builder's daughter – you should know that.'

'I know...I know. But, just a-lately I keep getting this funny feeling around the house. And sometimes I can hear a baby crying...it's weird.' Rose felt like sucking the words back in, in the hope that sensible ones would come back out.

'You're serious, aren't you?'

Rose nodded. She could feel tears of stupidity welling behind her eyes.

Seeing his wife's distress, Chris hobbled around the table to give her a hug, wrapping his arms around her shoulders. He kissed her on the top of her head.

'Hey, I'm not laughing at you, sweetie. Sorry...'

He tried to phrase his next words carefully in the hope of not sounding condescending or unbelieving. 'Having a new baby is exhausting, especially when you're tied to breast-feeding as well. Maybe the tiredness is affecting you more than you realise?' He kissed her again.

'Yeah, maybe.' She snuggled into his arms, relishing the secure warmth.

The secure warmth that was keeping the icy feeling from creeping up her spine – the icy feeling that had been very real in the darkness.

# Chapter 30

## Spring Awakening

The swathe of daffodils and narcissi glowed; the strengthening spring sunlight enhancing their golden-yellow brightness as they framed the postage-stamp of a lawn.

Mesmerised, Rose watched their gently swaying heads, shouldered by slender green leaves pointing skywards, like waving arms. Winter had finally given way to spring, and life was regenerating itself in the mid-April warmth. Early apple blossom, with its soft pink-white petals belied the gnarled, tired old branches that held them. She vaguely wondered if the apple tree would bear fruit so that she could make a pie from freshly picked apples. The view from the kitchen window was marred only by the ugly old coal-house and long-since disused outside toilet.

Alerted by the clatter of Chris's callipers, she turned towards him and put her index finger to her lips as he entered the kitchen.

'Sshh. Timmy's sleeping.' She pointed in the direction of his bouncy chair.

'Sorry, I still can't get used to these callipers. I swear they've got a life of their own!' Chris laughed, as he hobbled over to join Rose by the sink and share the view.

Rose wiped her hands on the tea-towel, then nodded in the direction of the old outbuildings. 'Maybe we should get Dad to knock them down and clear away that ugly pile of rubble, so that we can put up a neat, wooden shed...'

Chris nodded. 'Aye, that would make things look a lot smarter, that's for sure. And we'd see more of the view beyond. Much better than looking at the old brick lavvy. Crikey, to think people used to sit out there in the cold and dark.' He exaggerated a shudder.

Stirred by childhood memories, Rose laughed. 'Hey, my nanna and grandad had one of those. I spent many happy hours catching spiders and earwigs. There was something cosy about playing in the outside toilet.'

'If you say so...'

'But anyway, I think it's time for a proper shed – I'd like to get some gardening tools, and I'm pretty sure that Timmy will soon end up with a collection of push-toys and trucks and diggers and stuff. You know what Dad's like.'

'Timmy can't even sit up or walk yet!' Chris rolled his eyes and shook his head good-humouredly. 'I swear your dad wants to re-live his childhood through our Timmy. Then again, I look forward to the day when he buys the Hornby train set and Scalextric – no complaints there,' he laughed.

'I know – but Timmy is his only-daughter's only-child, if you get what I mean. He's bound to want to spoil him a little with boys-toys seeing as how I only had dolls and prams.' She grinned, knowing full-well that her dad's idea of "spoil" meant "lavish upon". 'Tell you what – it's Easter next weekend. I'll see if Dad can come then and start the demolition work. It'll stop him from getting antsy over the holidays.'

Chris nodded, then laughed. 'Sounds good. And don't forget to tell your dad that Timmy isn't old enough to eat Easter eggs yet...'

Rose shook her head then shrugged. 'Yeah, like that's gonna stop him!'

*\*\**

Rose looked around the bottom of the garden, or rather, what was left of it. The old brick outbuildings were now a distant memory, the site having been cleared of debris in readiness for the foundations of the garden shed to be laid, plus the inclusion of a little seating area. She nodded her approval, and gave her dad the thumbs up.

'It's going to look so much better, thanks, Dad.'

'Aye, lass, it's a big improvement, that's for sure.' He put the shovel and rake into the wheelbarrow before indicating the layout that he had in mind. 'So, we'll put the shed here, and the seating area there, where it gets most of the afternoon sun.'

Rose nodded. 'Sounds perfect. You're a genius.'

'I know that,' he laughed. 'But before I start all foundation work, what about this manky old apple tree?' He slapped the gnarly, moss covered trunk and gave it a shake, causing the blossom to fall like pink confetti. 'It's a bit past its best, I'd say. Should I cut it down and rip out the roots?'

'What! No, I love that old apple tree...' She gave her dad the pleading-eyes.

'Rose – it's old, it's rotten, and you'll never get any apples.'

'Why not?'

'Because you need a mummy tree, and a daddy tree, Rose,' he laughed. 'It takes two apple trees to make baby apples.'

'Oh, I didn't know that. But–'

'No "buts", Rosie. It's coming out. We can always plant two new ones, if you still want apple trees. We could put one here, and one over there, see.'

Rose pursed her lips, then shrugged. 'You're the boss...'

He elbowed her playfully before loading up the rest of his tools. 'Yes, I am, my girl, and don't you forget it.'

Alerted by something unusual in the pile of dirt, the workman raised his hands to form an 'X' towards the mini-digger being operated by Rose's dad. He then held up his right hand, rather like a policeman controlling traffic.

'Stop! Stop! What's that?' The workman went to the pile of dirt for a closer look, before giving the soil a nervous poke. 'Good God, Eddie! I think you'd better come and take a look at this...'

Rose's father turned off the digger and jumped out to investigate the commotion. There in the hole, tangled among the roots of the old apple tree, was what looked like small bones. The broken edge of some kind of plastic, makeshift coffin was also poking through the soil. A few small bones lay mixed in with the pile of excavated dirt.

The two men looked at each other, unsure of what to do next.

'Shit. What d'ya reckon?' asked Eddie. 'Aren't we supposed to call the police, or something, just in case they're human?'

His workman shrugged then looked around to see if anyone else had witnessed their discovery. 'They're a bit small for human bones... Here, take a look.' He picked up one of the freshly unearthed bones from the pile of soil and passed it to Rose's dad for a closer inspection.

Eddie cleaned off some of the soil, before shrugging. 'Maybe not grown-up size, but... Shit – you don't think they're kiddie-bones, do you?' He looked at his workman with wide eyes, eyebrows raised.

'Fuckin' hope not.' He looked around. 'Quick, pass me the little trowel. I'm gonna take a closer look before we hit the panic button.' With careful precision, the workman began scraping away some of the soil to reveal more of the bones. A small ribcage became visible. He looked up at Eddie for advice.

Eddie nodded solemnly. 'Keep going. But be really careful – for all we know, this could be a crime scene...'

Bone by bone, the little skeleton came to light. The workman shook his head then looked up at Eddie. His face was a mask of seriousness.

'I can see the skull...'

'And?'

'You're not gonna believe this...'

'What, for fuck's sake? C'mon man!' Eddie could feel nervous sweat beginning to run down his back.

The workman's face broke into a grin. 'It's a dog. It's somebody's fuckin' dog...'

'You're joking, right?'

'Nope, come and take a look...'

Both men peered into the hole then began to laugh – that strange kind of involuntary, sick-in-the-head laugh which comes through relief, shock, or disgusting situations.

Eddie headed back towards the mini-digger, shaking his head and still chuckling. 'Well, Fido – sorry old pal, but you're about to be exhumed. That old apple tree's coming out, whether you come back to haunt us, or not. And not a woof to our Rosie about our little discovery!'

'And what don't we tell our Rosie?' she asked, as she came down the garden path bearing two mugs of tea.

Her dad froze, then turned to look at his workman for moral support. The workman shrugged, and began laughing, 'She's your daughter, Eddie. You can break the news to her...'

Irritated by their subversive conversation, Rose pressed for answers. 'What news? C'mon, Dad, spill the beans.'

Knowing that there was no avoiding the situation, Eddie gave Rose the grizzly news of their discovery. 'We found the skeleton of a little dog under the apple tree. We were going to remove the bones when we took out the roots. I didn't think that you'd want to share your garden with old Fido.'

Rose pondered the situation for a moment. 'Nope, you have to re-bury him properly, Dad. If that's where he was laid to rest, then that's where he's going to stay. I don't want old Fido coming back to haunt me because he was disturbed from his final resting place.'

'Are you absolutely sure? I can take it all away,' he replied.

'I'm absolutely sure, Dad. Put him back so that he can continue to rest in peace.'

*There are enough strange feelings around this place without adding more, thank you very much!*

# Chapter 31

## A History Lesson

It didn't matter how much Rose contemplated, chewed over, or tried to make sense of the strange occurrences since they purchased the house, she felt – knew – that something was amiss. She twirled with her mug of coffee as though it would give her answers. She remembered back to when she first viewed the house, pregnant with Timmy. It was as though the house had called out to her, chosen her. During the initial building work, and even after they had moved in, she often felt Timmy rolling around – normal enough, but it was always strangely accompanied by a touching sensation on her swollen belly. But now the voice in her head, the more physical sensations – even hearing a baby crying... If this was Rose's descent into madness, then she felt like she was on a fast track.

A shadow passing by the kitchen window caused Rose to jump, knocking over her coffee mug.

'Shit!'

She quickly leaped up from her chair to grab the dishcloth before the stream of coffee cascaded over the edge of the kitchen table. A knock at the back door gave her heart a large dose of adrenaline.

*Pull yourself together, girl!*

Rose opened the door to find a smiling Mrs Barnett from next door thrusting a basket containing a dozen eggs towards her.

'I wondered if you would like some eggs, dear. Somebody gave Mr B two dozen this morning, and we ain't gonna use 'em all. We don't eat that many, on account o'Mr B's bowels. Eggs bind him up, you see.'

Finding it difficult to hold back a laugh, Rose allowed herself a polite giggle as she invited Mrs Barnett in with the basket of eggs.

'That would be great, thanks. I'm always baking. How much do I owe you?' Rose knew that Mrs B wouldn't take any payment, but she still offered out of politeness. 'In fact, I was just going to make a fresh cup of coffee. Silly me, just knocked mine over.'

'I'd prefer a cup o'Rosie…' Mrs Barnett made herself comfy at the kitchen table.

'I'm sorry, what's a "Rosie"? I don't know if I have any of that.'

Now it was Mrs Barnett's turn to laugh. 'Rosie-Lee – tea. It's Cockney rhyming slang for tea. Haven't you 'eard that one before?'

Rose shook her head. 'Is that where you're from? London.' She busied herself with the kettle and tea bags.

'Yep, born and bred within earshot o'Bow Bells. Both me an' Mr B. He came north first, up here to Derbyshire, as one o'them Bevin Boys. Had to help out with the war effort in the coal mines, you see.'

Embarrassed by her war-ignorance, Rose asked, 'What's a Bevin Boy?'

A smile of nostalgia caught Mrs Barnett. 'It was during the Second World War. A lot of the miners had been conscripted to serve in the services, but then the coal started to run out. The factories and such like were desperate; they couldn't operate without coal power. So this chap from Parliament, Ernest Bevin, had the idea of an additional kind of war conscript – to put young men in the coal mines. It was a bit of a lottery as to who got the call, and not many young men wanted to go. There was this stigma, you see – that Bevin Boys were just another form of cop-out, like those conscientious objectors, or "connies" as they were called.'

Rose poured the boiling water into the teapot and gave it a stir. 'Go on…'

'Like I was saying, Mr B's number came up, literally picked out of Mr Bevin's hat, so he had to come north to work in the pits. He worked at Creswell Colliery, and rented a room with a local family. Even after the war had ended, the Bevin Boys still had to stay on. Anyways, seeing as how everything had been blitzed to smithereens in London by the Jerries, I decided to up sticks and move north to join him. Take life a bit quieter, like. We had some lovely walks around Creswell Crags. But life down the pit wasn't for Mr B, so he got his lorry licence instead, doing haulage for a company in Woodcliffe, so we moved here. Been in the house next door ever since. Brought up six kids in that house, we have.' Her eyes took on a wistful look as she delved into her memory bank.

Hearing that her neighbour had lived here for many years, Rose seized the opportunity to politely grill her for information. She put the tea-pot on the table, together with a cup, saucer and milk jug – for some odd reason, Rose assumed that Mrs B would prefer her "Rosie" in a proper tea-cup.

'Shall I be mother?' laughed Rose, picking up the pot and pouring.

'That's one 'ell of an ugly teapot, if you don't mind me saying.'

Rose smirked, then confessed, 'It was a house-warming present from my mother in law.'

'Tryin' to give ya nightmares, is she!' Mrs Barnett couldn't help but laugh at her own joke. Rose joined in with her merriment, and took the word "nightmares" as a cue to question Mrs B about the house's history of occupants.

'So, I bet you've seen quite a lot of people come and go, then? Had quite a few different neighbours?'

'Uff, don't get me started...' But start, she did, and gave Rose the full run-down on what felt like the comings and goings of the whole street since 1945.

The sound of Timmy waking up from his late morning nap gave Mrs B an opportunity to replenish her tea-cup for the third refill, while Rose popped upstairs to get him.

'My, he's growing into a bonny lad, ain't he? Hello, young fella, what's your name again?' Mrs Barnett clucked and fussed under Timmy's chin causing him to grizzle.

Rose did the re-introductions. 'This is Timmy. Timmy, you remember Mrs B from next door, don't you?' The infant was nonplussed, preferring his breast-feed to a wrinkled old lady. 'So what about this particular house – in its more recent past, I mean?' Rose asked the all-knowing Mrs Barnett.

'Well, there's been all sorts of comings and goings these past few years. Last lot 'ere were some hippie people. Bloody noisy lot, they were; parties and such like. I heard that they were into that spooky Ouija board stuff, but got freaked out after getting in contact with the other side.' Mrs Barnett couldn't help but laugh. 'Smoking too much of the wacky-backy, I shouldn't wonder...'

Rose recalled the spray-graffiti on the walls when she viewed the house, testimony to the last occupants.

'And before that, let me think. Yes, there was a young couple. Always arguing, they were. Could hear 'em through the walls. She had a bit of a nervous disposition, didn't take much to get 'er all of a flap. They didn't say long either, maybe half a year, something like that. Kept saying the house was haunted. Ha!'

Waning a little by the endless stream of local history, Rose's attention was suddenly re-invigorated. 'What do you think they meant by "haunted"? Ghosts, you mean?'

Mrs B shrugged. 'Dunno, just said she had a funny feeling, mostly sat here in the kitchen. Like she was bein' watched or sumfin.'

'Interesting.' Rose could feel the hairs beginning to rise on the back of her neck and forearms, and her scalp prickle and tighten.

'And then there was the young lass – waif of a young 'un, she was, with black, spiky hair. Had a baby. Little boy, it was. Mind you, there was no young man around, if you get what I mean. Bit of a loner. I tried to speak to her if I saw her out in the garden, and offered to help her, like. But she just shook her head, and looked at me like I'd just come up the Thames on a winkle barge...'

Rose laughed, not quite sure of Mrs Barnett's meaning. 'What's a winkle barge?'

Now it was Mrs B's turn to laugh. 'It's another one of my Cockney sayings, dear. It means that she looked at me like I wuz from another planet, or sumfin. Distant, not altogether there.'

'Strange that she wouldn't accept any help.'

'Aye, you'd think so. Anyway, I reckon she was one o'them girls from the convent house from up the road – I often used to see a couple of young nuns come for a visit. Checking up on her, I suppose.'

Rose pushed some biscuits in the direction of Mrs B as an initiative to go on.

'Oh, I didn't know that there was a convent up the road.' Rose was beginning to feel decidedly ignorant in the company of her worldly-wise neighbour.

'Woodcliffe Grange – it's one o'them places where young girls go when they're caught in the family way. The Sisters look after the girls until they've had the baby, then they helps 'em to sort out the adoption afterwards.'

'Oh, I see.' Rose held Timmy close, protective. 'But you said she had a baby here at the house...'

Mrs B nodded towards Timmy, and answered Rose with a question. 'Could you give up your little mite?'

Rose shook her head.

'I think that was the case with this lassie, too. When push came to shove, she couldn't go through with it. Lordy, lordy, that baby had some good lungs on 'im, bless his little cotton socks. Could 'ear 'im crying and her shouting.' The old lady sighed. 'Poor girl. I don't think she coped very well. Ben, I think she called him. Anyway, one night they just vanished. About ten days before Christmas, if I remember rightly. It was December, anyways – bloody cold. Left a note to the landlord saying that they'd "Gone away". I presumed that she went back to her mother's. And here's me – I managed to bring up six 'o the buggers!'

'Well, motherhood isn't the easiest job in the world, eh. I guess it isn't for everybody,' Rose commented. A thought suddenly struck her. 'Did any of the neighbours have a dog, do you know?'

Mrs B rubbed her chin while she thought back. 'A dog? Let me think... Yes, years ago – there was a family who had a puppy. Yapped all day and howled all night, poor thing. The kids used to tease it mercilessly. Don't know whatever happened to it. That vanished as well.'

'Oh, I think I know what happened to it,' said Rose, rolling her eyes. 'We found some bones under the old apple tree when we ripped it out a couple of weeks ago. They were definitely from the skeleton of a small dog. I guess that's where the puppy ended up.'

'What! How could anybody do such a mean thing to an innocent little creature?' exclaimed Mrs B, her face aghast. 'I don't know what gets into people when there are other options available. Poor wee thing!'

A distinct aroma began emanating up from Timmy's nappy. This was Rose's perfect opportunity to politely bring matters to a close. She exaggerated a nose-wrinkle and wafted away the stink.

'Well, it's been lovely chatting, Mrs B. And thanks for the eggs. But if you'll excuse me and this smelly young man, I'm going to go and change his nappy!' She stood up and walked towards the door to show Mrs B out.

'Aye, I'd best get back and get Mr B's lunch ready. It's been nice 'aving a chat. We must do it again sometime.'

And it had been nice having a chat, or rather, having a "listen". Rose smiled – she assumed that her neighbour was making up for lost conversation-time, having only Mr B to converse with on a daily basis apart from when they went into town on pension day.

But what interesting information about the house. The strange happenings that she'd experienced (and she was damned sure that they were real occurrences), it seemed that the previous occupants had experienced them too. She thought about the girl and her baby, vanishing into thin air. What did Mrs B say? Around ten days before Christmas. That would be the fifteenth of December – the same date that Timmy was born. Rose shook her head as if to shake away the unrealistic thoughts that were creeping into her head as she recalled the moment that she went into labour, together with the improbable but invasive sensations which she attributed to the contractions.

*Unrealistic?*
*Improbable?*

# Chapter 32

## Going Somewhere Yet Nowhere

'The site must be around here somewhere. It feels like we've been driving around in circles for hours. I thought Bingo knew the way...' muttered Charley. She looked at the fuel gauge, then slapped the steering wheel in frustration. 'Damn! We're almost on red. I hope that we can find a petrol station before long, otherwise we're gonna have to get out and push it to Avebury!'

'There, look. He's pulling his van into that lay-by. At least we can take a look at the road map and see if we can figure out where we are,' noted Maggie, trying to ease Charley's frustrations.

The tribe of vehicles all followed Bingo's van into the lay-by in the hope of taking stock of their general location.

As Charley prepared to slow down ready to take the turn, the clutch struggled to engage gear, quickly followed by a crunching and grinding sound from the gear-box. Luckily the van still had enough momentum to coast into the lay-by, narrowly avoiding the back of Catweazle's minibus. She quickly feathered the brakes to bring the camper to a stop.

Catweazle appeared by the driver's side window and knocked. Charley wound down the window to speak to her potential mechanical saviour.

'That doesn't sound too good, my girl. Would I be right in thinking that you want old Catweazle to take a look at Hovis?'

'Would you? Could you? That would be awfully nice of you, Cat. Worth a cuppa and a biscuit, at the very least,' laughed Charley, with that manic kind of laugh set midway between humour and horror.

'You know me – anything for a cuppa and a biscuit. Sounds like it's either the clutch or gearbox. Either way, I'm afraid it didn't sound too good...' Catweazle patted the van. 'Put the kettle on, and I'll get my tool kit.'

'I think I'll go and see what Bingo's up to while you two sort out the tea and sympathy,' acknowledged Maggie, jumping out of the VW.

While the rest of the tribe used the opportunity to nip behind the hedges for a piss-break, or assist Bingo with his epic map reading failure, Charley busied herself with making a pot of tea. She re-joined Catweazle with two mugs of steaming Tetley's, once it had brewed.

Catweazle appeared from under the van, then wiped his hands on one of Charley's tea-towels, consigning it to his own collection of oily rags. He took the proffered mug of tea from Charley. 'It looks terminal, I'm afraid. Or massively expensive, at the very least. See here –' He pointed to a puddle of thick black oil under the gear box.

'But I don't get it. I always check the fluids and stuff. I know the basics of maintenance,' protested Charley.

'Sorry, old girl. This is nothing to do with maintenance. There's a big crack in the gearbox housing, so you've lost all the oil. You must have hit a big rock or something on the last site. No wonder you couldn't find any gears. It'll cost you shit-loads to get this fixed.'

Charley kicked the side of the van in frustration. 'Damn, damn, damn!' she screamed. 'I don't have the money to either fix it, or get another van...'

'Well, once we know where we're going, I could tow you to the site. Maybe the farmer would give you a few quid for the van? They're always looking for spare parts. Or at the very least, it would make a good chicken house...'

'A chicken house! You're saying that my beloved Hovis is only fit to be a chicken house!' She glared at Catweazle in mock indignation.

Catweazle shrugged then smoothed down his beard, effectively using it as a hairy hand-cleaner. 'It was only a suggestion, old girl. You two ladies can always bunk in with me until you find something else. You're always welcome in my love-shack.'

Charley patted him on the shoulder. 'That's really sweet of you. And thanks for all your help – you're a mechanical genius. Mostly...' She laughed. 'But I think I'll check with Penny first, if you don't mind. She has an awning for her van, so we could maybe stay in there. I'm sure something will turn up.' She looked up at the sound of Maggie returning, and half smiled.

'So, what's the diagnosis?' asked Maggie.

'Our home is dead on its wheels...'

'What! No way! Couldn't Mr Catweazle here fix it?' she clapped him on the back.

'Sadly, Miss Maggie, no. Not even I, the mechanical genius, could fix your old bus. Anyway, what's the verdict on our location? Are we well and truly lost?' he asked.

Maggie laughed, and shook her head. 'Nope. It appears that the farm is just around the corner. Bingo had the map facing the wrong way...'

'What a twat! Probably too busy fiddling with his balls to read the map properly,' snorted Catweazle. 'Well, I'm going to top up my tea, and have another biscuit before we go anywhere.'

'That sounds good; think I'll join you,' acknowledged Maggie, disappearing inside the now defunct camper.

Charley and Catweazle followed her inside, then sat at the table while Maggie topped up their mugs.

'Do you know what Cat suggested we do with Hovis, Mags? Sell it to the farmer so that he can turn it into a chicken house!'

Maggie grinned, then stroked the table gently. 'Well, let's face it, Charley – the van was already a million years old when you bought it. Well, quite ancient, anyway. All good things must come to an end...'

Charley's tone became defensive, as her voice wobbled and eyes filled with tears. 'Don't talk about my van like that! Yes, it might be old, but it was bought and paid for with honest money! This van was my home – our home, and our freedom,' she growled through clenched teeth. 'This means we're homeless.'

Maggie blanched at the sudden change in Charley's mood and character, then looked at Catweazle. 'Would you be able to drive me into the village later, once we've gotten settled at the site? There's something that I need to do.' She stood up and went to her personal belongings, and reached in to retrieve her old building society book. 'I have a small amount of rainy-day money in here. Just a little that I inherited from my dad, and wanted to save it for an emergency. Well – I think this is our emergency, Charley. I'll get us a new home...'

'What! No, I can't let you use that money,' she protested.

Maggie shook her head. 'I insist, Charley. We can't exactly go and get a car loan, can we? We have no choice but to pay cash. You took me in and gave me a home. You're the love of my life, and I want to do this for you – for us.'

Charley peeled herself from behind the camper table to hug Maggie, her eyes overflowing with tears.

'I think that's sorted, then,' said Catweazle. 'We'll tow this one to the farm, see if we can sell it to the farmer, and then go van hunting while we're here. I'd be happy to take a look with you, and make sure that you're buying something decent. Perhaps pick up a copy of Auto Trader too, while we're in town, and take a look in the small-ads.'

'Thanks, Cat. Yes, please. We'd really like that.' Maggie gave Charley a playful push, then laughed. 'Hey, we're buying our first home together!'

# Chapter 33

## Oh, to be in Monaco

"*Can you believe it! In the dying seconds of qualifying, Britain's Nigel Mansell takes third place on the grid for tomorrow's Monaco Grand Prix. Nigel Mansell, for Lotus Ford. So, the grid looks like this for tomorrow's race: Brazil's Nelson Piquet on pole position, Canada's Gilles Villeneuve in second, and our very own Nigel Mansell is in third. So, there you have it...*"

The hyperbolic exuberance of Murray Walker filled the front sitting room, his knowledge and enthusiasm spilling over, to be shared with all the Formula One fans who had tuned in to watch the Saturday qualifying.

Chris fist-pumped the air. 'Yes! Yes! Yes! Go get 'em, Nigel!'

His moment of joy was disturbed as the baby-monitor crackled into life, the gripes and groans of a waking Timmy competing with Murray Walker for attention.

'Ugh, nice one Timmy. Hang on, I'm on my way.' He turned down the volume of the television and tossed the remote onto the sofa before grabbing his calliper and heading upstairs to attend to his grizzling son.

By the time Chris had hobbled his way upstairs, Timmy was bawling incessantly, his face rosy and wet from crying, his little fists flailing the air.

'Sorry, pal, but it takes me a bit longer to get upstairs than your mummy. What's up, eh – those nasty teeth bothering you again?' He stuck his index finger inside Timmy's nappy. 'Hmm, better change you too. C'mon, mister, let's get you downstairs. A squirt of Bonjela and a clean nappy coming right up...'

Chris turned off Timmy's monitor before swinging his son up into his arms, and making sure that he was secure before hobbling down the stairs. He had developed a clever system of holding the crutch in one hand while holding Timmy in the other, and using the handrail as a sliding support for his elbow – a support system which works well unless a person steps onto a foreign object on the stairs causing a major slip and fall. Chris did his best to hold Timmy safe as he went down hard on his back on the treads, the carpet doing little to cushion the impact. His crutch-arm became tangled and bent as he slid and spiralled down to the bottom. He landed almost upside down, his head hitting the door frame to the dining kitchen, his legs splayed out, before his right knee crashed into the wall at the bottom. He lay stunned; eyes-open, eyes-closed, eyes-open, eyes-closed, eyes-closed, eyes-clo...

'Chris! Chris! Oh, my God, Chris. Wake up. Are you okay? Oh, my God, here let me take Timmy.'

Rose threw down her bags of shopping as soon as she came into the sitting room and saw Chris lying in a tangled heap at the bottom of the stairs, still cradling a screaming Timmy. She quickly took Timmy and soothed him before trying to rouse Chris. He groaned and opened his eyes as his senses returned, re-orientating himself with his surroundings. His eyes finally focused and fixed on Rose.

'My God, Chris, are you okay? Are you hurt...do you think anything's broken?' She tried to slide her arm under his shoulders to lever him up.

'Argh! Stop, wait, please. Just help me move my legs around, and move my crutch from under my arm and back.' He screamed as she tried to manoeuvre him as instructed. 'F-U-C-K! I think I've popped a couple of ribs. My side hurts...'

'Keep still. I'm going to call Dad to come over. Get him to take you to casualty.'

By the time Rose had returned from making her phone call, Chris had managed to lever himself to a reclining sitting position, lying with his back on the stairs, his legs crooked into a 'V' in front of him. He looked at his now-quiet son.

'How's Timmy?'

'He seems unharmed, thank goodness. Dad's on his way.' She checked Chris over as best she could. 'What happened, love?'

'I dunno. One minute I was on the stairs, the next it was as though I'd stepped on a toy, or slipped on something squishy. But there was nothing there. I'm sure of it. Yet, I definitely felt something... I'm sorry, Rose. I'm really sorry...'

'Hey, no harm done – Timmy's fine. We still need to get you checked over. Let's hope nothing's broken – maybe you've just bruised a few ribs?'

Chris tried not to breathe in too sharply, keeping his breaths steady and even. 'Yeah, let's hope that's all it is.' He turned his head as he heard the sound of a car pull up out front. 'Sounds like your dad's here. I should book a season ticket for the hospital!'

Once Chris was out of the house and on his way to hospital, Rose settled down on the sofa to feed Timmy. She allowed her mind to reflect on Chris's accident, trying to come up with logical "reasons-why". There was definitely no toy on the stairs, of that she was pretty sure. Yet Chris was adamant that he'd felt something squishy. How strange. He could normally manage getting up and down stairs using one calliper and the handrail as a guide, while balancing Timmy in his free arm. It can be easy to lose one's footing though – carpets can be slippery...

After feeding, she turned her attention to changing Timmy's nappy. *Poor little thing, he's soaking wet.*

As she wiped him down, she caught sight of some just-noticeable red marks on his back and legs. Only small marks – flea bites, perhaps? She ran her fingertip over the area. They were definitely bite marks or teeth marks of some kind. A cat, maybe? But how had a cat gotten into the house? She looked closer. The bite marks were flat and narrow; four little marks above, four little marks below. Almost like the small rows of a child's front teeth before they've cut all the others.

Rose's pulse quickened.

*What the fuck is going on around here...?*

# Chapter 34

## Solutions

Unable to settle her nerves after Chris's fall on the stairs, Rose grabbed her coat then bundled Timmy into his cosy suit before slipping him into the pram to take him out for a stroll. Goodness knows how long Chris would be at the hospital. She needed some fresh air, and she definitely needed to be out of the house.

As she strolled, Rose reflected on the short time that they'd been at Woodland Row. Whatever it was that had drawn her in was now making itself known in other, more sinister ways. She mentally chastised herself for having such thoughts – it was one thing to enjoy reading horror novels, or watching horror films, but really – c'mon Rose, you're being delusional...

Her walk took her past The Grange – the elegant convent retreat in which girls who were unfortunate enough to find themselves in a less-than-elegant predicament could be hidden away. Didn't Mrs Barnett once mention that one of these convent-girls was re-homed in the house where she now lived? She peered through the ornate wrought iron gates, and marvelled at the splendour of the well-tended gardens.

'Don't worry, Timmy – I'm not going to give you away to the nuns!' she whispered, as she looked into the pram. 'Mummy could never do that...'

Rose's thoughts lingered on the girl and her baby – she'd obviously chosen not to give the child up for adoption, which Rose could fully understand. There was no way she could ever give Timmy away; yet for some girls it was the only option. Strange that her only visitors were the nuns, never any visits from a boyfriend, or from her mother. Well, none that Mrs Barnett had ever witnessed. And then they vanished – poof! Just vanished into thin air. Most strange.

She took one more look at the old house then shuddered. 'C'mon, Timmy. Let's head home and see if Daddy's back from the hospital.'

Alerted by the sound of her dad's car pulling up outside, Rose opened the front door to take stock of her husband's injuries. She watched Chris intently as her dad helped him out of the car, then guided him up the path and the steps – Chris's face grimaced with pain despite his father-in-law's assistance.

Eddie looked at his daughter as she took Chris's arm. 'The good news is, nothing's broken – just a few bumps and bruises, and dented pride. Here's his prescription of painkillers.' He handed the pharmacy package to Rose.

'Thanks, Dad. You're a star! I was really worried – good to hear that nothing's broken.'

'Aye, happy to help. Anyways, I'd better head off home – got a stack of paperwork to get done; invoices and stuff.'

Chris tried to shake his father-in-law's hand, leaving his calliper dangling like a third arm. 'Cheers for the help, Eddie. Much appreciated.'

Eddie nodded and smiled. 'Anytime, lad. Right then, I'll be on my way. Take care now.'

Chris and Rose stood on the top step and waved as Eddie drove off, before carefully making their way inside.

Rose eased Chris onto the sofa before going to make them both a much-needed cup of tea.

She returned with the tray, her face taking on a serious outlook. 'I've been thinking – maybe it was a mistake to move into this house, what with the stairs and everything. It's difficult for you, isn't it?'

'Well, maybe a little. But the stairs are a good workout. I won't always be this incapacitated – it's just a long recovery, that's all. This house came just at the right time, remember? If it hadn't been for your dad, we'd have been out on the street because the lease wasn't going to be renewed on the old house. Plus it was right after my accident – being relieved of active service meant no money. I'm grateful to your dad, and for the house. It saved our backsides.'

Her eyes caught his, concern at their centre. 'True. But how can we make things easier for you until you're fully healed?'

Chris took a sip of his tea, washing the hospital taste from his mouth and easing the dryness in his throat. 'Getting up and downstairs is my biggest challenge, especially when I'm in a hurry to use the toilet.' He laughed at his own incapabilities.

Rose rubbed her chin while she thought. 'Maybe my dad could turn the pantry into a downstairs toilet area? That could be a solution, eh?'

Chris pondered the suggestion before replying. 'That would be a great solution,' he concurred. 'But I'm pretty sure that it's against building regulations. I don't think you're allowed to have a toilet next to a kitchen because of health and hygiene laws. There has to be an air-block with another door separating the toilet from the kitchen.' He waved his hands around trying to describe what he meant.

'Like a little square area, you mean? I'm pretty sure that Dad will be able to figure out what's needed. Besides, the pantry has already become a dumping ground for clutter, so it would make better use of the space. I'll talk to him next week and get him to take a look at it.

Chris squeezed her hand in grateful acknowledgement, then chuckled. 'What would we do without your dad, eh?'

# Chapter 35

## Digging the Dirt

A fine layer of white concrete dust feather-coated all visible surfaces in the dining kitchen. Rose surveyed the scene, her core jangling with every drrr-drrr-drrr of the jack-hammer being operated by her dad as he dug out for pipework in the old pantry-cum-toilet-to-be. On the floor lay a precisely drawn-out area where the little separating air-space would be. Crosses and lines, like some kind of noughts and crosses game for grown-ups, marked the direction of ground pipework and plumbing. All very organised. The jack-hammer drilled again, causing Rose to put her hands over her ears for protection, muffling the intrusive sound.

She watched her dad, marvelling in his ability to handle tools, whether it be a claw-hammer, jack-hammer or a paint brush. The tool became an extension of his creative mind and skilled hands. Realising that he was being observed, Rose's dad stopped his digging and broke out into a broad grin. He wiped away the sweat from his forehead with an old piece of towel, revealing a patch of sun-weathered skin from under the white dust.

'By 'eck, it's a bit dry and dusty in here. Gets into the back of your throat...,' he chuckled. He set the machine to one side, the compressor hissing as he turned it off. He coughed an exaggerated cough.

'Okay, Dad, I can take a hint. I'll put the kettle on,' laughed Rose. 'I might even give you a chocolate biscuit for all your hard work...'

'You spoil me, girl, you know that!'

Rose grinned and shook her head by way of a reply, as she went over to the sink to fill the kettle and make a pot of tea.

Eddie came and sat at the kitchen table, a cloud of dust puffing into the air as he sat down. 'Crikey, have you still got that ugly old teapot? Would you like me to accidentally jack-hammer it to death?'

'Sshh! Don't let Chris hear you say that – it was a present from his mother,' chided Rose, putting her finger to her lips.

Her dad rolled his eyes, then grinned. 'No comment... Where is Chris, anyway?'

'Hobbling around the neighbourhood with Timmy. He was planning to take him to the park for a stroll and feed the ducks while the weather's fine. Showers are forecast for later today. I don't think he fancied being bombarded with all the noise and mess while you're digging out.' Rose poured the boiling hot water over the tea bags then gave them a stir. She came and joined her father at the kitchen table, wiping off the chair before she sat down.

'Aye, good idea. Anyway, it's going well. I've almost finished cutting out for the shit-pipe so that I can break into the main drain. The pantry floor is quite uneven, what with the old brick steps and stuff, so I'm going to dig out to stabilise the ground, then backfill and level it with a new flood of concrete. And I've thrown out that manky old rug – time to let it go, Rose.'

Rose frowned. 'Yeah, but–'

Her dad finger-wagged not to argue back. 'Anyway, as you can see, I've marked out where the studding will go for the walls.' He pointed his hands in the direction of the lines, rather like an air-hostess showing passengers where the emergency lights and exits are. 'The first door will open inwards, with a sliding door into the toilet area. It'll look quite smart when it's finished.'

'I agree,' nodded Rose, pouring two mugs of tea. She pushed one in the direction of her father, along with a packet of chocolate digestives. 'I like the new layout that it gives to the kitchen – gives it more shape than just a boring square.' She pointed to the area where a new corner would be formed. 'I think I'll move the dresser to that wall there once it's all finished. Makes better use of the space.'

'You're such a little home-maker! Well, best get back to it – these walls won't build themselves.' Eddie stood and patted himself down, causing a cloud of white dust to form around him. He wafted the dust from his face, spluttering in the maelstrom. 'That was a bad idea!' he laughed, turning the compressor back on. 'Just a bit more noise for this last bit of digging out, then I can start shovelling up the debris and cleaning up.' He wriggled his ear-defenders back over his ears.

'Sounds good,' acknowledged Rose, giving her dad the thumbs-up. 'I think I'll go out into the garden for a while and do some weeding and tidying up. Get out of this noise and dirt.'

Rose topped up her cup of tea and grabbed a couple of biscuits to take outside, choosing to sit awhile at the little patio table in the recently revamped garden before starting on the gardening work. As with most living things, she automatically turned her face towards the sun, relishing the warmth of the longest-day sunshine – a welcome boost in between the rain showers. She cupped her hands over her eyes to form a shaded barrier, enabling her to scrutinise the flower beds. The borders either side of the lawn were a riot of early summer colour, and the newly planted apple trees had already established themselves. But even from this distance, Rose could see that the weeds had similarly benefited from the intermittent sunshine and showers. A grumble emanated from her throat. The weeds were winning the battle – for the time being, at least. She drained the last of her tea then forcefully put on her gardening gloves.

*Right then, you buggers – time to die!*

As Rose tugged and pulled at the weeds, she could sense a change in the atmosphere – that heavy, charged feeling in the air when everything falls silent before the onslaught of a thunderstorm. No bird sounds, no traffic sounds, not even building work sounds. Everything had stopped. An icy feeling began to worm its way up her spine causing her to shudder. She looked at the sky expecting to see gathering storm clouds, but there were none. Just the same few wisps of white clouds floating around as earlier, nothing that would bring imminent rain.

A sixth sense for movement drew her eyes towards the house. Her father was standing on the doorstep waving, beckoning towards her. There was something about his semantics that elicited a frantic urgency. Rose cocked her head on one side to catch what he was shouting, but despite the silent air she couldn't quite make it out.

*Did he just say "might be another dog"…?*

'Hang on, I'm coming.' Rose peeled off her gardening gloves and threw them down as she hurried towards the house. 'What is it? What about a dog?'

Even behind the coating of dust on her father's face, Rose could see the panic – his wild, darting eyes hiding nothing.

'In there. Don't look, don't go in. I've found something, Rose. It looks like something buried in there…' Eddie's hand was shaking as he pointed towards the pantry. 'I was just digging out the old brick steps and stuff, to try and level things. The jack hit something. I'm not sure what it is.'

'Here, Dad, sit down a minute.' Rose guided her dad towards one of the kitchen chairs and helped him to sit. 'Now, take a few deep breaths. That's better.' Rose gave him a few minutes to regain his composure. 'Start again. What is it, Dad? You're not making much sense.'

'Remember when we found the dog bones under the old apple tree? It was buried in some kind of plastic bowl, yeah?'

Rose cocked her head on one side, puzzled. 'Yeah, I remember. Why?'

'Well, I think there's another one in the pantry. The tone of the jack-hammer changed, like there was something different underneath, not just brick and rubble. Then it bounced into something plastic. Anyway, I got my torch to take a better look, and...and... I could see something strange. Like a blanket or something, inside the plastic.'

'Why on earth would anyone bury a dog in the pantry, Dad? Here, give me the torch.' Rose could feel the icy sensation creeping up her spine again, fingering around the base of her primitive brain.

She cautiously made her way through the rubble and debris of the pantry floor to take a look at her father's discovery. The torch-beam clearly picked out the edge of what appeared to be a bath – a baby's bath. She picked away some of the broken plastic and debris, revealing more of the blanket. Uncertain of her next move, Rose hesitated before moving the blanket to one side, her hands shaking as she did so.

'Dad...'

'What is it, Rose?'

'I think you'd better call the police...'

# Chapter 36

## Pandora's Box

Chris's brow furrowed as he turned the corner into Woodland Row. A police car and police van were parked on the street in the proximity of his house, making a sandwich either side of Eddie's Bedford flatbed truck. He sensed curtains surreptitiously twitching as neighbours peered with curiosity at the unusual comings and goings. As he neared, he realised that his own front doorstep was occupied by a young police constable. A wave of apprehension surged through his veins. Chris hobbled as fast as he could, his walking stick and pram hindering his urgent progress.

'What's going on? Why are you on my doorstep?' he asked, his voice tinged with rising panic.

'I'm sorry, sir, but I can't let you in,' replied the tight-lipped young constable.

'But...but, I live here – this is my house! What's happened to my wife? Is she okay?' Chris fumbled to get his wallet out of his pocket so that he could retrieve his driving licence. 'Here, look. See, this is me. Christopher Bradshaw.' He waved his proof under the constable's nose. 'This is my address. I live here...'

'Just a moment, sir. Let me check.' The young officer radioed inside and spoke with his superiors to get clearance for Chris's access. 'Okay, sir, you can go in.' The constable helped Chris up the front steps with the pram. 'But please don't touch anything.'

Chris could already sense the taut, charged atmosphere as he parked the pram in the front sitting room. His eyes widened as he entered the dining kitchen, the sight akin to something from a police drama series. A young WPC was comforting a sobbing Rose, while Eddie was sitting at the kitchen table deep in conversation with a note-taking police officer. Two white-suited forensic officers, armed with scraping tools and plastic bags were just disappearing into the now-out-of-bounds pantry, cordoned off by police tape.

'What the hell's going on here?' he asked, eyes still agog at the surreal scene set before him.

Rose looked up at the sound of his voice. 'Chris! Oh, my God, Chris, it's awful...' She broke free of the WPC's embrace and ran into Chris's arms.

'What is it, my love? What's going on? Why are the police here?'

'Dad found something while he was digging up the floor. We think there's a body in the pantry...' Rose's face was ashen as she spoke, her eyes red-rimmed from crying. 'There's a baby's bath with something in it. Oh, and the smell – it's awful. The forensic team is just in there now, trying to determine what it is. They might not be dog bones...' She began crying again, her words coming in-between the sobs. 'Oh, Chris, what if it's a baby! What if there's a baby buried in the house! All those weird happenings...'

Chris held her close. He could feel his own heart-rate beginning to increase at the prospect of a murder scene unfolding in his own home. Sounds of rubble being carefully moved and muffled voices emanated from the confines of the pantry. A bright work-light threw an eerie, otherworldly glow from the inner depths, interspersed with the lightning-bright flash from a camera. 'Let's hope for the best, eh. Let's just hope that it's another dog...'

The sounds of chairs scraping and a police officer slapping dust from his uniform signalled the conclusion of Eddie's statement-giving, as he and the police officer stood, then shook hands. The police officer indicated to Rose that it was her turn to come and give a statement. Chris released her from his arms, then took hold of his clearly-distressed father-in-law.

'I hope that it isn't a bairn. How the fuck could anybody do that to a little 'un, eh? It's beyond me...' Eddie wiped his eyes, his tears having streaked a pathway through the layer of grime on his face.

'What did you find exactly?' asked Chris.

'A little plastic baby-bath. And it had a blanket inside – one of those crocheted ones. Anyway, our Rosie took a bit of a closer look, and there was something under the blanket. A little bundle. And the stench – it turns your stomach right over...' He squeezed his eyes closed, as if trying to erase the gruesome mind-image. 'Anyway, we thought it best to call the police–'

Their hushed conversation was interrupted by the emergence of one of the forensic team, as he beckoned to the police officer interviewing Rose. Although they turned their backs towards her, whispers and nods intimated that something other than canine remains had indeed been found. The surreal, amplified noise of careful yet urgent scraping and more rubble being moved echoed around the dining kitchen. Rose felt goose-bumps rise on her arms and her scalp tighten, as she shivered. She swallowed hard, squeezing back the rising bile.

The police officer came over to Chris and Eddie, and motioned for Rose to join them. He lowered his head then clasped his hands together, right over left, as if in solemn veneration.

'I'm sorry to confirm that something suspicious has been found, so we'll need to take away the findings for a detailed forensic analysis. I'm afraid you're going to have to move out, as this is now a crime scene. Is there anywhere that you can go?'

Rose's hands shot over her mouth as she endeavoured to stifle a rising scream, her shoulders shaking with unreleased tension.

Eddie nodded. 'Aye, they can come and stay with me, officer. You have my address and details, so you know where to find us if you have any more questions.'

The police officer acknowledged Eddie's offer with mutual eye contact and a nod. He gently lay his hand on Rose's shoulder. 'I appreciate that you're in shock, Mrs Bradshaw, but if you could just come and finish giving me your statement, then we'll take over from here. You'll need to gather together some belongings to take with you to your dad's.' His radio crackled with a message from the constable outside. 'The constable says to be aware that the press have gotten wind of something – there are already a couple of local hacks hanging around. Probably alerted by the neighbours. Just remember not to say anything. We'll release a statement as soon as we have more details.'

Now on auto-pilot, Rose meekly returned to sit at the kitchen table, her face pallid.

Chris came and kissed her on the head. 'I'll go and put some things together,' he whispered.

The tone and mood of the house had now changed since the fateful nod of the forensic officer, creating one of quiet reverence. The fateful nod which suggested the grim likelihood of a body.

A baby's body.

# Chapter 37

## Jigsaw Pieces

Liz peered from behind the net curtains of the bay window as she watched Sergeant Gould walk up the front path. His hat was tucked under his arm, his steps heavy and morose. He was accompanied by another officer, tall and dark suited rather than in uniform. Déjà vu was playing out in Liz's mind. She went to open the front door, her hands shaking as she turned the latch and handle.

'Hello, Liz.' Sergeant Gould reached out to shake her hand. 'And this is DI Benson. 'I'm afraid this isn't a social visit – we're here on official police business.'

Liz guided the two officers into the hallway, and quickly closed the door behind them, eager to shut out the prying eyes of neighbours.

An uneasy feeling began rolling around her stomach. She ushered the policemen into the sitting room, proffering each a seat in the armchairs. 'Can I offer either of you a cup of tea, or coffee?'

Sergeant Gould shook his head. 'Not for me, thanks, Liz.' The DI shook his head. 'We'd best get on with this.'

Liz sat on the edge of the sofa, opposite the two official and efficient looking officers. A jelly-like feeling invaded her legs as she struggled to get her rising tension under control.

The sergeant took out his notebook then cleared his throat before asking, 'I suppose you've seen on the local news that there's been the discovery of a baby's remains in a terraced house in Woodcliffe?'

Liz nodded her mute acknowledgement, her throat constricted by nervousness. She swallowed, the hardness hurting.

His eyebrows furrowed together as he began reading from his notes, a welcome diversion from making eye contact with Liz. 'Well... Anyway, erm, house-to-house inquiries and investigations made by the Woodcliffe police lead them to believe that a young girl was the occupant of this particular house during 1977. And that she lived there with a baby, a little boy.' He looked up from his notes, but Liz's face was unreadable. 'According to their investigations, the young girl stayed at The Grange convent until she'd had her illegitimate baby, then – unable to give the baby up for adoption – moved into this particular house with her child, under the pastoral care of the nuns.'

Liz's heartbeat shifted up a gear, and she could feel the colour rising in her cheeks under the now watchful scrutiny of Sergeant Gould and DI Benson.

He continued. 'The young girl's name was given as Margaret Braithwaite, originally of Millers Common. So, naturally, the Woodcliffe police passed a request to our station to make some local inquiries. I only know of one Margaret Braithwaite – did your Maggie have a baby, Liz?'

Liz looked at Sergeant Gould eye-to-eye, her face suddenly taking on a careworn expression, as if the weight of all her burdens and worries had descended at that very moment. Her shoulders sagged, barely supporting her nod of affirmation.

She spoke in a low voice. 'Yes, she did. And I was so embarrassed that I sent her away to the convent home in Woodcliffe until after the birth.'

'Well, I'm sorry to be the bearer of bad news, Liz, but there's now a warrant out for Maggie's arrest – she's a wanted person...'

Momentarily stunned, Liz just stared at the policeman like he'd just punched her in the belly. Tears began welling in her eyes, as she spoke in a low, shaky voice. 'Just a minute, Sergeant Gould – I need to show you something.' Liz left the room briefly, returning moments later with Maggie's Bible. She opened the black leather cover to take out the letter that Maggie had written but never sent, together with a series of photographs of baby Ben. She passed them to Sergeant Gould.

'I found this a couple of years ago when I was cleaning Maggie's room. I never took her to be a Bible owner, so curiosity got the better of me. Don't ask me why, but I couldn't resist taking a look.' Liz sighed as she recalled the moment of guilty discovery. 'I've never said anything to her – I didn't want her to think that I'd been snooping.'

He scanned over the letter, his eyes widening with every word. Liz noticed that his hands were shaking, and that his face now bore the same beleaguered appearance that she had worn only moments before. He looked from the letter to the handful of photos of Ben – photos that tracked the few months of his short life. Myriad thoughts whirred around his mind. As he spoke, his voice became softer.

'This is quite some accusation, Liz. And if, as Maggie says here, that our Jimmy is responsible for this, then I'm really sorry. The baby's body that they recovered from the house – although quite badly decomposed – allegedly had the remnants of sandy coloured hair, just like on these photographs.' He fanned them open like a hand of playing cards, and shook his head. 'There's no denying that this little fella certainly looks like our Jimmy did at this age – like two peas in a pod, that's for sure.' Realising that he was now speaking like a concerned father rather than an on-duty police officer in front of his superior, he took a deep breath in order to regain his official composure. 'I'm going to have to take these as evidence, Liz.' He tapped the Bible and secretive contents before slipping them into a plastic evidence bag. 'This doesn't look good for Maggie, I'm afraid.'

Liz closed her eyes and nodded her silent acknowledgement before speaking.

'But...but, Maggie told me that she'd finally given up Ben for adoption – that she couldn't cope anymore. She told me that she'd taken him back to the convent. They had people willing to adopt him...It all sounded so plausible – I didn't think to follow it up.'

Sergeant Gould shook his head. 'I'm sorry, Liz, that doesn't seem to be the case. The Reverend Mother's records are very precise – there's no record of a male child being returned for adoption at that time, nor any other adoption having taken place. The forensics team has identified a male infant, aged approximately eight to ten months. They're still working on the cause of death.'

Liz blanched and put her hands over her mouth, while her stomach lurched and rolled. She endeavoured to steady her breathing.

The sergeant took up his pen in readiness for more note-taking. 'Do you know of her whereabouts, Liz? Like I said earlier, there's a warrant out for her arrest – we're going to have to bring her in for questioning as our main suspect.'

Liz shook her head. 'No, sorry, Sergeant. She went on the road a few years ago, just after her eighteenth birthday. Went to live with one of those New Age Traveller groups. She lives in a camper van with her boyfriend, Charley – Charley Green. I presume that it's short for Charles. They just travel from festival to festival, especially in the summer months. Funny how she's with a boy now, after all that fuss she made about being one of those lesbians...'

'Do you know of her most recent whereabouts?' asked the DI.

'I'm sorry, I've no idea where she is – I haven't heard from her since she sent me a birthday card. She always sends me a birthday card. We have, at best, what could be described as an estranged relationship.'

'Do you know where she posted them from?' asked DI Benson.

'Yes, I still have the cards in the envelopes.' Liz went to the bureau to retrieve the bundle. 'There are three birthday cards, all with postmarks from Salisbury. So she must be somewhere near there towards the end of June – my birthday is 1st July, you see. She sent me Christmas cards too, but the postmarks are random, look – Edinburgh and Cardiff.

Maybe Charley's parents could help. They live in the Salisbury area, in Barrowfeld, near Stonehenge. Charley and Maggie often stop by there when they go to the festival at Stonehenge in June.'

The DI took over the questioning, his tone slightly more gruff than the sergeant's. 'And where can we find Mr and Mrs Green?'

'She – Mrs Green – has the coffee shop in the village. The Willow Tree, I think it's called.'

'That's really helpful, Mrs Braithwaite. We'll get in touch with our colleagues in the Wiltshire area, so that they can set up a line of enquiry. We'll also need the most recent photo of Margaret that you have, to help with identification.'

Liz nodded towards the DI in cold affirmation, 'I'll go and get one for you.'

His reply was equally terse. 'Thank you. By the way, do you know whether your daughter has a valid passport?'

'Not that I'm aware of – we've never been abroad. Not as a family. No passport paperwork has ever come here for Maggie since she left home, let's put it that way,' she replied.

Liz then turned to look directly at Sergeant Gould as she spoke, snubbing the DI. 'Will you keep me updated, Sergeant? This is quite a to-do, isn't it? I really can't believe that our Maggie would be capable of doing such a thing as this. But well, we never really know our children, do we?' Her hands fiddled nervously before asking, 'Did you know about the rape? She told me that she'd been experimenting with a boy. Why would she do that? Why would she protect your son, eh? Why would she cover it over?' Buoyed by a sudden rush of maternal instinct, she continued her tirade. 'Did you know that your son raped my daughter? Your son and his sick friends. Did you know that your daughter bullied Maggie at school, just after Maggie admitted to being different? Surely this letter will vindicate her?' She began to cry – huge, choking sobs racked her body. 'There's no wonder she ran away…'

Aware that his superior was privy to these personal accusations, Sergeant Gould coughed to clear his throat before speaking, effectively cutting off any further dialogue from Liz. 'I'm shocked and ashamed to hear these things about my kids, Liz.' He reached over and took her hands in his, as he mentally recalled the last time in which he'd visited Liz – bearing the news of her husband's death. 'I'm so very sorry. My God, life has not been kind to your family...' After allowing Liz a few minutes to regain her composure, he took up the statement paperwork. 'We're going to have to take an official statement from you, with you having a connection to Maggie, you understand. Everything that you remember.'

Liz dried her eyes with a tissue and nodded, then began recounting all that she could bring to mind, right from Maggie announcing the pregnancy, up to the moment of her return, just before the Christmas of 1977. 'Isn't it strange – I remember when she told me that she'd returned Ben to the nuns that I said it wasn't like returning a puppy to the RSPCA.' Her shoulders sagged. 'It all seems to add up though, doesn't it?'

Sergeant Gould finished writing then passed the statement to Liz so that she could read it over before signing. 'We have to present all this evidence and statement to the Woodcliffe station. They'll obviously contact the Wiltshire area as a part of their enquiries, and put out a search for Maggie to bring her in for questioning. But no, it doesn't look good for her...'

'I feel sick, Sergeant Gould. I still can't believe the calm way that she returned home with this story. It was all so believable. I never even thought to check it out. How could she do such a thing?'

'Who knows what drives people to carry out these acts, Liz. I've seen some things in my time on the Force. Believe me, she must have been going through hell, and felt under immense pressure or depression, carrying all this mental baggage. And speaking from experience, you'd best prepare yourself – things will get tricky for you too. You know how quickly gossip and speculation can escalate. Once people start putting two and two together, you'll come under the spotlight.'

The DI intercut. 'That's right, Mrs Braithwaite. Beware of talking to the press, or answering the phone. Those slime-balls will try every trick in the book to get a story from you. You might want to pack a bag and go to a hotel out of town for a few days. But make sure that you let us know where you are. We'll need to keep in touch with you.' He stood up to shake her hand, in readiness for leaving.

'I understand,' acknowledged Liz. 'Yes, that sounds like sensible advice, thank you.'

Sergeant Gould stood up and began gathering his papers together. 'Again, I'm sorry to be the bearer of bad news...'

Liz smiled wanly, before asking, 'One thing – will Jimmy be charged for his part in all this?'

'Only if Maggie presses charges for rape. There's no statute of time limit for presenting such charges. And if she does, then I'll have to step to one side from the case. I might have to step aside, even now, on the basis of this letter. I can't be seen to be protecting Jimmy. These kids, eh! You think you've done your best to bring them up well, give them everything that you can...'

They looked at each other, a look of mutual understanding.

No reply was needed.

# Chapter 38

## Needle in a Haystack

DCI Partridge eased the unmarked police car to a stop by the kerbside and took a few moments to observe the Greens' cottage; typical of the area with thatched roof and ornate brickwork.

'Nice place they've got – can't be short of a bob or two. Right, remember what the Guv said at the briefing – "Keep the questioning light and simple". We just need to find out what van they're travelling in so we can keep a lookout around the festival sites.'

The accompanying sergeant crushed out his cigarette, the curl of dying smoke and ash puffing over the edge of the ashtray. He quickly flicked away the debris from the dash console and his trousers under the analytical glare of his superior, before double-checking his notebook. 'True. The last thing we want to do is for the parents to give them a tip-off and put them on the run. Be like trying to find a needle in a haystack among all those hippies and Stone Age Travellers. Dope heads that need to get a bath and get a job...'

'New Age Travellers, you clot. They're called New Age Travellers.'

'Well, whatever they're called, it's costing the taxpayers a bloody fortune cleaning up after them. And police man-hours–'

'Bloody 'ell – aren't you a grumpy shit this morning,' interjected the DCI, effectively cutting off Simmons mid-complaint.

'Sorry, sir. The little 'un kept us awake last night. Started teething.'

DCI Partridge laughed and shook his head. 'Ah, the joys of parenthood – I remember it well. Just wait until they're teens – it doesn't get any better. You spend their early years teaching them to walk and talk, then their older years wishing they'd shut up and sit down! How many kids have you got now, Simmons?'

'This is the fourth, sir. Think we'd better put a stop to it, otherwise we'll need to move house,' he laughed. 'Right then, shall we go in?'

The DCI looked at his watch. 'And just in time for morning coffee...'

Hillary Green poured out two cups of coffee for their unexpected guests, her hands shaking as she set the tall pot back on the tray.

'Help yourselves to milk and sugar, officers. So, what's this all about?'

The DCI took up the reply. 'We need to contact a girl by the name of Margaret Braithwaite in connection with some of our enquiries, and we have reason to believe that she's travelling with your son.'

'My son? He's at university, not travelling.'

Sergeant Simmons quickly checked his notebook. 'Your son, Charles. Charley Green.'

'Charley – that's our daughter! Her name is Charlotte, but goes by Charley. Thinks Charlotte is too prissy.'

The two police officers looked at each other, before DCI Partridge interjected. 'Your daughter? Ah, Margaret's mother seems to be under the impression that Charley is male...' He scribbled some notes in his notebook.

'Really? I wonder what gave her that idea. Maybe she got confused by the name. Mind you, I don't think they communicate much these days, her and Maggie. Same with us and Charley – once a year, if we're lucky. Free spirits!'

'So, are they, you know, a couple, then – Charley and Maggie?' asked DCI Partridge.

'Yes, they've been together for about three years. Maggie was working for me at the coffee shop when she first met my Charley. They've been together ever since.' She began pouring a cup of coffee for herself, slopping it over the edge onto the tray.

'Do you know where the girls are at the moment? You say that they travel around a lot...' asked the sergeant, still irked by the thought of free-loading, free-loving hippies.

Noting that his wife was still showing signs of nervousness in the company of the two officers, Kenneth Green cut in before she could answer. 'They stopped by just recently, while they were at the Stonehenge festival – didn't stay long though. They'd been given a ride into the village while a friend of theirs came for supplies, so they said. Anyway, they just stayed long enough to each take a shower and have a bite to eat, then walked back to the site later in the day.'

'And how did they seem?' continued the sergeant.

'Just fine. They seemed to be in good spirits. Is there any reason why they shouldn't have been?'

'No, none at all. Do you have any idea where they could be now?' asked DCI Partridge.

'No, sorry, I'm not sure. They tend to follow the festivals and the weather. I remember Charley saying that they were en-route to Glastonbury rather than staying here at the Henge for the solstice. The girls are also into this CND thing, or whatever they call it. Ban the bomb. So they're probably roaming those festivals and rallies as well. I can't remember all the places that she mentioned–'

'Make sure that you're writing all this down, Simmons,' interrupted the DCI. He deduced that now would be a good time to deploy his "keep mum busy" tactic, so poured himself a top-up of coffee. 'Do you have a biscuit, Mrs Green? I'd love a biscuit, if you have one.'

The request snapped her back into the moment. 'Of course – I'll go and get some.'

The DCI turned his attention back to Kenneth Green. 'It would be very useful to our enquiries if you could let us have a photograph of your daughter, as well as some details of her camper van.'

'Yes, of course.' Kenneth went over to the wall unit to retrieve a pack of photographs. 'Here are some taken from last summer when she stopped by. I didn't get any this year.' He riffled through them, then selected one of her posing at the side of Hovis. 'Here, you can take this one – it has a picture of both her and the camper, if that helps you.' He passed it over to Sergeant Simmons, who seemed to be dealing with all the secretarial note-taking.

'This is great, thanks.' The sergeant looked at the photograph. 'Pretty girl. Ah, the VW camper – the travel choice of thousands.'

Kenneth laughed. 'That old bus! Hovis, she calls him – thinks it looks like a loaf of brown bread. They're quite the duo, aren't they?'

Hillary Green returned with a pack of chocolate biscuits and some side plates. 'Who are a duo?'

'Charley and Hovis.'

'Well, they're a trio now, aren't they? Anyway, if I might ask, why are the police searching for Maggie – Miss Braithwaite? I hope our daughter isn't in any kind of danger. You never know, these days.'

The two police officers stood up to leave.

'We can't say at this stage of our enquiries, Mrs Green,' elicited DCI Partridge. 'There's no reason to believe that your daughter is in any danger, let's put it that way. But thank you both, anyway. Your information and the photo will help us greatly.'

'Well, that's a relief. What about your biscuit? I thought you wanted a biscuit,' she twittered.

The DCI patted his rotund girth. 'On second thoughts, Mrs Green, I think I'd better give the extra calories a miss. But thanks for your hospitality. Right then, Sergeant – time to head back to the factory...'

# Chapter 39

## Unwelcome Visitors

'Ugh! I don't believe it. Not again!' Maggie ruffled her fingers through her hair, and grimaced as a handful of head lice fell out and scuttled across the white Formica of the camper table. She quickly thumped them with her fist in a bid to crush their escape. 'Creepy! Crawly! Bastards!'

Charley stepped up into the camper with the rinsed-out piss bucket just as Maggie was venting her frustration at the unwelcome visitors. 'What is it? What's all the fuss about?'

'Head lice – again!' exclaimed Maggie. 'That's the third time since we got this van. I swear there must be some nits or something in the cushions.

'Noooo! Not again,' Charley protested.

'Here, sit down and let me check your hair.' In an almost primal manner, Charley sat still while Maggie systematically picked her way through her long hair. 'Sorry, my love, but you've got them again, too...'

Not usually one to become riled, this was the last straw for Charley. 'Oh, for fuck's sake! That's it – it's coming off.'

'What!' Maggie's eyes were wide with shock. Charley's long, golden locks were her pride and joy.

'Seriously! I'm going into Newtown to get some hair clippers and a gallon of that lice shampoo. I'm going to shave off all my hair, and give this van a good scrub. I think you're right – we've had nothing but lice trouble since we bought this van.' Charley began scratching involuntarily.

'Well, if you're shaving off your hair, then so am I,' declared Maggie. 'We're in this battle together,' she laughed.

Shocked at the sight of a shaven-headed Maggie hacking off Charley's hair with the scissors, Penny let out an involuntary shriek.

'Good God! What the hell are you two doing?'

'Stay back – stay back,' laughed Maggie. 'Unless you want head lice…' She wielded the scissors like a battle sword towards their green-haired friend.

Penny shuddered, then began scratching her head as an auto-response. 'No way – don't tell me that you two've got lice again.'

'Afraid so,' sighed Charley. 'But this time it means war. Gonna get rid of the little buggers once and for all. So, we're having a haircut. All of it; every last strand is coming off!'

'No way! You can't cut off your hair, Charley…'

'Too late now,' laughed Maggie, clutching a pony-tail handful of Charley's hair. She held up the hair clippers. 'We're going all the way!'

Penny's eyes widened at the sight of the clippers.

'And we've got three bottles of lice shampoo. Going to shampoo the whole, bloody lot – us and the camper. Like Charley said, this means war!' Maggie declared.

'Maybe we should try disinfecting Catweazle as well; the old fleabag!' snorted Penny, amused at her own joke. 'So I guess you missed getting a visit from the cops earlier today? They paid a less-than-social call to the site.'

'We saw a couple of police vans heading this way while we were en-route into Newtown, but they didn't stop us. So what did the boys in blue want? Same as last year's raid, I guess?' asked Charley.

'Yup. Mostly just drugs searches, checking around the campers and tents for any illegal substances or weapons. That said, they seemed to be taking quite an interest in number plates this year – maybe they were looking for people who were driving without tax and insurance, that kind of stuff.'

'Did they find anything on Bingo and Catweazle?' asked Charley, knowing they were usual targets for searches.

'Nah. Lucky for them, they were up in the woods looking at the wildlife to see if there was anything worth poaching. Either that, or they were running around the fields worrying the sheep,' she laughed.

Maggie took a step back to look at her hairdressing handiwork. Charley's hair, or what remained of it, stood out in uneven clumps and tufts, while the once glorious, now-detached golden locks lay on the floor around the stool. 'I don't know whether to laugh or cry,' she declared. 'You don't look like you anymore.'

'Pass me the mirror – I want to take a look...'

Quick as a flash and in resounding unison came a loud and firm 'No-ooo!' from Maggie and Penny.

Once Penny had regained her composure, she pulled up a camping chair to sit with the girls. 'Oh, and while I remember, Daisy and Pippa from the CND tent stopped by to remind everyone that there's going to be a campfire ceilidh tonight over by their place, so we need to take our instruments. Starts around eightish. Sounds like it's going to be quite a gathering, with a few guest-speakers and stuff, as well as music. Should be fun.'

Charley looked up from being shorn with the clippers. 'We'll definitely be there. All this threat from nuclear war and nuclear weapons is freaking me out. What kind of game do the governments think they're playing with our lives? Why can't people just live in peace?'

'I hear you, sister – it freaks me out, too. I wish there was more that we could do,' replied Penny. 'Surely the superpowers must realise what a deadly game they're playing?'

'Well, that's their whole point, isn't it?' Maggie interjected. 'They're using the nuclear threat as a weapon against each other, effectively holding millions of innocent lives to ransom. Let's just hope they don't get itchy fingers and press the red button, eh. Thank goodness for the CND movement. They get my full support.'

'Hear, hear, and hallelujah, sister!' snorted Charley, raising her hands upwards. 'Ouch, go steady with those clippers!'

'So, sit still, and save the hallelujahs and protests for later,' Maggie chortled, trying to hold Charley's head upright. 'We need to work on banning the head lice before we can ban any bombs!'

# Chapter 40

## Twisted Hypocrisy

Over the summer months, a strange, and at times strained, atmosphere had descended over the tribe. The constant travelling between festivals, bad weather, and growing objections from local communities, was beginning to have a profound effect on their collective psyche. At their most recent meeting, called at the behest of Bingo, the tribe had voted to disband and go their separate ways. While some of the group had decided to continue their nomadic lifestyle, others had chosen to immerse themselves fully into the CND cause at rallies and festivals; such was the impact and escalating fear towards the growing nuclear threat. During their stay at the Pontardawe Folk Festival, word had come through via the CND network that a group of women planned to march from Cardiff in Wales to the RAF Greenham Common airbase in Berkshire. The base was reportedly going to take delivery of ninety-six nuclear cruise missiles – each one fifteen times more powerful than the bomb which had raised Hiroshima to the ground. The British public had not been given any say in the matter, so the women felt duty-bound to raise awareness of this growing threat. Humbled and inspired by this simple, yet persuasive gesture, Maggie, Charley, Penny and the twins, Pinky and Perky, felt similarly compelled to join the protest march. The march was to be a peaceful one, setting off from Cardiff on 27th August, with the aim of delivering a letter of protest to the base, while quietly spreading the message for a unified, nuclear-free existence.

\*\*\*

'Well, old Catweazle's gonna miss you girls, that I am.' He peered out from under his unkempt hair at Maggie, Charley, Penny, and the pig-twins. 'But good luck to yerz. The tribe won't be the same without y'all.'

Charley gave Catweazle a reassuring hug. 'Hey, it's for a good cause, Catweazle. We're going on a peaceful protest march – we'll be safe.'

'That's right – it feels good to be doing something meaningful,' cut in Maggie. She reached out to embrace the human equivalent of a living scarecrow.

Penny lined up to take her turn in hugging Catweazle. 'We'll have two camper vans with us, so we can leapfrog the driving and marching, and have shelter. We'll be fine.'

'I know, I know...' grumbled the old man. 'It feels like I'm letting my daughters leave home, that's all.' He took a deep breath. 'You girls just be careful, d'ya hear.'

Bingo appeared behind the group just as they were climbing into their campers. 'Namaste, girls. You heard the man...Y'all take care. Hopefully we'll find each other again, if destiny allows.'

'Namaste, Bingo. I'm sure we'll meet again,' smiled Charley.

Maggie wiped a tear from the corner of her eye as she settled into the passenger seat. 'He's such a sweetie, old Catweazle. I'm really going to miss the old fleabag.'

'I know, me too,' concurred Charley. 'He can be a grumpy old cuss at times, but you couldn't ask for a better friend.' She patted Maggie on the shoulder and gave her a reassuring smile. 'But our time has come to move on – we have a new direction in life. What we're doing is important, Mags. The future of mankind is becoming more uncertain day by day.' Charley shifted the camper into first gear before releasing the handbrake, then giving the remainder of the tribe one last goodbye-wave.

'True. Who knows what the future will bring?'

'Exactly! It scares the shit out of me. And that's why we're going to join the march...'

\*\*\*

The group marched forward, their footsteps heavy, measured, yet resolute; each weary footstep was a step closer to their goal. With grim determination, the "Women for Life on Earth" proudly marched to deliver powerful words on behalf of the nation – a nation that had been denied the right to have a say in the prospect of an ominous and insecure future; a future driven by governmental acceptance of nuclear weapons. It was beyond comprehension that the government was prepared to allow the US Air Force to install nuclear warheads and weaponry on British soil. A government who had not consulted their nation in whose back garden they were going to be located.

Enough was enough.

Day by day, the marchers had received support from well-wishers; whether by roadside cheering, local hospitality, or inspirational speakers providing words of encouragement to the would-be dissenters. But blisters, drizzle and a lack of media coverage can have an abject way of stripping the spirit and will, no matter how important the cause. The collective band of strong, proud shoulders were beginning to sag, as the once-vigorous march descended into a tired, dogged plod.

Despite the pain from the raw skin on her heels, Maggie felt a sense of honour being allowed to bear the banner aloft, sharing the left flank with Charley, swapping every few miles once the weight and pain became intolerable.

Suddenly sparked with an idea, Charley nudged Maggie to take the banner.

'Here, take this. I'll be back in a jiffy...'

After a short while, Maggie could hear the strains of Charley's voice, accompanied by her guitar, moving forward through the group. As if by some mutual instinct, the group stopped dead in their tracks and evolved into an impromptu choir, with John Lennon's *Imagine* being their song of choice.

Maggie looked around and smiled at the lady next to her, then held out her arm to link them together; one by one, arm by arm, the unit came together as one – their voices and message strong –

"We are here, we are marching, and we are going to be peacefully heard!"

\*\*\*

Miles and miles of tall, grey wire fencing greeted the women on their arrival at the airbase – a thin line not to be crossed; a thin line dividing madness from sanity. The women knew that they were on the side of sanity. The leaders of the group, proudly bearing their standard, "Women for Life on Earth," moved forward, the rest of the assemblage falling in behind. Save for a few local hacks and a few curious onlookers, there was little in the way of media coverage or attention. Where were the big news crews? Why did only a handful of people seem interested in highlighting the cause? Surely this affront on the nation warranted more than this? A mood as grey as the sky above began rippling through the marchers, their restless frustration evident.

Charley looked around and scowled.

'I don't believe it – is that it! We've walked all this way, and for what? A few local news reporters and nosy neighbours. I expected a bigger welcome crowd than this. What a let-down! Where are the national news teams? I really feel for the girls...'

'I feel for them too, Charley. Maybe once they've delivered the letter, things will start hotting up. What if you get out the guitar and start a rousing chorus of *We Shall Overcome*? Surely that will get some attention,' suggested Maggie, her frustration equalling that of her partner's.

'No, I don't think this is the right moment for something like that, Mags. Let's just wait and see what happens. Believe me; we haven't walked all this way and suffered sore feet and blisters without the organisers trying to engage the base in some kind of dialogue. It isn't our place to intervene, Maggie.'

Maggie hung her head like a chastised child, grateful for her partner's logic and level-headed maturity. 'Sorry, you're right. But I get the feeling that they're not going to accept any kind of defeat – I think this is going to turn into something much bigger; you just wait and see.'

Eager to see what was happening up front, Charley strained on her tiptoes. 'Look, they're delivering the letter now. Let's move over there to get a better view.' She ushered Maggie over to one side, giving them a clearer vantage point, and joined the other women that were beginning to seat themselves on the grass verge. 'I think you're right, Mags – judging by the look on their faces and body language, I'd say this is going to spiral upwards. I can already feel the heightened tension...'

The mounting strain and emotion of the women's group was further fuelled when word was returned to them via the base officials that the government was not prepared to engage in any kind of public debate regarding the deployment of missiles at the base.

Not to be cheated or robbed of the opportunity to highlight the governmental injustice to the British public, the women's group felt duty-bound to bring global media attention to the cause. Word spread through the group as to the next line of defence.

It was time to raise the stakes a little higher...

"*A number of arrests were made today at the RAF base at Greenham Common in Berkshire. At least thirty-six women were cut free from the gates and fencing, having chained themselves as a mark of protest. The group, who call themselves "Women for Life on Earth" instigated a peaceful march from Cardiff in Wales to Greenham Common in Berkshire, a journey of some ten days, in order to highlight the growing public concern over nuclear weapons. A spokeswoman for the protesters said that their chains and shackles were a symbolic gesture towards the British government for holding the nation to ransom over their agreement with the United States of America to house a significant number of cruise missiles at the base. Those women who were not arrested said that they will remain defiant, and will set up camp at the base as an on-going peaceful protest until the government agrees to their request for a public debate."*

Liz watched the news report with interest as the police officers wrestled with the protestors, pushing them unceremoniously into the back of waiting police vans. A wave of panic and realisation suddenly coursed through her veins.

*What if...?*

She moved closer to the television screen and scanned the fast-moving news images, searching for a familiar face.

Old women. Young women. Ordinary women. Rebels...

*Oh, God, don't let her be there – it would be just like our Maggie to get caught up in something anarchic like this...*

She swallowed hard and willed the telephone not to ring.

# Chapter 41

## ...But You Can't Hide

Sergeant Gould browsed his way along the array of framed photographs on the highly polished teak sideboard; family photographs from happier days. He selected one in a silver frame – a family portrait of Liz, Joseph and Maggie; most likely on a family cottage holiday to the seaside judging by the background.

The swish of the sitting room door opening and the clatter of crockery on the tray caused him to look up as Liz entered. He nodded towards the photograph.

'I never realised that Maggie and Joseph had the same colour eyes –'

Liz's gaze became wistful.

'Aye, crystal blue; they were his windows to the soul. He could never hide anything from me – those eyes always gave too much away, Sergeant. Pity I can't say the same about Maggie – it's impossible to read Maggie through her eyes. They might as well be black.'

Sergeant Gould sat down and began pouring coffee for the two of them.

'Have you heard anything from Maggie since the search was put out for her?'

A perturbed look crossed Liz's brows. 'You know that I haven't, Sergeant. I would have been in touch with you if I had,' she reprimanded. 'I was rather hoping that you have some news for me...'

'Yes, and no, Liz. The camper van that they were travelling in, the old VW belonging to Miss Green, has been located.'

Liz looked up, mid-sip of coffee, her eyes wide. 'Miss Green? You said "*Miss* Green".

'Yes, that's correct. You seem puzzled, Liz...' The sergeant cocked his head on one side, his face quizzical.

Liz's mouth fell open as she struggled to find her words. 'But...I thought Charley was a he – short for Charles?'

Sergeant Gould looked at Liz and shook his head. 'No – Charley is a girl. Charlotte. It's Charlotte Green, not Charles Green,' he corrected.

'Well, I never! I always thought that Charley was a boy. Maggie never said one way or the other...' She zoned off, her eyes distant, while she contemplated her faux-pax.

The policeman waited a moment while Liz digested this new information, before intentionally clearing his throat as a way of bringing her back to the present moment. 'Anyway, as I said, the camper has been located. However, it's being used as a chicken shed. Turns out that it suffered some kind of mechanical failure while at some pop festival in Avebury, so a nearby farmer paid them a few quid to tow it away, saying that he would be happy to take it off their hands. Anyway, a search by the DVLA shows that Miss Green purchased another van – bought it privately from some people in that area. We have the registration details, so the local forces around those festival sites are keeping their eyes peeled. She's used her parents' address though, as the registered address – presumably because she's classed as NFA, or No Fixed Abode.'

'That's good to know. Maggie has to face her justice, Sergeant, as much as it pains me to say that about my own daughter.' She shifted uneasily in her chair before continuing. 'Is there any news on, you know, the fate of little Ben?'

The sergeant nodded sagely. 'Aye, Liz – I was just coming to that. The forensics report from the Paediatric Pathology Department confirms that he was most likely asphyxiated. No other injuries were revealed by the autopsy – no signs of any physical abuse from what they could make out.' He wanted to add, "allowing for the rate of decomposition", but thought better of it. 'Apart from that, he appeared to be in reasonable health. A bit on the small side, but then again, Maggie's only small.'

Liz shook her head, her eyes full of sadness. 'I can't imagine what drove her to do such a thing. She must have been desperate–' Tears began welling in her eyes.

'That's usually the case with something like this, Liz. Apparently he was well-wrapped when they found his body, plus there was a soft toy with him. It was almost ritualistic, the way that she had buried him.'

A silence hung in the air, each locked in their private, momentary thoughts.

Sergeant Gould coughed as if to clear his throat. 'Anyway, we've been notified that Ben's remains can be released to you for burial. And – seeing as how Ben is most likely my grandson too – I would like to share the cost of the funeral with you.'

Liz looked at the sergeant. 'No, I couldn't possibly let you do that. What would your Barbara say?'

Sergeant Gould shuffled uneasily. 'She doesn't know about the connection. Until Maggie makes a formal accusation of rape and paternity, then there's only really you and I that know about Ben's likely parentage. Even Jimmy doesn't know.' His eyes clouded over and his face became stone-like. 'Do you know, Liz – I can barely look at our Jimmy these days, knowing what I know.' He poured himself another cup of coffee before continuing. 'I have my own money, my own savings. Seriously, Liz, I'd like to help you. It's the least I can do.'

'Thanks, Sergeant. Yes, I'd like that. I have to confess, I feel very alone at the moment, so your support is most welcome.'

'Like I said, Liz, it's the least I can do. In the meantime, if you have any communication from Maggie, please let either me or the station know, so that we can follow up any leads as to her whereabouts. I suppose one plus-point is that the festival season has pretty much come to an end, so these travelling groups usually try to find somewhere more fixed over the winter months.'

'I've been thinking about that. She'll more than likely send me a Christmas card – she always does. At least we can check the postmark on the envelope; see where it's come from. Plus, the annual statement from her building society account always comes here – Maggie is still registered here as her home address. Maybe it will show if she's made any recent withdrawals, and the branch location.'

Sergeant Gould made a few notes in his notebook regarding this new information and possible leads. 'That would be great, Liz. Yes, by all means let the station know. All leads are vital to us and this investigation. Anyway, I'd better get back to the station.' He stood up to leave and popped the notebook into his jacket pocket. 'Let me know when and where for Ben's funeral, and, of course, how much, and I'll be there to support you.' He stretched out his hand to shake Liz's, holding it a moment longer than he needed to – a bond of solidarity.

Squaring her shoulders, Liz took a deep breath, filling her lungs to capacity, before allowing a long, deep, stress-releasing exhalation. She briefly closed her eyes, then nodded.

'I'll be in touch.'

# Chapter 42

## Santa's Magic Key

Feather-soft flakes of ambient snow clumped together and swirled gently to the ground, creating an almost mystical looking blanket over the sinister components of the airbase – the purity of white cloaking an enclosure of potential death.

Vapour clouds formed over the five steaming mugs of hot chocolate, competing for space with the vapour trails of exhaled breath. The group huddled closer, shivering. Charley turned to close the curtains of the camper, prompting the others to do the same.

Pinky sneezed, her pig-like nostrils rupturing with an explosion of slime and snot. She wiped her nose on a handful of tissues before speaking.

'Oh, for fuck's sake! – excuse my vernacular. Sorry, ladies, but I'm going to call it quits on the protest, at least for the winter. I can't risk getting bronchitis again.'

Perky draped a woolly blanket over her twin sister's shoulders, before taking up her sister's thread of conversation.

'Mum and Dad have insisted that we go home for Christmas. I think we have to concede that it's the best thing for Pinky's health. We're going to head off tomorrow.'

The other three murmured their reluctant agreement.

'Where do you live? Maybe we could drive you home?' suggested Maggie, looking at Charley for support.

'Milton Keynes,' came the twinned, stereo reply.

Charley blanched. 'Oh. That's quite a way from here–'

'Don't worry, I'm sure there's a train from Reading to Milton Keynes,' snuffled Pinky, before sneezing again. 'A lift to the railway station would suffice.'

Maggie nudged Charley and scowled at her, her eye-message clear.

'No, we'll take you,' said Charley. 'We could use the trip to do some Christmas shopping, and send Christmas cards to our families before the mad rush. What date is it today, anyway?'

Maggie looked at today's window on their Advent calendar. 'I opened number 11 today...'

Penny blurted out an incredulous laugh. 'You girls have an Advent calendar! I thought they were just for kids...'

Charley scowled in mock indignation. 'Hey, chocolate is chocolate – of course we have an Advent calendar. We take it in turns to open a window – sharing a calendar means that it's only half the calories,' she laughed.

Unseen by the others, Maggie returned her gaze to the Advent calendar to do a mental count of the windows. If she had opened number 11 today, then it would be her turn to open the window for number 15.

*15th December...the fourth anniversary of Ben's...*

A hearty clap on the back from her partner brought Maggie back into the moment. She blinked, unsure of how much conversation she had absently missed.

'And what's more, Maggie would eat too much chocolate if I didn't restrain her!'

Realising that a joke had been made at her expense, Maggie blushed then grinned. She held her hands up in defence. 'So, I'm a chocoholic...'

Even with the blanket over her shoulder, Pinky shivered. ´But, getting back to your offer of a ride home, thanks, that's really kind of you. We'll gladly accept.'

'No problem,' said Charley. 'Happy to help. Besides, I've heard a lot about the shopping centre in Milton Keynes, and I'm curious to see the grid-system of roads.' Her face lit up as another idea came to her. 'Perhaps I could do some busking and make some extra money for the cause? It would be great to get something for the women here at the site – maybe some hot water bottles – something to help keep them warm. I think that we could all do with a bit of Christmas cheer in this bloody weather!'

'And I could use the trip to get some chocolate – sorry, I mean cash – out of my account, and send my mum a Christmas card,' chuckled Maggie. 'Plus, I'd love to see those famous concrete cows.'

Pinky rolled her eyes. 'Oh, yeah, the famous, controversial cows! We can give you a grand tour of Milton Keynes, and show you where everything is. Make a day of it.'

'We'll chip in with the cost of the fuel,' added Perky. 'At least Santa will know where to find us this year,' she laughed.

Maggie's crystal blue eyes sparkled with nostalgia, as she zoomed back in time to reminiscing mode. 'My dad used to tell me that Santa had a magic key to let himself in – the fireplace at my mum's house is blocked off by a gas fire, you see. So he had to have a magic key, which my dad always hid under the front door mat on Christmas Eve.'

'Wasn't that an open invitation for burglars?' quipped Charley.

'Nah, it was just some old door-key that he'd sprayed silver then painted with glitter. Genius solution to keep a kid excited at Christmas!'

Penny cupped her hands around the mug of hot chocolate, relishing the warmth. 'Actually, this snowy weather has just given me an idea. Not everyone here is lucky enough to have a camper or caravan – I could offer a rotation for people to have a warm night inside, seeing as how I'll have the extra space. Might be an idea to get some big cooking pots, too, when you go shopping, so that we can start making some winter-warming soup to hand out.'

'Agreed. That's a brilliant idea,' acknowledged Charley. 'We'll take it in turns with you on the cooking, won't we, Mags?'

'Definitely. The season of goodwill to all men...well, women, but you know what I mean,' she laughed. A yawn escaped, setting off a chain reaction of yawns around the group. 'Well, we've got a long day ahead tomorrow – time to get some sleep, I'd say...'

# Chapter 43

## No Room at the Inn

Birthday balloons and coloured paper chains vied for space with the Christmas decorations, while birthday cards stood alongside Christmas cards on the sideboard and mantelpiece in her father's living room. Rose looked around at the array of mismatched ornaments, her mood torn between one of celebration and one of frustration.

'Happy first birthday, Timmy!' She came and sat on the floor by the gurgling child, and tickled him under the chin in a bid to lighten her frame of mind.

Chris came over to join them, and pulled a few funny faces to make Timmy laugh. 'Wow, I can't believe that it's a year since this little chap came into our lives.'

'And what a year – what a horrible year! Shame that we're not having his birthday party in our own house.' Rose's voice turned to a low growl. 'I hope that they bulldoze the place.'

Sensing that a bout of hostility was about to be unleashed, Chris sighed quietly under his breath. 'Have you seen Mrs Barnett or any of the other neighbours since "the incident"?' he queried, knowing that there was no hope of deflecting Rose from the subject.

'No, but I often think about her. I do wonder how the neighbours are coping with everything – having to live with a "death house" in the street. It must be a nightmare for them. Probably reduced the value of the whole street, not just our house. Woodland Row is worthless.'

'Why don't you look up her telephone number and give her a call? Perhaps arrange to meet her somewhere for a coffee and a mince pie.'

'Rosie... She only drinks Rosie Lee – tea,' she corrected.

'Okay, so a cup of tea and a mince pie. But I'm pretty sure that she'd love to hear from you, and find out how you are since we moved out.'

'If only that girl knew the trouble she's caused,' hissed Rose. Her voice began to rise in frustration. 'Maybe Dad will be able to write-off the house to business losses. And to see a big man like that reduced to a nervous wreck – doped up with antidepressants or tranquilisers, or whatever they're called. My dad – on tablets! He can't even take on a job that involves digging a hole.'

'Sshh, keep your voice down – he'll hear you! He's only popped upstairs to get changed.' Chris tried to soothe Rose's tirade with a positive note. 'At least you're sleeping better since we moved out. The bad dreams seem to have stopped.'

'Aye, that's one blessing. Maybe spirits are tied to the house in which they died? I still feel guilty, though – maybe I should have looked more closely into the dreams. Perhaps I should have got a psychic or someone to come and assess the vibes, or whatever it is they do? We might have found his little body sooner – his spirit was obviously reaching out to me.'

'If you believe in that kind of thing...'

Rose scowled at Chris for his mocking tone. 'At least the poor child can be laid to rest in peace now. I hope that girl burns in Hell for what she's done!'

'Have you heard anything from the police recently? Any updates?' he asked.

Rose shook her head. 'Nothing of late. How hard can it be to find someone?'

Chris threw up his hands in exasperation, making Timmy jump. 'Hey, come on – this isn't like some TV episode of *Dixon of Dock*

*Green*, or *The Sweeney*, where every crime is solved before the end of the programme, you know. This is real life. The police told us that she lives like a gypsy, remember? Always on the move.'

'I know, I know,' she retorted, perhaps a little more sharply than she'd meant. 'But it's been months since, you know, the body was found.'

'Don't worry – I'm sure that she'll trip up and make a mistake. They'll find her. Anyway, let's try and change our mood – after all, it's Timmy's special day.' Chris gave his wife a reassuring hug, and then looked at the clock. 'Besides, my parents will be here any min–'

Rose laughed at the sound of the doorbell. 'As punctual as ever! Let's get this party started...'

*Crystal clear stars twinkled in the inky blue-blackness of the night sky, but one star shone brighter than all the others. A sign – it must be a sign. Maggie followed the bright star, stopping only to caress her swollen full-term belly. The innocent child within slept, unaware of his mother's predicament.*

*'Don't worry, baby – we'll soon find somewhere to rest... Look, there's an inn just ahead – maybe they will have a room for the night.'*

*Maggie's weary steps carried her forward, desperation driving her on. She knocked at the door. A woman's voice came from within, the tone sharp and impatient.*

*'Who's there, and what do you want at this time of night?'*

*'It is but a weary traveller, heavy with child, who seeks a room for the night.'*

*The door opened just a crack, as the innkeeper shone a lantern. The yellow glow revealed the haggard crone's features – the features of Kate. She scowled when she saw Maggie at the door.*

*'Oh, it's you! We don't give rooms to pregnant dykes. Move on, and find somewhere else. There's no room at the inn for you, Maggie Minge-Muncher.' Kate the innkeeper hastily slammed the door in Maggie's face.*

*Maggie hung her head and sighed.*

*'Don't worry, baby – we'll find somewhere. Look, the bright star is shining, guiding us on. I can see a path through the woods, and a little house.'*

*And there in the little house a child was born that night. A boy with golden hair.*

*After swaddling her newborn son in a white blanket, Maggie laid the sleeping child in a manger, on a bed of straw. A manger which morphed into a white, plastic baby's bath. She kneeled beside the manger-bath, and bowed her head.*

*Three kings entered the scene, each bearing a gift for the newborn child. One by one, the kings stepped forward; Jimmy held a giant sperm, its head and tail thrashing like that of a newly caught trout.*

*'I bring you the gift of life,' he said. He bowed, then took a step back.*

*The second king stepped forward; Mick held out her folded umbrella.*

*'I bring you the gift of evidence,' he said. He bowed, then took a step back.*

*The third king stepped forward; Jason held out her knickers.*

*'I bring you the gift of decency,' he said. He bowed, then took a step back.*

*The bright star in the sky moved downwards, earth-bound. It hovered just above them, blinding them with light. Maggie could see the face of the angel, and it looked like Charley. The angel spoke, and it had Charley's voice.*

*'For each of your sins, I smite you down! For each of your sins you will pay!'*

*One by one, the angel cast a bolt of lightning at the three kings; each one evaporating in a ball of flames.*

*The angel looked kindly at Maggie, and with hands outstretched, she spoke. Except that the angel had now transformed into her mother, and had her mother's voice.*

*'Let me take the child, for I can take him to a better place. A place where he can live free and in peace among the angels.'*

*Her wings filled with blinding light as she took Ben from his baby-bath manger, before ascending into the night sky.*

*Slowly, slowly, the light faded, leaving Maggie cold and alone...*

'I had one of my "Ben dreams" last night.' Rather than calling them nightmares, or dark dreams, Maggie had taken to calling them "Ben dreams". 'It was really weird,' she continued. 'You were in it, and so was my mum. You were both one and the same angel, and took Ben up to heaven...'

'Me – an angel! That's a new one. Perhaps there's hope for me yet,' laughed Charley.

Maggie's brow furrowed. 'But what can it mean? Isn't there some kind of psychology connected to dreams?'

Charley put the teapot onto the camper table, then slid into the seat opposite Maggie. 'Everything that is earthbound is connected in some way to the cosmos and our psyche. Tell me about your dream, and let's see if we can analyse it...'

Maggie recounted what she could remember of her dark version of the nativity to her partner.

'Wow, you do have some weird dreams, Mags! Perhaps the angel is connected to the Advent calendar? You got a chocolate angel in your window yesterday morning, remember?'

'Maybe it's a sign to stop eating chocolate,' laughed Maggie, trying to make light of the torment and sense of foreboding that was raging in her mind.

Charley's face clouded over as she had a sudden realisation. She put her hands over Maggie's. 'It was the fifteenth yesterday. Isn't that the anniversary date that you gave Ben up for adoption? Do you think that something's happened to him? Something bad? Perhaps this is his way of reaching out to you, as his birth mother?'

Maggie could feel her heart hammering within her chest causing her pulse to quicken. Her throat constricted, blocking off any words. Her mind raced for answers. Yes, she knew that it was the fifteenth yesterday. Yes, she knew it was a message from Ben. But she wasn't just his birth mother – she was also his death-mother…

She shook her head, and shrugged non-committedly to her lover. What could she say?

She retreated into her psyche –

*What does it all mean? What is the dream telling me?*

# Chapter 44

## A Secret Wish

Liz picked up the collection of post from the doormat – a large, red envelope bearing Maggie's handwriting was tucked into the stack. She checked the postmark – Milton Keynes. Liz kissed the envelope before carefully tearing it open to read the card and the little note. Maggie always enclosed a little note:

*"Charley and I are just fine – looking forward to a chilly but cosy Christmas in the camper. Don't worry – Santa will know where to find us, and I'll put the magic key under the mat so that he can get in!*

*Miss your mince pies!*

*Happy Christmas, Mum, and wishing you a wonderful 1982.*

*All my love,*

*Maggie xxx (and a hug from Charley)"*

Her stomach lurched as she looked at the telephone in the hallway. She shook her head then blew a kiss into the air.

*Merry Christmas, my darling – wherever you are. Sergeant Gould can wait until the New Year to get an update...*

# Chapter 45

## A Message of Peace

To be part of the women's anti-nuclear movement was the niche that the three girls had been looking for; to peacefully air their views together with other like-minded women. Camping out in all weathers in the middle of winter in campers, caravans – even tents; showed a true spirit of commitment. The group had been able to find their own voice; their own way to protest in a gentle, non-confrontational way. Mothers, daughters, sisters, aunts, grandmothers; all united in a common cause against a very real threat. Yet the government still refused to talk about this very deadly issue. And so the women remained at Greenham Common.

Christmas brought a special time of togetherness – of sharing all that they had, be it food, warmth or camaraderie. Evenings were rarely without spirit-lifting music and story-telling.

The New Year brought renewed hope – maybe the governments and super-powers of the world would see sense and bring an end to this madness. To unilaterally disarm was a vain hope; but to locally disarm would at least be a step in the right direction.

Many other women joined the grassroots movement, swelling their numbers on a daily basis. Others joined whenever they could to show their support, be it for one day or for a weekend. All were welcome, providing their activism was kept to a calm, quiet minimum; a unified energy to shame those who peddled in war-mongering.

For these courageous women, peace was the key word in their desire to make their voices heard.

# Chapter 46

## Black, White and Red

The long, white, windowed envelope stared at Liz. It was addressed to Miss M Braithwaite, and was from her building society. Another piece in the puzzle which could help to guide the police towards Maggie's whereabouts. Possibly.

Mercifully the gossip and stares had reduced to almost nothing – the news story was old, replaced on a daily basis with something more shocking or tragic. It seemed to be the way of news stories these days – everything had to be sensationalised to get the reader's attention. And yet... Liz inwardly wished that it was all over and done with – give the matter closure and move on with life. As much as she loved her daughter, she knew that it was the only way forward – for both of them.

With reluctance, Liz took up the bladed letter opener and slit open the envelope. Her eyes scanned over the black and red text, showing places and cash withdrawals. Only withdrawals, no pay-ins.

...April: Whitby, May: Avebury – quite a sizeable cash withdrawal (didn't Sergeant Gould say something about a new camper van around this time?), June: Glastonbury, July: Newtown (Wales!), August: Cardiff (Wales again, and another sizeable withdrawal), October: Reading, December: Milton Keynes. No other withdrawals since this date.

Maggie had certainly been well travelled, if the statement was anything to go by – mostly in the South of England, apart from one spring excursion up to the North East. She could be anywhere...

She went over to the letter rack to retrieve the Christmas card, still in its bright red, festive envelope. The post-mark was also from Milton Keynes, dated at the same time as the last cash withdrawal.

Last known whereabouts: Milton Keynes.

But that was about three weeks ago.

Liz sighed, knowing what she had to do next – with heavy steps, and an even heavier heart she made her way into the hallway to the telephone.

# Chapter 47

## The End of the Road

### 22nd March, 1982

Despite the cloying, sticky drizzle, an almost carnival atmosphere and tangible energy resonated throughout the camp. Today would see a pivotal change in tactics by the women; the first blockade of the gates. Since the planning meeting in February, word had spread among the CND groups in support of the action. Along with the intermittent drizzle and rain showers, came a steady stream of women in a bond of solidarity – difficult to estimate their numbers; two hundred, two hundred and fifty – maybe more.

It had been agreed at the meeting that the protest at the base would be "women-only", in preparation for the blockade. Men would be welcome at the base over the daytime, but would have to leave at night. The plan was simple – the blockade would be a peaceful protest with gentle action. No banners. No men (at the risk of inflaming or inciting the gate officials and police). If the workers couldn't get in and out of the base, then the building work in preparation to receive the death missiles couldn't go ahead. Disruption in its simplest, most peaceful form.

In contrast to the positive, yet grim determination of the women, an element of external negativity had begun creeping in from the media and the locals, stirred up by the now ever-present body of police. The traditional, female role of home-maker and care-giver was being twisted to negate what the women were doing. Many outsiders were now implying that the women should be at home with their families, not dancing around at the base and causing trouble, wasting tax-payers' money. They didn't understand the bigger picture; that the women were not only trying to protect their loved ones, but protect the nation from this most unwelcome threat. They were not dissenting against family life, but dissenting against the government and its take on nuclear weapons. And they were grimly prepared to suffer all manner of hardships in support of this belief.

At the allotted time of 6:30 pm, the women worked their way around the nine-mile perimeter fence of the airbase, and peacefully placed themselves at each of the seven gates.

The sit-in had begun.

Rain poured steadily; a threat that could dampen the spirits unless resilience was strong. And it was strong – resilience and resolve, blended with adrenaline and passion, held the women fast. Tea was brought, and instruments were played, as the women rotated in four-hour shifts throughout the night – a collective resistance supported by collective unity.

Anxiety and adrenaline coursed through Maggie's veins as she lay in front of the gates, Charley alongside her. A few of the women in their group had already been hauled away by the police as a way of setting an example to the other dissenters. Contractors needed to get in and out, and these silly women were blocking the way...

She reached out and sought Charley's hand, entwining her fingers in those of her partner.

'I'm starting to get nervous. Have you ever been arrested?' she murmured.

Charley turned her head towards her so that she could keep her voice low.

'No, I've only ever been nicked for speeding. Have you ever been arrested?'

Maggie shook her head ever so slightly to indicate that she hadn't. 'No... But I think we're about to find out what it feels like...'

'Remember to go limp...' whispered Charley.

The desk sergeant looked up with disdain as yet another van full of women was brought into the police station; a rough looking, mud-spattered group of smelly hippies and dykes who were playing at being peace-loving eco-warriors. Another bunch to be charged with affray and resisting arrest. The station had been put on alert that tonight was likely to be busy...

He yawned, then winced when he caught a whiff of his own breath. He picked up his pen and grabbed a charge-sheet.

'Name.'

'Margaret Braithwaite.'

'Address.'

'A camper van. Greenham Common...'

'Don't get facetious with me, young lady...'

'Here, Guv – I think you'd better come and take a look at this...' The young officer tapped the computer screen after keying the latest round of charge-sheets into the system. His instructions had been clear; tonight will bring a load of paperwork, so make it worth the effort – keep your eyes peeled for those who've got any previous, or who have been red-flagged with warrants out for their arrest. Anything to ramp up the entertainment value of the mundane.

The senior office leaned over young Ferguson's shoulders to take a closer look. He looked at the screen and grinned, eyes wide.

'Ho-ly fuck! Good work, Ferguson. Good work, my boy.' He clapped the young officer on the back, then picked up the charge sheet from the tray on the desk. 'Get me the telephone number for Woodcliffe Station, would you. I'll take over from here…'

# Chapter 48

## Angels

The two women faced each other, each with the instinctive realisation as to who the other one was. The older of the two women spoke first, extending her hand for a cautious handshake.

'Hi. You must be Charley? I'm Liz, Maggie's mum.'

Charley returned the handshake then pulled Liz towards her in a hug, uncontrollable tears exploding down her face.

'Oh, Mrs Braithwaite – the police have taken Maggie and they won't let me see her.' She clung to Liz like a child would cling to its mother after a fall.

Liz rummaged through her coat pockets to find some tissues for the stricken young woman.

After drying her eyes and blowing her nose, Charley battled to recompose herself. 'The Woodcliffe police have had me in for questioning – they say that Maggie murdered Ben. They wanted to know what I knew about it – whether Maggie had ever said anything to me. They said that if I did know, I could get into trouble for harbouring a criminal.' Unable to hold back another round of sobbing, Liz led the distraught Charley over to some chairs near the front desk of the station.

'The police told me that, too,' acknowledged Liz. 'Maggie always maintained that she'd given up Ben for adoption...'

'Yes, that's what she also said to me,' snuffled Charley, stemming her tears.

Liz glanced up at the station clock. 'I've got a meeting with one of the officers in a couple of minutes. Here, take this address.' She quickly scribbled an address onto a piece of paper. 'It's the guest house where I'll be staying for the next few days. Go and book a room for yourself, and I'll meet up with you there a little later. We've obviously got a lot to talk about.'

'Oh – but I don't have any money on me. I've just had to pay a huge fine for taking part in the blockade demonstration at the airbase the other day. That's when we both got arrested.'

'Don't worry, I'll pay for it,' said Liz. 'Go and get cleaned up, and get some sleep. I'm sure that you need it.'

Lost for words, Charley hugged Liz by way of thanks.

'Anyway, I'd best let the front desk know that I'm here.' Liz took Charley by the hand to lead her in the same direction. 'And you'd better tell them where you'll be staying, in case they need to contact you.'

They both looked up as a set of heavy doors opened to the inner sanctum of the police station, only to be glared at by an officious, tweedy-looking senior officer.

'That's one of the officers who interviewed me,' whispered Charley. 'Good luck...'


By the time Liz returned to the guest house from the police station, Charley was already curled up on the sofa in the communal sitting room. Both women had red-rimmed and puffy eyes, testimony to an afternoon of tear shedding.

Charley gave Liz a weak half-smile. 'Did they let you see Maggie?'

Liz nodded. 'Briefly, just for a hug. Oh, my poor girl... It tore me apart, leaving her there.' A tray with a fresh pot of tea was on the little sofa table, prompting Liz to pour herself a welcome cup, before continuing. 'The police pressed me again about my knowledge of Ben's death. I honestly knew nothing about it – Maggie always maintained that she'd put him up for adoption. It was as though she'd blanked the reality from her mind, and had a different perception of events.'

'I know, that's the way she told it to me, too.' Charley's gaze became distant as she retreated into her thoughts, searching for Maggie's image, by way of comfort.

Liz took a sip of her tea, allowing herself a similar moment of private contemplation. Her jumbled conscience spilled out, releasing her guilt. 'Do you know, I feel like the worst mother in the world – how could I have missed all the signs that my child was living a lie? How could I have missed the signs that my child was distressed and crying out for help? But sometimes we don't see what's right under our nose, do we? Sometimes parents can be so blind. We think our age and wisdom counts for "knowing best". We find it so hard to admit when we're wrong; that we've failed in the eyes of the children we're supposed to be taking care of.'

Charley shook her head and looked directly at Liz. 'Don't feel bad, Mrs Braithwaite. We do what we think is right at the time.'

'I know, but...well...I guess hindsight is a wonderful thing.' Liz shrugged and sighed. 'So, I suppose that's it for you two, then?'

Charley looked at Liz, her face wide-eyed and incredulous. 'I'm made of tougher stuff than that, Mrs Braithwaite–'

'Oh, please, call me Liz...'

'Maggie and I have been together for almost four years. I love her with every fibre of my being, Liz. She's my soul-mate. And though I can't condone what she's done, who knows what depths a person can sink to at their lowest point of despair unless you've ever been to that point yourself. Who are we to judge? I can't imagine what torment this must have been for her, especially with the other issue, too.'

'Do you mean–?' Liz cautiously left the question open ended.

'–The rape? Yes, she told me all about it. The whole matter tortured her with nightmares for years. She's had many sleepless nights, Liz, believe me.' Charley sighed as she mentally recalled the nights that she'd held Maggie until her mind and body had calmed from the dark dreams that invaded her very soul. 'I remember one dream that she had – must have been around Christmas time – she dreamt that we were both an angel, like in the nativity. We were one and the same angel – I came down and you went up, and you took Ben with you, up to Heaven.'

'I suppose I did, in a way. Ben's remains were released to me for burial. Maybe I can take you there one day? I've arranged for a little marble angel for his headstone.'

'Thanks, Liz – I'd like that. I'd like to have a connection to Ben.'

Liz looked wistful. 'I had thought about laying Ben to rest with my Joseph – Maggie's dad. I suppose you've heard about Maggie's dad, and how he was killed?'

Charley nodded solemnly. 'Yes, she told me all about it. Such a tragic accident.'

'Anyway,' continued Liz, 'I decided to get Ben his own plot in the Children's Garden at the cemetery – be with other little ones, rather than with a grandfather he never knew, if you get my meaning. But there is one good thing to come out of all this – the police told me that Maggie is going to press charges for the rape.' Liz smiled a half-smile; a blend of despair and justice.

Charley closed her eyes and took a deep breath before replying. 'That's the best news I've heard in all of this, Liz.'

'She's been assigned a good solicitor who deals in these types of cases: rape, infanticide, and the like. The solicitor's going to arrange for all kinds of mental assessments, so obviously the rape will play a big part in all that. It's going to be a long and painful journey, but it will be good to see justice done,' said Liz.

'Hallelujah to that, Mrs Brai– I mean Liz. I'm so pleased that she had the courage to finally speak out about the rape. At least it goes some way towards helping people understand her spur of the moment act...'

Liz looked at Charley, her eyes full of compassion. She had seriously prejudged and misjudged this young woman. 'Where will you go while the trial is on? Do you have anywhere to stay?' she asked.

'My camper – I'll find somewhere to park up.'

'Won't you go home to your parents?'

Charley sighed, her breath deep and heavy. 'Not an option. I've been pretty much ex-communicated by them – persona non-grata. They've made it clear that I'm not really welcome. Besides, there's no way that I could go back to Barrowfeld – I would be stoned out of the village. My life would be made a misery.'

'Well, that settles it then,' declared Liz. 'Come and stay with me – I'm sure that we could both use the mutual support.' She smiled at Charley; her smile one of benevolent warmth, before adding, 'I guess that makes me your mother-in-law!'

# Chapter 49

## Contempt – Compassion – Confusion

*T*he police came to let Chris and I know that they'd arrested the girl who murdered the baby – the one whose little body was found in our pantry. It fills me with horror every time I look at our Timmy. How could anyone hurt an innocent child? Did she really have to resort to that? Surely there were people that she could have reached out to: the nuns, her mother, social services...? I just don't understand it.

Local rumours say that the girl had been raped, and by more than one man... Isn't that awful? Apparently that's how she ended up pregnant. What a dreadful situation to find yourself in. I can't begin to imagine what she must have gone through. Without doubt, it thrust a very warped view of life upon her. Does it justify what she did? Who can say? Who knows where the mind can push you after you've endured something so vile?

So, what does all this mean for Chris and Timmy and me? Despite everything, I still feel drawn to the little house at Woodland Row. Could we ever move back there? I really don't know. We'll have to go back soon anyway, to put things right – maybe that's when we'll make our decision. See how we feel. But on the other hand, I doubt that anyone would want to buy or rent it from us, no matter how much work we do to it. Rumours *will always follow its history – it will always carry the stigma of being "that house". Maybe we're destined to keep it.*

*We're still living with my dad for the time being. His health is improving, but he keeps getting flashbacks to "that day". It's going to take a while for us to overcome what we saw.*

*Where do we go from here? What does our future hold?*

*Only time will tell.*

# Chapter 50

## *Remorse – Regret – Retribution*

*I* sit here and I look at my hands – the hands that took the life of my child. Yet I barely remember anything of the event. The mind is a powerful tool when it takes over – it can create the worst in people, as well as the best.

Of course I feel remorse for what I did – I'm not that cold-hearted. I took the life of my own flesh and blood. Yet I did it without any conscious awareness... It's a terrifying thought; knowing that you've been in a situation in which you became something other than your rational self. But when you've been put into a situation over which you had no control – well, it unleashes a monster of the worst kind, and gives you a very slanted view of the world. I can only offer my most heartfelt apologies to Ben.

If only I had chosen to wait for the bus – fate is such an unpredictable mistress. But then again, life is just so full of "what-ifs", isn't it? Of being in the wrong place at the wrong time. I often think what if my dad had been a couple of minutes earlier or later going about his business, would he have avoided the spot where the drunken driver lost control of his car? Would he still be alive today? Or what if I hadn't accepted a lift from Jimmy Gould? Would life have been different for me? I'm pretty sure that it would have been.

*As tough as it's going to be, I'm glad that I made the decision to press charges against Jimmy and his mates for what they did to me. I know that I'll have to face them again in court, and I know that their solicitors will try to tear me down and discredit me. But my legal team are confident that they'll get long sentences – the evidence and odds are stacked in my favour. The paediatric forensics team only had to take a look at the photos of Ben and the remains of his copper-coloured hair then match them against photos of Jimmy as a baby. There could be no question of his paternity. After the police carried out a search of the old Miller's Cottage, they found my lost umbrella. It had most likely fallen out of the car when I was wrenched out, before...before... At least it helped to back up my statement.*

*Besides, I have to stay strong in honour of Ben – the innocent child who entered and exited this world through the vilest means possible. I owe it to him, and I owe it to myself – we both deserve our retribution.*

*Mum took care of the funeral for Ben after his body was released to her. At least I will have somewhere to go; a place where I can apologise. She's been my rock through all this. And Charley. Both have stood by me; their support strong, their love unconditional. I was pretty sure that Charley would have given up on me, but I obviously misjudged the depth of her love; of our relationship. She sees beyond the proverbial blood on my hands; she knows that I'm not a cold hearted killer. But that's the basis of soul-mates – inextricably intertwined through invisible bonds. We'll see what life throws at us once I'm free. We've vanished before, and we can vanish again if we need to – reinvent ourselves.*

*"Adapt or Die"; that seems to be our life motto.*

*I often reflect back on my other period of confinement – the time that I spent with the nuns at the convent all those years ago. Though I neither realised nor appreciated it at the time, they gave me a sense of inner peace and personal strength when faced with adversity. And I draw on those teachings now, while I am detained in the hospital. When I was lost for words, Sister Theresa encouraged me to write down my feelings. Writing has now become a constructive vent for my emotions: poetry, short prose, letters that I'll never send; every word releases a personal demon.*

*Life will never be the same for any of us; we've all been tainted in some way. Mum has already put the family home up for sale and is getting ready to move out. We're also going to change our surname back to my mother's maiden name – Glover. At least it will give us a modicum of anonymity.*

*Mum told me that Mr and Mrs Gould are getting a divorce because of the strain that it put on their marriage, and that Jimmy's fiancée broke off their engagement after he was charged with rape. As for Kate, I hear that she's abandoned her dreams of joining the police force in favour of joining the Royal Navy. Now it's her turn to run away; to experience shame.*

*Karma.*

*Justice.*

*Retribution.*

*Call it what you will – but what goes around, comes around.*

*My solicitor has been a tower of strength, as have the counsellors here at the hospital. To be honest, the level of compassion has surprised me. They have not only helped me through the darkest days of despair and remorse after my arrest and trial, but are now preparing me for the impending rollercoaster ride of questions, accusations, and best answers for the upcoming rape trial against Jimmy and his cronies. I am ready to look those bastards in the eye, and watch them go down. At least Jimmy's confession, and that of the other two, helped reduce my sentence to infanticide on the grounds of my "vulnerable state", as they called it. I'm grateful that my case was looked upon with compassion.*

*I'm not the cold-hearted monster that the local news reports are portraying me as. I bear the scars of trauma, and carry the burden of my deeds; of exposed secrets and lies. The dark dreams might have subsided now that Ben has been laid to rest, but his memory will never fade. And nor do I want it to – I owe him that much. Ben had every right to enter my psyche and tear down the mental barriers that I used as a shield against my actions.*

*I'm no longer hiding in the shadows.*

*I no longer fear the future.*

*And I no longer fear my dreams.*

*Thank you, Ben.*

# Epilogue

Satisfied that Timmy was now asleep, Rose parked up the pram on the little lawn. Daffodils and narcissi framed the patch of grass, their stalks heavy with forming buds. She dusted off some winter debris from one of the wrought-iron chairs before sitting at the nearby patio table, allowing herself a moment to absorb the spring warmth. It felt good to be shaking off the cloak of the damp, grey winter. Her eyes traced the creepers of the tangled ivy on the old brick wall dividing No 23 from next door; fascinated by the way that it wove around itself, and the determined way in which the roots fingered a hold into the crumbling mortar joints. Was the ivy holding up the wall, or the wall holding up the ivy?

She toyed with the keys in her hand. Chris had offered to come back to the house with her, but Rose felt compelled to make this first visit alone. After all, she would be the one making the final decision. To Chris, it was just a house. To Rose, it was...

A familiar sensation tickled the bottom of her spine; an icy feeling. An unwelcome feeling.

She tensed and closed her eyes, then tried to regulate her breathing, steeling herself for the impending mind-intrusion. Vertebrae by vertebrae, icy little fingers crawled upwards, until they reached the top of her spinal cord. The icy sensation paused, chilling her primitive brain. Rose could feel her scalp beginning to tighten.

A voice she knew well entered her psyche.

*"Sorry I scared you lots..."*

The humble, simplistic tone of the little voice caught Rose off-guard. She paused for a moment before forcing words into her consciousness. *"You don't need to say sorry for anything."*

The mind-voice sighed. *"I do. I was lonely. And I just wanted a mummy..."*

Rose felt her heart skip a beat. That was all the poor child wanted – a mummy. She thought of her own child, and swallowed hard, fighting back tears. *"I'm sorry – I should have listened to you... But..."*

Almost as quickly as it had arrived, Rose felt the coldness beginning to recede. Sensing that this might be his last visit, she seized the opportunity to send one final thought – an instinctive, maternal thought.

*"Will you be okay?"*

The fading, tiny voice replied. *"Think so... Bye, nice lady."*

Rose opened her eyes and kissed the tips of her fingers, before gently blowing the kiss and the words into the air.

'Bye, Ben. I promise we'll take good care of your house...'

-oOo-

*Benjamin Braithwaite*

*12.02.1977 – 15.12.1977*

*Adopted by the Angels*

-oOo-

# About the Author

Originally from Chesterfield, England, Ann Thorsson now lives on a farm by the sea, nestled under the iconic Snæfellsjökull (Snaefells-glacier), in the beautiful West peninsula of Iceland. She shares this idyll with her Icelandic husband, their two bilingual sons and a bilingual Siberian husky.

*Dark Dreams* is Ann Thorsson's second novel.

Gabriel Rutenberg
Photography, Iceland

Her debut novel, *Downhill*, is a gritty drama set in the 1980s' coal-mining North of England (published 2019; UK Book Publishing).

She is currently working on an anthology of poetry – *Sunflowers: a collection of specially chosen words*.

**For more information about Ann Thorsson:**

www.annthorsson.com
@ann.thorsson.author
**Facebook:** https://www.facebook.com/ann.thorsson.author/
**Instagram:** https://www.instagram.com/ann.thorsson.author/

# Acknowledgements and Thanks!

Hawkwind, (1973), *The Space Ritual Alive*, United Artists Records
King, C. (1963), *Stig of the Dump*, Puffin Books
Smith, P. (1975), *Horses*, Arista Records

Grateful thanks go to my pre-readers: to Lucy, Kay, Gemma, Henriette and Lisa. Your feedback and suggestions were invaluable!

To Ruth, Jay, and the team at UK Book Publishing, for getting *Dark Dreams* out into the world. You're the best!

To my dear friend Heather Burns, of Heather Burns Photography – for her artistic genius and creativity on the cover-work of *Dark Dreams*.

To all those who have supported me along the way with *Downhill* and *Dark Dreams*.